MAYBE THIS TIME

MAYBE THIS TIME

Robert E. Dunn

Published by Tate Publishing & Enterprises, LLC
127 E. Trade Center Terrace | Mustang, Oklahoma 73064 USA
1.888.361.9473 | www.tatepublishing.com

Tate Publishing is committed to excellence in the publishing industry. The company reflects the philosophy established by the founders, based on Psalm 68:11,
"The Lord gave the word and great was the company of those who published it."

Cover design by Arjay Grecia
Interior design by Caypeeline Casas

Published in the United States of America

ISBN: 978-1-62854-109-0
1. Fiction / Religious
2. Fiction / Science Fiction / Apocalyptic & Post-Apocalyptic
13.08.30

DEDICATION

To my English teachers Mrs. Forrester at Schuylkill Consolidated School in Phoenixville, Pennsylvania; Mrs. Groff, who taught the whole school of four grades in a one-room schoolhouse in Intercourse, Pennsylvania; and Charles J. Joseph and Alice M. Kendig at Upper Leacock High School in Leola, Pennsylvania.

Because of poor eyesight and hearing, I never did well in school, but somehow these teachers managed to instill in me a love of our language and writing. These folks are probably all gone from us now, but they all made a great impression on my life. Especially Mrs. Groff, who discovered that I could not see well and advised my parents to get my eyes checked. Also Ms. Kendig, who introduced me to Ernest Hemingway's writing enough for me to recognize that famous writer when I ran into him in a hotel in Valencia, Spain.

I give special thanks to my wife, who transcribed most of my book, which I scribbled onto tablet paper while on lunch breaks at work. She also put up with my joking that I would someday be rich and famous like Hemingway and my fussing and fuming over my editing out all of my errors. Of course, I did not eliminate all errors. I am sure the Tate Publishing Company will find a million or more and send the manuscript back covered in blood for rework a time or two!

A very special thanks to Carolyn Green of Brooklyn Center, Minnesota for reading my manuscript and correcting many many mistakes that I had made in grammar and sentence structure. She also bolstered my confidence that the book is viable.

WEDNESDAY, JUNE 13, 2102

"Charlie! Your breakfast is ready. Come and get it while it is hot."

"I'll be there in a minute, Barb."

"Well, hurry up. I made pancakes, eggs, and scrapple, and you know how this toast gets after it lays around for a while."

"Okay! Here I am in all my glory. How do I look?"

"Like a million bucks. Sit down and eat now before this gets cold. Oh, I better put a bib on you. I don't want you to mess up that fancy suit. What or who are you getting all dolled up for anyway? Do you have a new secretary or something?"

"No. I have a new client, I hope. SEC, that space exploration company that has been in the news for skimping on launch vehicle fuel and lost a ship and three scientists has really been catching a lot of flak lately. Their communications people think that someone has intercepted their satellite data and leaked the news of their financial problems and penny-pinching to the media.

"Our company has a new satellite interface unit that has thirty very secure channels and one open channel for maintenance. We call it the flying thirty-one. Those secure channels are so tight that nobody has been able to hack into them yet. SEC has three hundred stations around the world so I have a chance to sell that many of our units. If I can make this sale today we will be able to afford that motor home and take some time off to get you out of Binghamton and see some of the world."

"Charlie, you are flying around the country all the time, but I sure would like to go to Sacramento to visit my sister and her new baby. Do you want some more scrapple? Oh, by the way that old man called us again."

"What old man?"

"The old guy that lives in the place that used to be deep in the woods, the place your great-grandfather, Damian, told us about."

"Oh, that old relic! Does the old geezer still want me to change the world?"

"I don't know. He just said he needs to see us both."

"Barb, that sounds scary! Where is that place?"

"In a little park where Avignon Way crosses 128th Avenue South."

"Here in the city?"

"Yes, but when it was built, about a hundred years ago, it was in a forest. Do you remember that big fight about street alignment when the city expanded into that region? The chapel was in the wrong place to match the streets. I think they finally just put a traffic circle around it."

"I still don't understand why Granddad wanted us to find it. Actually, I forgot about it. I guess I forgot it because everyone says Granddad was crazy as a loon. I don't even know if he was ever there."

"Oh, Charlie, you fell asleep when he was telling about it. He was there all right, but he wasn't directly involved with whatever happened. His father was though. He helped to build the little chapel way back in the early part of the twenty-first century."

"What are we doing on Sunday, Barb? We're both off work then, aren't we? I wonder why my great-great-grandfather had a chapel built. Grand mom said that old coot was some kind of mad scientist or something. Why would a scientist build a chapel?"

"I don't know, Charlie. I just know I have a really strong feeling we should go there."

"Okay, let's pack a lunch Sunday morning. If nothing else, we can have a picnic in the park. You have a really strong feeling, do you?"

"Charlie, I guess I never told you that your great-grandfather and I had a real long talk after you fell asleep. He didn't think his dad was crazy at all. He was a scientist all right. He made major discoveries about magnetism and other forms of energy. He was published in every scientific journal in the world. Your great-great-grandmother, Marie, was a well-known scientist too. I'm surprised you don't know more about them."

"I know that my mom says my ancestors were some kind of religious nuts. I don't know how they could be that and scientists too. Dad doesn't like to talk about them at all. I guess he's ashamed of the old coots."

"Charlie, your great-grandfather said that his parents actually heard God talk. God told Marie, your great-great-grandmother, that Damian would be a fine man."

"Well, I guess he is quite a man. He discovered a cure for that disease that used to kill people. Oh, what was it called?"

"It was cancer, Charlie. Everyone was afraid of it until your grandfather found the cure."

"He also invented the fuel we run our transporters on. I guess he is a great man, but I used to get tired of his preaching all the time. I don't see how he could figure out how things are when his head was so full of religious junk. You say Old Tony and Marie talked to God? Man, those old coots must have been really nuts to tell their kid something like that! I wonder where they got the name Damian."

SUNDAY, JUNE 17, 2102

"Well, here is Avignon Way and 128th South. Wow! Is that the chapel? I expected a one-room shack. That place is more like a cathedral. A bunch of monks could live there. Where can I park this thing? Ah, there's a spot."

"One old man, the caretaker I talked to on the phone, does live there. His name is Aaron Fisher. He is waiting for us. Oh, that must be him there."

"Good morning, Charlie and Barb. I have been waiting forty years for you two. Come in, and I'll show you around. Please forgive the dust and things that need repair, like that window. Some young punk shot it out three years ago. I fixed that boy. He is learning to be a preacher now. I am too old to fix that window, though, and keep out the dust like Lorraine and I did for all those years.

"This is more than just a fancy church. God himself ordered us to build it, way back in the beginning of the last century when I was a little boy. Charlie, you don't have to give your wife a look that says, 'That old coot is nuts.' I am as sane as you are. I also know that you think all your ancestors were nuts too, but when this day is over, you will know the truth.

"Come on in with me, and I'll show you around. This little room is for coats and shoes and hats. Hardly anyone wears hats anymore, but we all did when we built this place. The hats were mostly baseball caps. We don't wear shoes inside to show our reverence to God. Also, it helps keep out a lot of dirt.

"The other side of this coatroom is an office. It is full of old-fashioned computers, printers, fax machines, and other gadgets that were quite modern fifty years ago. Now let's go through the office and along the south side of the building. This hallway runs to the rear between the sanctuary and all these classrooms here.

"Now back here is where I live. I have these three rooms at the rear of the church. This room was supposed to be a living room for the caretaker, but I use it for a laboratory. I still like to learn how things work. This is where I learned to dissolve the failed disks in backbones and then clone a new one from the cells of the old. That way, there is no rejection by the immune system.

"Getting the new material to grow into the shape of a good disk was tricky until Lorraine invented a mold that could be dissolved away by an enzyme after the bone was formed around the spinal cord. I guess thousands of doctors around the world made millions of bucks from my procedure, but I never made a cent. I wasn't much of a businessman. Oh, that is my collection of stuff that I made as a little boy. I used to keep it in a chicken house at Dad's farm a mile or two north of here. When Pop got too old to farm anymore, he sold the place to a developer and moved to Florida. I really had to scramble to get my stuff out of my old museum. That developer wasted no time leveling the farm and throwing up those flimsy houses that make up the Fisher Farms neighborhood now. You'll learn more about my collection in the writing.

"Now along this north wall are more classrooms. The more we tried to teach people what happened here and in Chicago, the more they were convinced we were nuts. After Tony and Marie died, Lorraine and I carried on the effort. Two of Tony's sons worked with me for many years, but all the established religions on earth called us heretics and nuts. Your great-granddad spent three years in jail because of trying to convince people we don't dispute their religion, we explain it. He rocked the boat too hard. You two are our last hope, Charlie. Now let's go into the sanctuary.

"This is the altar that God told us to build. It is built to the specifications we found on a piece of paper left behind after God talked to us. This is the writing I mentioned earlier. Sit here and read this. Do you drink latte? I'll go make some while you two read this journal. Your great-great-grandmother kept this and eventually made it into a story."

"God talked to you?" Charlie asked.

"Just read the journal," Aaron answered.

SUMMER 2066: THE JOURNAL

My name is Marie Matheson. I have been writing this journal for more than fifty years. I finally put it all together in story form. Until eight years ago, when he died, my husband Tony helped me to remember and write down the events of this strange story. Now I, my first son, Professor Aaron Fisher, and a very few scientists from around the world who are still living have been trying to convince the whole world of the truth of what we saw and experienced about sixty years ago.

We have been called cultists, wierdos, nuts, and other names I refuse to write. Some of us have been hanged, some shot, and some just disappeared. My own son, Damian, spent three years in jail because of our effort to convince all the established religions in the world that we are trying to explain, not dispute, their religions.

To my great sorrow, my second son refuses to believe my writing and is active in trying to prove we are just hallucinating. He is convinced that our effort is the result of having lived through the age when drugs were used for recreation. He swears that Damian is the result of drug-induced paranoia that came from my drug use while carrying him.

That is not true at all. I have been a biochemist all my life. I know what drugs do to our brains and to the epigenetic marks on our DNA. I know and have always known what drugs do to our cells. I have never taken anything but aspirins, and those reluctantly.

Damian is able to quote, in any language on earth, a speech I heard fifty years ago. He was still in my womb when I heard that. It was with Damian's help that I was able to reproduce it in this writing. That speech was recorded, but so far, no machine has been invented to decode it. Not even the most sophisticated computer system can do that.

Read my story, and be prepared to change the way you think about those around you and those around them and beyond, to everyone, and be prepared to know God.

SUMMER 1998

It all started hundreds of years ago. Nobody ever noticed that something was creeping through the forest like the creeping crud or cancer or something even worse.

School was out, and nine-year-old Aaron Fisher began an adventure that eventually involved people from all over the earth. Aaron was about to become the second victim of a deadly affliction. The boy and his dog were exploring. It was their favorite activity, and they often wandered miles from home through the forest that covered most of New York and Pennsylvania. Aaron's home was a small farm south of Binghamton. Many times Aaron walked to Hawleyton where one of his school classmates, a girl named Lorraine, lived. She too loved to wander and explore, but today it was just Aaron and Jinx.

Aaron often amused his father with his tales of the discoveries he made. The boy made a collection of arrowheads and even pottery pieces. He glued each piece to a plywood sheet and very precisely labeled each with the location of his find and a short description. His mother often looked at the collection and wished it were all still out in the forest. Aaron had so much stuff in his room that she could not clean it well.

Sometimes though, she looked at it with a wistful expression. She was Native American. It was her ancestors who had lived in the area south of Binghamton. Of course, there were no towns or borders then.

There had been a legend about a big pile of dirt. The legend was handed down from one generation to the next but was largely forgotten in modern times. Aaron's mother only remembered that it was a place dangerous to children, and she warned Aaron never to go there. Of course, this was an invitation for Aaron to seek out the strange mound of dirt. He never found it. He knew every fallen tree, every deer trail, and every little brook that ran through the woods, but he never saw a big heap of rocks and dirt that was higher than a man. He finally decided it was just an old wives' tale made up to frighten children.

This fine summer day, Aaron crossed an open place in the woods. Jinx ran around the place through the trees. Nothing seemed to grow in that bare spot. Aaron never found anything of interest there, but he noticed the soil felt soft and fine to his bare feet. He was watching a woodpecker in a nearby tree as he walked. He stubbed his toe on a rock.

"Ouch! That hurts! What's that rock doing in the middle of this big bare spot? Ain't nuttin' else out here. Nuts! Now I scared the woodpecker off.

"C'mon, Jinx. Let's get out of here. Where are you, Jinx? Oh! There you are. Why don't you ever step on this bare spot? Do you know sompin' I don't know? Ouch! My toe hurts. I better find someplace to sit down and see if there is blood coming out of it. I'm sure glad Mom didn't hear me cussin' at that rock. I would taste soap if she had.

"Ah, there's a spot to sit down. If my toe ain't busted, I can cross this ditch and sit on that old tree that fell down.

"There ain't no blood comin' out, but what's this? The tip of my toe is a different color from the rest of it. It still hurts too. Oh well, it'll go away.

"I wonder what made that big bare spot over there. I used to think a flying saucer landed there, but I was younger then. That was a year and a half ago. I was just eight. That spot was a lot smaller then. It was only as big around as the bottom of the haystack behind Lorraine's barn. Now it's bigger."

Aaron got down off the log, walked over to the edge of the bare spot, and pulled out his pocketknife. He knelt down and dug up some of the soil in the bare spot. He found the soil to be soft, almost like powder, and no bugs. None at all. No bugs, no worms, and no flies or any other bugs were flying around over the bare spot. Even tree roots stopped at the edge of the bare spot. Aaron dug as deep as he could with his knife. He found roots, but all of them ended at the edge of the bare spot.

"Jinx won't get anyplace near that spot. Maybe I shouldn't either. I don't know how a dumb ol' dog knows that place is bad, but I guess I better trust him and stay off of it too. Jeez! I walked all around in there. I hope nothing bad happens to me. Damned toe still hurts."

He finished his candy bar, and Jinx finished his dog bone, and they continued to explore. There was much to see because the forest always looked different each summer. Aaron thought about that place where he stubbed his toe. "It seems to be a much bigger spot with no growth this year. What's killing all the weeds and stuff? That spot even has a different smell from the rest of the forest. It doesn't have that smell of new life and rotten old life underfoot. It doesn't even sound like the rest of the forest, the rustling of leaves when the wind stirs them, and the creaking sound of two branches rubbing each other. The place has the feeling of death. No, not even of death. With death, there is bad smell and a feeling of stuff that used to be alive. This place does not even have that. It doesn't stink at all."

Aaron studied that spot for an hour or more then followed Jinx to a hole under a fallen tree where it looked like a bear had hibernated. Sure enough, he found tracks nearby. As he looked at paw prints, he noticed his toe was hurting a little more. Looking at it closely, he could see right through the tip.

Six days later, when his mother made him take a bath, Aaron was looking at his toe again. Nothing had ever bothered Aaron much, but that toe was still hurting a bit. Also, he could see through the end of the toenail, and back farther, he could almost see through the nail. It no longer covered the toe. It was shorter.

After his bath, Aaron told his mother about his toe. She examined it and declared, "I have never seen anything like that. I'm calling the doctor." There was something nagging at her memory. It was something strange, but not strong enough to come to the surface of her memory. She shrugged it off then called their family doctor in Binghamton.

The doctor was an older man with a number tattooed on his wrist. Aaron's mother thought he was old enough to retire. He really seemed to enjoy working with children. Donna was glad that he was still practicing medicine.

They made the appointment for three days later. By the time Dr. Staneck looked at the toe, the nail and most of the hyponychium were almost gone. That which was left was transparent. Aaron said the toe hurt just a little bit, so the doctor gave him pills to ease the pain and asked him to return in three more days.

Dr. Staneck suspected some kind of cancer, and he needed time to study all he could find concerning that condition. He also scheduled an MRI at the local hospital. MRI is short for magnetic resonance imaging. It gives us a three-dimensional view of the inside of our bodies.

Dr. Staneck could find nothing in his books that described Aaron's problem. Even though he was an old doctor, he kept up on all new information on conventional medicine as well as some of the holistic treatments. He read up on copper bracelets and magnets. He could find no description of Aaron's problem in any conventional medical journals.

When Aaron returned to the doctor's office, there was no toenail at all! Most of the tip of the toe was gone too. Dr. Staneck asked Aaron, "Are you a brave boy?"

"As brave as they come, I guess," Aaron said.

Then the doctor addressed Aaron's mother and said, "I would like to have a small sample of that toe to examine under a microscope."

He cut a very small piece of the toe and put it on a microscope slide. When he examined it, he could see nothing! He sent that slide to a chemistry lab.

The lab called Dr. Staneck after they had examined the sample and asked for another sample. The doctor said that could be done. He called Mrs. Fisher and asked her to return with Aaron.

She and Aaron came back to the office immediately. The doctor asked for another sample.

Aaron said, "I soon won't have any toe left if you keep slicing and dicing."

"You won't have any toe left anyway if I can't figure out what is going on here," the doctor replied.

He actually made two cuts this time. He sent the second sample to another laboratory that he knew had an electron microscope. The cutting did not hurt Aaron. In fact, he felt nothing at the tip of his toe. There was no bleeding.

Aaron and his mom arrived early for the MRI. The wait in the hospital was excruciating for the boy. There was not much in the waiting room to interest him. The magazines were all for grown-ups and sports fans. He finally did find an outdoor magazine someone else had put back on the little rack. Aaron was engrossed in an article about beavers when a nurse called his name.

The nurse led Aaron into a room with a big machine that looked like the waffle iron at home, but bigger. It had a narrow bed on a track and lots of tubes, wires, and stuff. Aaron was never so afraid of anything as he was of that machine.

The nurse, whom Aaron thought was very pretty but rather old (about twenty, he guessed), told him to take off his clothes and put on the robe she handed him.

"You never know what a little boy will have in his pockets, and some metals can really hurt Aaron or even the machine," she explained to his mother.

Aaron was fearful and slow to undress. The pretty nurse helped him. He was never so embarrassed in all his life. He would not let her take off his underpants. He did that himself as she turned around and grinned at his mom.

When he had the robe secured as tight as he could get it, he asked, "What next?"

The nurse pointed at the monster machine. Aaron stepped up to the thing and bravely lay down as instructed. He was brave on the outside, but never in his life was he so fearful, not even when he turned the crank on the potato-digging machine and the engine came to life. Aaron had run out of the barn screaming for his dad. He just knew that digger was going to crash through the barn wall and come after him! Actually, it was not self-propelled. The engine operated only the conveyor belt, but Aaron didn't know that.

Then he had been able to run away from danger. Now he had to face it head-on! The pretty nurse smiled as she explained the machine and the noises Aaron would hear. Aaron thought, *She is the worst kind of monster! She can smile so pretty while she's committing a boy to his terrible fate.*

The nurse and Aaron's mom left the room, and then the thing started up, and it ate his whole body. He was inside the thing, and he was not allowed to move at all. The monster hummed; made tapping noises; then went *zert, zert, zert, zert, zert, zert*; then was quiet for a little while. In the quiet times, the anxiety level in the boy went through the roof. The machine hummed again and went *tap, tap, tap, tap, tap, tap*. It sounded like a small jackhammer, then it got quiet again. By this time, Aaron realized he wasn't being hurt at all. His insatiable curiosity took over. He began to look around at the inside of the machine. He moved his head to look to the side of him. The nurse reminded him not to move.

Aaron wondered, *How come I can hear her? She's in another room.*

"Just one more picture," she said.

Hum, tap, tap, tap, tap, tap, tap, zert, zert, zert, zert, zert, zert. Then it was quiet. Aaron felt the board he was on start to move out of the machine.

The monster is spittin' me out. I guess I don't taste good, Aaron thought.

When the board stopped moving, Aaron asked, "Can I get off this thing now? Can I get dressed?"

"Yes, you can get dressed now," the nurse said. "We are all finished. Can I help you?"

"No! I'll put my clothes on myself. I only have a sore toe. I don't know why I had to take all my clothes off!" Aaron had no knowledge of the danger he was in. He just wanted out of there and back to the farm, with a stop for ice cream, of course.

Two days later, Dr. Staneck examined the toe again and could find no difference in it. The disintegration had stopped. One week later, the toe was again slowly disappearing.

The technician who read the MRI, his supervisor, and Dr. Staneck all agreed that the result of the test was questionable. The sore toe and part of the next toe and even part of the foot simply did not appear at all! Another MRI was scheduled.

When the doctor called Aaron's mother to tell her of the need for another MRI, he said there had been a problem with the machine the day Aaron had his test. Aaron's mother was not fooled at all. She realized that there was something wrong with Aaron, something much worse than a sore toe. She began to feel frightened.

When Aaron was told he had to go back to the monster, he immediately left the house and went through the cornfield and into the woods. He took Jinx and walked all the way to Hawleyton. He asked Lorraine to go exploring with him. The girl's mother noticed that Aaron was unusually quiet and had no food with him. She insisted that the children take a lunch with them. She made them sandwiches and also packed fruit, candy bars, and bottled water.

She sent the brave explorers off with her usual "Have fun, and be careful, kids." Fifteen minutes after the children disappeared into the woods, the phone rang.

"Mary, this is Donna Fisher. Have you seen Aaron?"

Something is wrong! thought Mary. "Why, yes, he just left here with Lorraine. I think they headed south this time. Donna, what's wrong?"

"Aaron has a sore toe," replied Donna in her matter-of-fact voice. But beginning to cry, she added, "His toe is slowly disappearing, and the doctor doesn't know why. He had an MRI on Tuesday, and now they want to do another one. They said the machine malfunctioned, but I think they are hiding something from me. Something is bad wrong." Then she completely lost the ability to talk and just cried.

Mary covered the mouthpiece of the phone and called her husband. He was in the garage working on a small boat with two of his friends. He came into the kitchen, and from the look on Mary's face, he knew there was a problem.

"Go find Lorraine and Aaron. They went south, I think," Mary said.

He left with his friends, and they headed into the woods. The children rarely followed trails, so the men knew they had a difficult search ahead.

Donna finally got her crying under control and tried to explain that the MRI was to be done that afternoon, but Aaron ran off when told of it.

"Mary, I don't know why I am so afraid for Aaron. Dr. Staneck always knows what is wrong with someone, but not this time. There is something at the back of my mind, something from the ancients, but it just won't come forward. I can't remember what it is."

"Oh, Donna, this is the twentieth century. Those old legends are no longer true, are they?" asked Mary. "Sometimes Joe gets a weird look on his face, and I know he is thinking of his ancestors. He too is from the tribe, you know. I can usually get him over it by asking how his latest project is progressing."

"The legends don't die," replied Donna. "Oh, I have to find Aaron and get him to the hospital."

Mary, who was Irish-American, knew nothing of old legends, not even the old ones of the Celts, her ancestors. But she was a woman. She was able to ease Donna's fears and give her some comfort. They spoke for nearly an hour.

Aaron and Lorraine headed south for a while then turned west. Aaron was going to the big bare spot in the woods where he had stubbed his toe. They walked fast. Normally, Aaron was very careful to avoid disturbing anything, but today he was upset. He did not like having to get in that machine again, even though it didn't hurt him at all. Going through that was merely unpleasant, so that isn't what made him run away today.

His fear was not of that *tap, tap, zert, zert* thing, but of whatever it was that was happening to his toe. He just had to talk to someone who would understand him. The grown-ups just pooh-poohed everything. They never really listened to his concerns, so he normally hid any fear that he had. Lorraine always understood. Neither child had reached the age when boys and girls begin to think on different channels.

The children walked on and on, straight toward the big bare spot. When they got close to it, Aaron stopped and sat on a fallen log. Lorraine sat beside him and gave the boy a questioning look. "Aaron, what is wrong? We have never walked straight to anything before. We always explore, except today."

"I'm scared, Lorraine. See that big bare spot over there? In the middle of it is a rock. A few weeks ago, I bumped my toe on it. Now my toe is disappearing." He lifted his foot up to show her but warned her not to touch it. "In fact, don't even touch me at all.

I think that rock put a spell on me for cussing at it when I kicked it. That's why I didn't hold your hand like I usually do."

"But, Aaron, it is only a rock. How can it put a spell on you?" Then she really looked at his toe, and sure enough, it was half gone. "Oh, Aaron, I am sorry!" she cried.

Aaron said, "First the toe, then the foot, then the leg, then all of me! The doctor can't seem to find out what 's wrong. He keeps sending me to the hospital. They make me get in some big machine that takes pictures of my insides and stuff. They won't let me look at the pictures though. They think I am too young to see my own body."

Lorraine agreed. "Grown-ups are so dumb sometimes. They think we don't know anything."

"They don't wanna scare me, but I can tell Mom is terrified. So is Dad," Aaron replied. "I brought you here to show you the place. Don't ever go near it. When I saw it the first time, it was about as big around as that haystack behind your barn. It's getting bigger. Someone put a spell on that place, and it put a spell on me! Do you remember how to get here?" Aaron asked.

"Yes, I remember. We were here before, so I know the spot. I'll stay away," Lorraine promised.

"Good! Let's get out of this spooky place," Aaron said as he got up. Lorraine held out her arms to Aaron, and he nearly took her hands to help her up, but then he remembered not to touch her. Lorraine sat back down, and both children cried. They feared that they could never touch each other again. They could not play tag. They couldn't help each other up hills, over logs, or under fences. They could not hold hands.

When both of them were cried out, they headed east away from the spot but did not go straight home. They walked awhile then stopped to talk for a while and sometimes cry. They stayed in the parts of the forest that were familiar to both of them. They wandered far and were a long way from either of their homes.

"Are you afraid to spend the night in the woods?" Aaron asked.

"No, not as long as you stay close to me," Lorraine replied.

"I'll stay as close as I can without touching you," Aaron promised. "So will Jinx."

Relief stops were no problem for the children. They knew they were different and just simply accepted the differences. They were explorers and buddies, and the difference in their bodies was just not important to them—not yet. They went to a favorite copse of young evergreen trees where they could see the stars, and there they bedded down for the night.

"I wish we could hold hands," Lorraine lamented. "That bare spot in the woods reminds me of a story my great-grandma told me last winter. She told me there was a big pile of dirt where sick people were buried when they died. They had some weird kind of sickness that kept them confused about who they were or something. They were so confused they didn't know if they were boys or girls. They couldn't have babies, so when they died, there was nobody left. They all disappeared. I'll ask her more about it when we visit her again."

"Did she say where it was?" Aaron asked.

"Yes, she said it was where two creeks came together near a giant oak tree. She said if you stood by the tree and looked at the moon at dusk on a summer night, the pile of dirt was in front of you. It was not near any of the trails that her ancestors used. It was a bad place, and no one wanted to go near it. She told me other stuff too, but I don't remember it all."

"Oh my gosh!" Aaron exclaimed. "Oh my gosh!"

"What's wrong, Aaron?"

"Remember that log we sat on when I showed you the bare spot? Remember we had to go down in a big ditch, then climb up to the log, and on the other side of the log was another ditch? As we looked at the bare spot, we could see the moon. That bare spot is where the big pile was! Those ditches were the two creeks that came together! That fat old log was the giant oak tree! But what happened to the big pile of dirt?"

"Aaron, that was a long time ago. Maybe that pile of dirt just disappeared." She began crying. "Like your toe."

"That would take much more time for all that dirt and bones and stuff to go away," Aaron replied.

"But, Aaron, it didn't happen just in my grandmother's lifetime. She told me it was a legend from long, long ago."

"What's a legend?" Aaron asked.

"A legend is a story that a father tells his son. Then the son tells it to his son, and that son tells it to his son, and it goes on like that forever. It could have been a hundred or a thousand years ago," Lorraine explained.

"Wow!" Aaron said. "Am I being haunted by a ghost that is a thousand years old? Wow!"

Eventually the children fell asleep, side by side, with Jinx at their feet. They awoke when the sun came up. After relieving themselves and eating the remains of the lunch Mary had packed, they started toward Hawleyton.

Mary's husband and friends, the volunteer fire company, and other friends and neighbors searched until dark for the kids. Lorraine's father, a member of the old Seneca tribe, occasionally found traces of the children's passage, which gave him a general direction of travel.

When it became too dark to track, the search was called off until morning. No one, not even Mary or Donna, was worried about the children's safety. They thought Aaron was upset about the MRI and was trying to avoid it. The test was necessary for the diagnosis, so the search was resumed in the morning.

Late in the morning, Lorraine recognized her father's voice.

"Should we hide or run away?" she asked.

"No, I guess we better go home," Aaron said. "I have to go into that machine again sometime. I just needed to be with you and Jinx for a while."

Lorraine whistled three birdcalls then repeated the calls and chirped like a chickadee. It was a signal her father had taught her. Soon he joined the children by the side of a stream.

"Did you both have a pleasant night?" he asked.

"I guess so," Aaron replied. "We were both sound asleep all night."

The MRI was rescheduled for later that day. Aaron knew what to expect, so he was not worried or frightened this time.

When Dr. Staneck got the results, the machine again showed nothing of the toe or the affected area of the foot near the toe. That area just looked like a bright spot on the display.

One thing the doctor noticed was that the disintegration stopped again as it had after the first MRI test. He studied all he could find on the MRI machine and found that it was magnetic energy the machine used to create the image.

Dr. Staneck tried an experiment. He taped a magnet to Aaron's toe. He wrapped it in gauze to keep Aaron from knocking it loose. He asked Aaron to come back in three days. Aaron smiled and said he would. He actually enjoyed these trips into town. His mom always took him to the ice cream store after his visit with the doctor.

When Dr. Staneck saw the disappearing toe again, there was no noticeable change. He measured the length and circumference of the toe and recorded the findings then put the magnet back on for another three days.

Aaron noticed that Dr. Staneck put on two pairs of rubber gloves before he touched the bad toe and threw them away as soon as he was finished.

Aaron said, "This is a good experiment, but it sure is hard to walk with this big ball of stuff around my toe."

At the end of the three more days, there was no change. The measurements were as before. Dr. Staneck again put the magnet back on and sent Aaron home. He then called a friend in St. Marys, Pennsylvania, who had a factory that made electronic parts and very powerful magnets. He ordered a magnet of a specific size and shape that would stay on Aaron's toe without much bulk. He never did notice that the rubber gloves he wore whenever he examined Aaron's foot disappeared from the trash can.

When Dr. Staneck received the odd-shaped magnet, he called Aaron in again and put the new magnet on his toe. He changed the visit schedule to once a week, then once a month. There was no more deterioration.

The magnet seemed to solve Aaron's problem, but Dr. Staneck was not satisfied. When he tried to call the labs he sent samples to, one of the labs claimed that they never received the sample.

The electron microscope lab did not answer the telephone. The calls seemed to be transferred to another location, but after several calls over several days and then two weeks without any answer, Dr. Staneck finally gave up on that and continued to study any and all medical journals for past history of disappearing flesh.

DISINTEGRATION

Jacob Sczymzack unpacked the sample he had received from Dr. Joseph Staneck and mounted it on the viewing plate of the electron microscope. He turned on the scope then went to the lab's kitchenette to make coffee and wait for the scope circuits to warm up and stabilize. He drank a cup of coffee then went back to the lab. He activated the scope and proceeded to focus the image.

The focus controls did not work. Jacob changed the range and tried again to focus. There was still no changing the image. It just looked blurry. Jacob changed the range switch to another level, and there was still no ability to focus. The image was smoky. Smoke? Smoke! The smoke was coming from the electron microscope. Jacob hit the emergency off switch, but smoke continued to pour out of the internal circuits of the scope.

When it finally stopped, Jacob removed all the screws from the cover plates of the scope. He found the circuit board that was smoking and, with an ohmmeter, tried to diagnose the problem. This scope was the only source of Jacob's income, so he worked at trying to repair it until late at night. He finally recorded the identity number of that board and wrote up an order for a replacement board. He put the order into the outgoing mailbox then took another quick look at the circuit board. He noticed that all the smoke came from just two resistors and a capacitor. The circuit board itself was not burned at all.

In the morning, Jacob made coffee. While it was brewing, he looked at the circuit board again. This particular board was connected directly to the transducer that actually looked at the sample. The circuit board was smaller than it had been the night before. Jacob looked for the sample, but the scope was devoid of any sample. In fact, the glass and steel mount were mostly gone. There were no burn marks or scratch marks or anything. The area around the sample had simply disappeared. Jacob went back to the scope's maintenance manual and looked up part numbers of all the affected parts. He called the manufacturer and ordered replacement parts. Since the scope would not work, Jacob closed the lab and went to a ball game, then out for dinner, then home for the night.

The next morning he went to the lab to update his paperwork. He took a look at the scope, and the entire viewing area was gone! There were no scratch marks or tool marks on or near the edges of the remaining mounting parts. Jacob broke the smoky circuit board into two pieces and mailed them to two different testing laboratories for analysis. He wanted to know why that board failed and why it was getting smaller.

KILABREW

One of the labs that received part of that circuit board was the Kilabrew Testing Laboratory in Chicago. Marie, a young assistant at Kilabrew, unwrapped the board and read the cover letter that accompanied the sample. It only indicated that the board seemed to be disintegrating. Marie broke off a small piece and reduced it to powder. She tried several chemical tests on the sample. To her surprise, none of the tests were either positive or negative. It was as if the powder had not been touched at all. She tried two more tests and then asked Tony, the other assistant, to test the powder.

Tony had the same luck Marie had—none. They tried several more tests together and got the same results. Finally, they reported to their employer, the scientist who owned the testing laboratory.

Emil, an elderly chemist from Germany, said with a twinkle in his eye, "I don't know why I have two assistants who can't do simple tests."

Actually, he knew that both Tony and Marie were among the best in their field. They did 90 percent of the testing at Kilabrew, so Emil knew before he even looked at this sample that he had quite a challenge with it.

Emil tried all the standard tests on the material and was rewarded with the same results that Tony and Marie had—none. He began using chemicals and physical tests that were not standard. He tried to break off another small sample, but the remains of the circuit board were too small to use.

Emil went to the lab's kitchenette for coffee and discussed this new problem with Tony and Marie. When he returned to the workbench, the sample was even smaller than before.

By then he noticed that much time had gone by. It was already two hours past closing time, but Tony and Marie were still there with him. Emil asked Marie if there was any more of the sample available.

"Yes, I have more in the box it came in," she said as she picked up the box to hand to Emil. The remains seemed to be smaller than when she had broken off the small portion they had been testing.

None of the three testers had any desire to go home until the mystery was solved, but Tony complained, "I'm hungry enough to eat that circuit board and the box it came in."

Marie and Emil laughed as Marie picked up the phone to order pizza. Then the three of them sat down to discuss the facts they did know about the sample.

First of all, it was an electronic circuit board. Second, the board used standard electronic components, like the ones in millions of television sets, radios, computers, and other household gadgets. Thirdly, the board was part of an older model electron microscope. Fourth, the operator of the scope, Jacob Sczymzack, reported that the sample he had been trying to look at seemed to diminish in size. That was really all they knew. They discussed these facts until the pizza arrived, and then they tore into the food. They were all very hungry. Marie got root beers out of the refrigerator for herself and Tony and a beer for Emil.

After their meal, Emil asked the youngsters to clean up the office a bit. He had a strange feeling about this problem they were faced with. He wanted to be alone with it for a while. Emil proceeded to repeat every test they had done before. He subjected the sample to every chemical that should have a predictable reaction to the combination, but always there was no reaction. He broke off a piece of the board from the intact side and repeated several tests on that small sample. The reactions were quite normal. He again tried the same tests on the disintegrating side, and again there was no reaction.

Emil worked until midnight then remembered that Tony and Marie were still there. He opened the lab door and told the kids to go home to get some sleep. They both left then, and Emil kept working another hour with no positive results. He finally clipped another piece of the circuit board in a hands-free device that consisted of two clips mounted to a heavy base. He left the board there then went to the telephone to call his wife.

"*Gut abend zucker*. [Good evening, Candy.] I will be quite late getting home tonight," he said.

"You are already quite late. Did somebody give you a thousand samples to study?" Martha asked. Then she filled Emil in on the latest news at home. "Joey is home from Detroit. He got the job he wanted there, so now he and Liz have to pack up and move there by next Friday."

Emil said, "I sure hope he is happy there. He talked of nothing else but getting that job for about six months. No, I do not have a thousand samples to study. Just one, but it sure is a difficult one. Tony and Marie could not figure it out, and neither can I."

"Ah, but if I know you, you will be there until you do solve that great mystery. Won't you?" Martha asked.

"Yes, I will fight this bear until I get it into the frying pan," Emil answered.

"That's my Emil. I'll see you when you get home, *Schatz*," Martha said.

"Yes, I'll see you then, *S?sware*. Bye."

Emil didn't really call to tell her he would be late. He really called to hear her familiar voice. He needed to know he was not dreaming or had not lost his mind. He worked until 4:00 a.m., when he was just too tired to continue. Just before he turned off the lights, he noticed that the clip holding his sample of the circuit board was changing color.

In the morning when Tony and Marie arrived for work, they found the hands-free clip had completely disappeared. The bar that held the clip was shorter than before, by about one centimeter. The circuit board itself, or what was left of it, was lying on the laboratory bench. Where the edge of the circuit board contacted the bench, there was a small crater in the surface of the bench.

When Emil arrived at the laboratory in the morning, he still looked tired and sleepy. He had not slept well at all. Never had he seen anything so strange as the problem he now had in his lab. He looked at the circuit board, the hands-free device, and the workbench without touching any of them. He instructed Tony and Marie not to touch anything at all in the lab until he should tell them otherwise.

HANS

They stopped taking any more analysis jobs. Emil closed the lab. He called a friend of his in Germany, his old professor of physics. He described what he was seeing and all the tests he had performed on that circuit board. He told the old physicist that any tools that touched the circuit board were disintegrating before his eyes!

Silence, then laughter. "Emil, you always were a joker, but *ach du lieben* [oh, you lover], this is too much. You made a long-distance call just to play a trick on me!"

Emil had to laugh when he remembered some of the practical jokes he had tried on his old friend, but then he said, "This is no joke, no trick. If I buy you a plane ticket, will you come to Chicago and look at this?"

"Yes, I will fly to Chicago. If you are willing to pay the fare, you must have a real problem there."

"Yes, I do," said Emil. "But it is not just my problem. It is bigger than that."

"If it is so bad, then I will leave right now," said the old professor. He had never known Emil to get emotional about any of his discoveries, but he definitely heard a bit of waver in his friend's voice.

Hours later, Emil picked up Professor Gossel at the airport. Both men had gotten some sleep, Emil on a couch in his laboratory office and Hans Gossel on the airplane. On the ride to the lab, they discussed common friends and their whereabouts. They discussed their families, the economy, the weather, but not a word about the problem that lay before them.

When they arrived at the lab, they found the crater in the lab bench was now a hole about ten centimeters in diameter, and the small remains of the circuit board were on the floor under the bench.

The two scientists went to work immediately. The circuit board was reduced to powder then subjected to every physical and chemical test the men could think of. None of the tests had the expected results. Strong acids had no effect on the material. Strong alkali had no effect. All through the night, Emil and Hans worked. When they ran out of the circuit board remains, they conducted tests on the hole in the lab bench. At eight o'clock in the morning, they heard through the intercom, which always monitors the office, that Tony and Marie had arrived. Emil asked Marie to find something to eat and to make some strong coffee.

Marie went to the nearby fast-food restaurant and purchased breakfast meals for all four of them. Tony made the coffee. When Marie returned, work was stopped, and they all went to the little lounge area to eat and discuss their problem. Emil, Tony, and Marie always did this whenever they took a break from work. But today, every time one of the three brought up the subject of the disintegrating circuit board, Hans asked a question or stated a fact completely unrelated to their problem.

"Marie," he asked, "how did you become a laboratory technician?"

"I liked chemistry and got good grades in high school and college. I had other jobs after school, but none of them were very interesting. When I saw the help wanted advertisement for this position, I came here and took Emil's test. There were six other applicants, but I was chosen."

"How about you, Tony? Did you reply to the same advertisement?"

"No, sir. I attended the School of Mines at Golden, Colorado. I did well there. Emil called me and offered me the position."

"Do you both enjoy your work here?"

"Yes, we do," Tony and Marie replied in unison.

Emil said, "These two are the best assistants I have ever had. However, for the time being, I do not want either of you in the laboratory until I tell you otherwise. Please come to work each day, but stay in the office. Work on the files and clean up, but stay handy in case I need something, like food for the four of us. We have no secrets to keep from you. We do have a very strange thing going on, and until we know what it is, I don't want either of you near it. It may be dangerous!"

Marie said, "It's dangerous to you too, isn't it?"

"Yes, but you two are so young, and we are so old, like this old couch that squeaks and groans," Emil said as he and Hans got up to go back to work.

Later, Emil asked Hans why he hadn't wanted to discuss the problem with the two young assistants.

"Because I am beginning to think this is something different from anything ever seen on earth before. Something like a subatomic change brought about by some external force—or lack of it. Where did that decomposed circuit board come from?"

Emil said, "It came from an electron microscope in Binghamton, New York."

"We need more of this microscope so we can do more testing," Hans proclaimed.

Emil pushed the intercom button and asked Marie to call the microscope operator to ask for another sample.

"Yes, sir," Marie replied then immediately looked up the phone number of the Binghamton laboratory that had sent the circuit board. When she dialed the number, she heard the phone ring three times, but the third ring was aborted. Then there were two more rings. It sounded like the call was transferred to another location.

A sleepy-sounding man received the call. Marie asked if he was Jacob Sczymzack, the microscope operator.

"I used to be," he replied, "but not any longer. There is no microscope anymore. The darn thing just slowly disappeared, and it ate a hole in the floor where it was mounted. Any of the scope that is left is in the basement eating a hole through the foundation."

Marie asked if it was possible to get another part of the scope.

"If you want any of it, you better come and get it yourself. I ain't going near that building ever again! The door is open. I was so frightened I left in a big hurry when I saw that hole in the floor."

"Do you remember when all of this disintegration started?" Marie asked.

Jacob replied that the last sample the microscope was used for was a piece of a boy's toe. "It was sent to me by some doctor here in Binghamton. His name is on a letter that came with the toe sample. Maybe the letter has disintegrated too."

Marie confirmed that Jacob's lab was at 3410 Robinhood in Binghamton and then asked him if he were having any strange symptoms himself.

"I am fine," Jacob said. "I wore latex gloves the day I tried to examine the boy's toe. I took them off and threw them away as soon as I realized the scope was not operating. I tried and tried several adjustments on the instrument panel, but I never touched the toe sample."

Marie thanked him. Then she called Emil on the intercom and reported her findings.

Emil thanked her and complimented her thoroughness. Then he turned to Hans and said, "If we want another sample of that scope, I guess we have to go to Binghamton and get it ourselves."

It was then that Hans realized they did not have to go anywhere for a sample. All the tools used to examine the circuit board were disintegrating before their eyes. It was a slow process and could not be seen by watching. It took several hours to become evident, but surely every forceps, every cotton swab, even the glass slides of Emil's microscope were disintegrating. The two old scientists went back to work with renewed vigor. They began testing every bit of disintegrating equipment.

Tony and Marie went back to work in the office. They checked every file, cleaned out any unnecessary paperwork, and rearranged some of the files. They dusted and cleaned until both were becoming bored. Besides boredom, fear was growing in both youngsters. Fear of the unknown danger that prompted the two scientists to ban them from the laboratory. Seeking comfort from one another, they were soon together on the old couch in the lounge, the squeaky old couch that groaned and squeaked whenever anybody sat on it or got up from it.

Hans raised his head from the microscope he had been peering into and asked, "Was ist das? [What is that?]"

Emil, grinning from ear to ear, replied, "Das ist nicht, nur Tony und Marie. [That is nothing, just Tony and Marie.]"

"Ach, so! They are so young and so full of life. Emil, do you think those two could safely find the letter that accompanied the toe sample to Jacob's lab and bring it to us?"

"I think so," said Emil. "If they don't touch anything there."

When the squeaking of the couch stopped, Emil waited about twenty minutes, then he opened the lab door and called, "Tony and Marie!"

They both went to the lab, but Emil stopped them at the door and said, "I would like you two to go to Binghamton and retrieve that letter that arrived with the toe sample. I do not want you to touch anything there unless it is absolutely necessary. It will probably be in a file cabinet. Don't touch the cabinet. Use something like these pliers to open the drawers. Buy new pliers at a store before you get to that lab. Also, I want you both to buy new clothes and shoes to wear to the Binghamton lab then throw them into a trash Dumpster as soon as possible after you retrieve the letter. Drop the letter into a folded newspaper, then put it into a plastic cooler like you would use for beer. Also, wear rubber gloves so you do not touch anything in the lab. If that letter is still intact and you find it, I want it as soon as possible. Both of you drive, so one can sleep while the other drives. I know that all this seems melodramatic to you, but Hans and I just don't know what we have here. I love both of you, and I don't want you to get hurt by this strange…strange -I don't know what!?

"Remember to get all new clothes and tools then throw them all away as soon as possible. Get money from our petty cash fund. Also, take my credit card just in case you need it. Take my old Volkswagen, and be off with you, and be careful!"

WHY

Later, back at work in the lab, as they were examining and measuring all the tools that had been in contact with the now nonexistent circuit board, Hans paused and smiled at his old student and friend. "Did I hear you right, that you love those kids? That is a very unscientific display of emotion."

"I have worked for three years with those kids. I think it only natural to feel love for them."

"You know the names of every bone in their bodies. You know the approximate size of each organ in their bodies and even the volume of excretion from each organ. You know how their brains work and how their nerves carry messages. Are they not mere specimens?" Hans asked. "Are they not just tools?"

"Why, Hans, we have been friends for nearly fifty years," Emil replied. "You know all that about me. Am I a mere specimen? I have loved you and respected you. You have been my hero since I first began to study under you in Darmstadt. Have I loved a mere computer, a collector of facts with no emotion at all?"

Hans collapsed into a soft armchair that Emil called his thinking chair. "I had felt love once, for a girl named Marianne, when I was in school. I adored that girl, but she merely tolerated my presence. She went to dances and parties with the school's soccer heroes. I was merely a fly on the wall to her. Later, I did marry a girl I found interesting. She was a girl I could discuss science with. But after just two years, she said I drove her crazy. She ran off with a collector of garbage. I think he had no brain at all. Together they had three children and seemed happy. I joined the Nazi Party and became accepted there. The party got me a laboratory and allowed me to do experiments. I learned so much there. I am convinced there is no room for emotion in the life of a scientist. Only facts are important, only facts!"

"Oh, Hans, I am sorry you have missed so much of life," Emil commented. "I was married for fifty years to Krystal until she died of cancer. She was my constant companion and my laboratory technician. It was after she died that I went looking for help here and found Tony and Marie. At first I thought of them as merely employees, but they are such delightful youngsters. I can't help but love them. They are in my will, along with my three children."

There was silence for a few minutes while each man's thoughts wandered in different directions. Emil noticed a tear in the eye of Hans, just before Emil said, "Of course, if this whole laboratory disintegrates, there would be nothing left for any of the kids."

Hans replied, "I think that is reason enough for us to solve this great mystery. Let's get back to work."

"First, let's just discuss the facts we have," Emil said. "Why would anything just disintegrate? What is it that holds everything together? We can smash a cookie into dust then separate a particle of dust into its basic elements, of which there are 112 now known, but why do those elements exist as they are? Why is there just one electron in the hydrogen atom? What keeps that electron in orbit around the nucleus? Why does it not fly off on a tangent? Or crash into the nucleus? Of course, it is energy that propels the electron to orbit the nucleus and a different kind of energy to keep the electron from spinning off on a tangent. These two energies must balance one another. If I spin a top, it spins for a while. Then friction overrides the inertia, and the top falls over. If, as the evolutionists say, the universe is millions of years old, why does the earth not run out of inertia as it spins around the sun? Where is the energy coming from to sustain the action? We measured no heat from the disintegration of that circuit board or from our tools. If one gram of carbon is burned, it gives off eight thousand heat units. Each of these heat units can do forty-five-thousand-gram centimeters of work. The subatomic energy is even greater. But we measure no energy, no heat, no light, and no radiation. Nothing! *Vas ist unrecht?* [What is wrong?] Why is this disintegration passed on to anything that comes into contact with that board?"

"*Langsam*, Emil! [Slow down, Emil!] Einstein himself said that he misnamed $E = MC^2$ his theory of relativity. He later said he should have named it the invariance theory. He meant that the laws of physics do not vary. That which varies is the way we observe or compare an action or reaction. The Doppler effect can affect the way we see an object moving through space or even around the nucleus of an atom. Another experimenter may see it differently, but the law governing that action does not vary. The little formula could just as well been even shorter: $E = M$. Even light is mass! We just have to keep looking at this disappearing stuff in different ways until we see the energy or mass moving away.

"Einstein's theories have never been proven wrong -never! His theory of gravity still stands one hundred years later. But here we detect nothing, neither mass nor energy, as our samples and equipment disappear before our eyes. It is like looking into the galaxy M87, where there is intense activity at the core. We can't see it because it is a black hole, and light cannot escape. Do we have miniature black holes here? Einstein told me that matter is frozen energy. If that is true, why can we not detect the released energy? We see no light, no sign of electricity, no sign of radioactivity or anything.

"Who am I to refute Einstein 's theory? He made these great discoveries when he was in his twenties. That is the age I was when my greatest effort was in finding the most effective ways to torture people. I'm but a slimy worm compared to Albert Einstein. I have no right at all to question his theories. I am so ashamed! Sometimes I want to go to Tel Aviv and tell the world what a beast I am.

"Perhaps my past is keeping me from seeing what is there at the end of that disappearing forceps. Is there really a God, and is he punishing me by blinding my mind? Einstein was a good man and could see things as they are. Why can't I?"

"Hans, I can't see it either. Neither can Tony or Marie, and you know how those two are always talking to God."

Hans responded, "What is this God? I see no calf made of gold or any other idol. I see no saintly man in radiant robes or even just a bright light. But often I hear Marie talking to somebody that I can't see, like he is standing right next to her. Is this one of those relativity things that must be observed correctly to see and understand? Am I blind, or has Marie been so brainwashed at church all her life that she thinks she sees this god? I tell you, Emil, this thing has me so confused, I don't know which way is up. I thought I had suppressed my past, but my brain is like the food in a blender. The evil things I did are no longer hidden in some closet but instead are throughout my body. In contrast, I see the unabashed love between Tony and Marie, and that love seems to flow to others around them. It is not diminished but grows greater. Such turmoil inside me is like a black hole consuming a whole galaxy of stars.

"Einstein made his great discoveries in his early years. Later he got bogged down in trying to unify electricity and gravity. I can understand why he was trying to do that since gravity seems to be the same as magnetism and a wire passed through a magnetic field generates electricity. The point is that he never got it figured out. Was he like I am now, past my prime? Will I never again make any discoveries? Am I, how do you say, 'washed up'?"

"No, Hans, you are not washed up. If you are, then I am too. I cannot see that which is happening here either. I have been looking at these disappearing tools, instruments, and workbench for weeks, but I see nothing I can read about in any physics book.

This thing is something that has never happened before. We are pioneers in this phenomenon.

"You are not washed up, but perhaps you are observing this disappearing act through smoke-clouded glasses like a welder uses. I think that your worrying about your past may be clouding your vision. I have done rotten things too, things I would like to forget. Perhaps there is something to this God that Marie talks to. She once told me she is always happy because she knows her sins are forgiven. She doesn't have to worry about where she will be after her death. She accepted the fact that Jesus died to pay for her sins. You know, Hans, that is not a dream or conjecture. It is history written in the oldest book, the Bible."

"Ach, Emil, I have never read that. I have always thought it was just garbage dreamed up by some ruler to help him control the masses. I have heard some of the wild tales about dead people coming back to life and about men inside a furnace without being burned up. The scientist in me knows these things can't be true. How could they be? Such junk defies physics! No, Marie is happy because she is in love with Tony, and she is carefree because their copulation releases stress and tension."

"No, no, Hans! She was a happy, carefree girl before she ever met Tony. That is why he fell in love with her. That is why I love her. Tony has always been a happy, carefree person too. Neither one of them has any problem with a conflict between God and science. If you ask one or the other, they will tell you that science explains the way God does things. God explains science too! One day I was teasing them about that, and Marie ran out and got her Bible. She turned to First John, chapter four, verse eight. I remember the numbers because the sentence hit me like a hammer. It says 'The one who does not love, does not know God, for God is love.'"

"Emil! Emil! What has love got to do with science? Science is about things that really exist, things I can see and touch. Love is just emotion!"

"Hans, can you see heat? You can look at the results of the presence of heat, or the lack of it, but can you see the heat? You can see the results of love in a life or the lack of it, like that niece of yours you once told me about. But can you see love? Is it possible that love is another form of energy? Is love an energy that fills in all the blank spots in our understanding of science? Is love all encompassing, and does it explain, and indeed control, all the other forms of energy? Does this not make it easy to understand how a virgin can give birth or a dead man come back to life? Think about it!

"I even heard that Albert Einstein once advised a student to write a thesis on prayer. That was in his latter years when he was at Princeton. Did that great thinker, who understood the universe better than any other man, finally come to the conclusion that God created the whole thing and still controls it?"

"Ach, Emil, now you have wasted your money on my airline fare. How can I concentrate on solving this problem I came here to help you with when you have my head full of that other stuff? Yes, I must think about what you have said. Why didn't Einstein think of this much sooner? Why didn't I? Have I been so evil that your God doesn't even see me?"

"Hans! Hans! Forget your past. We all have a thing or two we would like to forget, something or other in our past that we fear will become known. We all live and learn."

"Yes! We live and learn. When did you first have this crazy thought that love is energy?"

"I first heard this from Krystal, my first wife. We talked of religion, science, and even politics often. She had an insight that was different from mine. She saw things that never even passed through my brain in an instant. You probably have fleeting thoughts too. Thoughts that come and go so quickly you don't even consider them at all. Krystal would freeze-frame the fleeting thoughts then analyze them from every angle. One night about three o'clock, she woke me up by shaking me. She insisted that I wake up and listen to her. We ended up discussing the merits of Harry Truman and Eisenhower for hours.

"It was after she was found to have cancer that she first suggested that God is love. She said it has been in the Bible for hundreds of years, but she never heard any preachers give a sermon on those three little words. To Krystal, those words made the whole Bible clear and simple and true. They explain everything! She once told me, 'Oh, Emil, you don't have to believe in God. He just is, and your thoughts can't change that at all. The way you see the Bible is different from the way I see it, but our views cannot change one bit what is written there. God is as real as this coffee cup and this kitchen table, and neither of us can change that and—'"

"Wait a minute, Emil! What was that she said about different views of the Bible? Did she say it stays the same, no matter how we look at it?"

"Yes, Hans. Nobody can change that which is by thoughts or opinions. God is, was, and always will be, no matter how we choose to view him or his word."

"Hmm."

"Hmm what?"

"I'm not sure. I must think about this a bit. Why do preachers not preach about the three little words 'God is love'? Is it not the heart of religion? Is only the carrot and stick important? This is not my field of endeavor or yours. Perhaps we need to talk with Tony and Marie about this."

"Yes, I agree, but you seem to have something in mind."

"Yes, yes, but I am not ready to discuss it yet. Perhaps I am forming a theory, but I must consider it thoroughly. I must understand it fully before I discuss it with you. However, I would like to discuss my question about preachers not preaching those three little words."

"Hans, how do you know what they preach? If you don't believe in God and don't go to church, how can you know?"

"You just told me that Krystal said that. Ever since Dachau, I have been deeply troubled. I have tried many religions, even Judaism and some Asian religions, but never have I heard anyone discuss in detail 'God is love.' Also, I have never found solace for my troubled mind. The religions all seem to be just sugar-coating. Is it because nobody really believes in love? Is it because they really don't believe in God? The things I learn about science I don't believe in—I know! I can touch and see and measure. How does one measure love? How can we see God? How many preachers really know God? How many are preachers because it seems to be an easy way to make a living or a way to wield power? Have I ever met a preacher who has no doubt at all? Have you?"

Hans continued, "The Christians make such a big deal out of the sentence in their Bible that says God made this universe in only six days, even though they can dig up dinosaurs that have been turned to rock for millions of years. Verse eight in the third chapter of second Peter says as plain as day, 'That with the Lord one day is as a thousand years, and a thousand years as one day.' Were those six of our days or six of God's days? On the other side of the controversy, has science proven which ape we evolved from? How can I, having studied science all my life, prove something that happened millions or even just thousands of years ago? Why bother? The Bible explains our origins very plainly. Everything else that book says makes sense, so why question it?

"Scientists study how God's universe works. They do not study to disprove the Bible. It is not a book of religion but a record of man's life. It gives instructions about how we should be living here so we can be in harmony with God, the creator of it all. At the same time, we the people ignore the Bible's advice to love your brother and to forgive seventy times seven. God rested on the seventh day? God has been forever, and six of our days would be like six-hundredths of a microsecond. Why would he need rest already? I think your Christians do themselves no favor by concentrating on that 168-hour period and seem to forget that God meant for us to rest one day of the week. That is what works. Just try working day after day, with no day of rest. Very soon you will be making so many mistakes your work will be useless.

"Your God is a practical being. He does not violate his own laws of physics, even when he does something we think is a miracle.

"Is love so equated with sex that preachers fear to discuss it? And what is wrong with sex anyway? You Americans are really weird about that subject! You use women's breasts to sell anything from soap to cars, but breast-feeding an infant is done in secret places like it is a crime. Sex is in every television commercial, but does anyone ever tell a young man or woman how to do it? Sex is not all instinct. It is an art that provides joy and pleasure to a marriage and a lifelong commitment, and it must be learned. Is it more fulfilling to eat hamburger or gourmet cooking? Ach, you Americans have allowed the Puritans to take the joy from your lives. However, casual sex without any commitment is empty and void of feeling and soon forgotten. It is throwing gourmet food to the swine!"

"Hans, don't lecture me on that subject. I am much too old for it to do me any good. Perhaps I should have sent you along with the kids to give you a rest from this research. I thought you said you never read the Bible! Help me to set up this spectrometer. That forceps is our specimen now. It is disintegrating like everything else around here, so don't let it touch the scope."

On through the day and late into the night, the two scientists worked with no rest and little to eat.

THE ADVENTURE

On through the day and late into the night, Tony and Marie drove to Binghamton.

"Tony, why did we make love today?" Marie asked. "We have worked together and gone to restaurants, movies, ball games, and stuff together, but never did you touch me like that before. And why did I respond so quickly?"

"I don't know, Marie," Tony answered. "Maybe we finally realized we love each other. Or maybe because we are both scared silly of whatever is going on in the lab. I have never seen Emil act like this before. He is always so careful with every penny he spends. But today he gave us his credit card and all the petty cash. We're to buy new clothes just to wear for a few minutes or an hour."

"I think you're right, Tony. I have never been so afraid in all my life. But, Tony, our loving was the greatest thing that ever happened to me."

"Me too, Marie. It made me feel so whole, so complete. I hope that whatever is loose in the lab allows us to live to enjoy that again and again for many years—you and I together."

Marie moved closer to Tony and laid her hand on his leg. They drove on in silence until they got close to the Binghamton exit, and Tony suggested they stop for gas.

"Once we have that letter, I want to be on the way home as soon as possible."

"Yes," agreed Marie. "I have to use the restroom anyway."

At the convenience store they bought a street map of Binghamton then proceeded into town to find the electron microscope lab. They passed a thrift store that looked like it would sell secondhand clothes, and Marie suggested they return there to buy their temporary clothes. "It will be a lot cheaper," she said.

Daylight was just barely beginning, so Marie could not see the big grin on Tony's face. She was really surprised when Tony pulled over to the curb, parked the car, then took her in his arms and kissed her.

"Wow! What was that for?" Marie gasped.

"I just love you," Tony replied. He was thinking that if Marie was so careful with Emil's money, she will be careful with theirs too. What a wife she will be! Tony was one happy lab assistant. He was on an adventure with his girlfriend in a strange city, and a new day was just starting. Tony's heart felt like it was going to burst from being so filled with love. What a beautiful day this promised to be!

Marie was just a little bewildered by Tony's sudden show of affection. Along with love, that kiss conveyed the promise of warmth and a secure future that they would share. She could not figure out why a thrift shop should evoke such emotion. She too, however, felt the excitement of their adventure and the dawning day.

After their impromptu embrace, they wrote the names of the cross streets where they found the thrift store then continued on to find 3410 Robinhood. They located the lab just two blocks from the thrift shop. They drove around the back of the building to locate a Dumpster. They found it in the alley almost directly behind the lab building. The lab itself was a red-brick building partially covered with ivy. The windows and back doors, one a walk-in door and the other a garage door, made the building look more like a house than a business.

Tony noticed that the walk-in door was slightly ajar. He hoped that the high hedge between the lab and the alley kept thieves from noticing the open door.

Tony and Marie went back to the thrift store to await its opening. Marie got out and walked to the door to find the opening time. She learned that they had to wait only about a half hour. During that time, they planned how they would go about looking for the letter. Marie suggested that only one of them go in to limit exposure to whatever was in there. Tony thought they both should go because the technician had said there was a huge hole in the floor. They might have to help each other get around that hole. Marie wrote a list of what they had to buy. Emil had said, "Buy all new clothes, even underwear."

"Also," Tony said, "write down burglar tools." These he wanted in case they had to break into the file cabinet. While she was writing that down, Tony noticed a policeman glance at them as he drove by in his patrol car.

When the store opened, they went in and bought blue jeans, shirts, shoes, and socks but could not find underwear. They would have to find another store for that. On a table in the rear of the store, Tony found two screwdrivers, a crowbar, a hammer, and two pairs of pliers. Marie found rubber gloves, a plastic picnic box, and a road atlas.

While checking out, Tony remarked, "Binghamton seems to be a modern city and is waking up early with lots of cars on the street already."

The clerk said, "It is a modern city with industry and business. I have been reading a history of the area, and the original people here were the Seneca Indians. They were known for the Seneca trot."

Marie laughed and asked, "What kind of dance is that?"

"It was not a dance," the clerk said. "It was a way to run that was steady, and the Indians could cover a great distance with little fatigue. They were the ones that ran all the way around the land mass that became Pennsylvania, when the king of England settled a debt to William Penn's father."

Two minutes after Tony and Marie paid for their purchases and left the store, a young police officer approached the clerk and asked what the two customers had bought.

"Clothes that won't fit them and a set of burglary tools, I think," replied the clerk.

"Thanks," said the officer. He left to see if he could find his two suspects again.

Tony and Marie drove around the town until they found a store where they bought underwear and a newspaper. Then they proceeded to the car. That was where the young officer spotted them and resumed following them. It appeared that they were taking evasive action because Marie made several turns that didn't make sense. Actually, they were trying to find their way back to the abandoned laboratory. Tony was reading the map and finally got them on the correct path. They drove into the alley behind the lab then into the parking area, which was mostly enclosed by an ivy-covered chain-link fence. The officer didn't see them turn into the alley.

Sheltered by the ivy, Tony and Marie stripped off their clothes. Marie was really enjoying this adventure even though she was aware of the gravity of the search. She decided to tease Tony by slowly removing each piece of clothing.

Tony, however, was quite apprehensive and in no mood for play. He did not like the looks of that police officer. He had spotted the black-and-white squad car again while they were trying to get reoriented after the stop to buy new underwear. He really hurt Marie's feelings when he said, "C'mon, hurry up. We have to find that letter and get out of here."

Marie did hurry to undress then to dress in her temporary clothes. But Tony noticed there were tears in her eyes as she worked.

"What's wrong?" Tony asked. "Why are you crying?" He couldn't figure out why changing clothes should make a girl cry. Tony and Marie were on two different tracks by then. Marie could think only of her love for Tony, and he could think only of fear and the knot in his stomach. They had done nothing illegal, but he just had a bad feeling.

Marie replied, "Oh, just forget it. Let's just get the damned letter."

Dressed in their ill-fitting clothes, Marie was upset and confused, and Tony was fearful and confused. They entered the abandoned laboratory and passed through a small hallway with restrooms on the right and a small lounge on the left. Next was a big room with a chart on one wall, and on the opposite wall was a workbench with some instruments, glass beakers, test tubes, Bunsen burners, and some papers on it. The bench extended from wall to wall on that side of the room. The ceiling had two big skylights and plenty of fluorescent lights. The floor, however, was mostly gone. A gaping hole in the center left the workbench intact on the west wall and about three feet of floor around the other three walls.

Tony and Marie looked down and saw the remains of the electron microscope. It looked like a big blob of metal with a few instruments and knobs, but even those were distorted.

Hugging the east wall, the two adventurers made their way through that room and into the office area. They began searching immediately for the precious letter. For hours they searched the offices. First they checked all the desktops then began the laborious task of going through the file cabinets. They had to look in every folder since they had no name or subject to reference. It was not a lackadaisical search. They had to find a letter or bill of lading or something that would show where the microscope's last sample came from. All they had to go on was the approximate date. Working with rubber gloves and pliers made the job harder.

TERRORISTS

Meanwhile, a young police officer kept his eyes open for a blue Volkswagen with Illinois plates. After a couple hours, he returned to the area where he last saw the VW. He searched every street and alley but missed seeing the little car.

Later, on a hunch, he checked the alley behind the lab again, but in the other direction. He finally spotted the blue Volkswagen. He parked the cruiser down the alley and walked back to the lab.

He noticed the back door was open. He could hear Tony and Marie talking and noises that sounded like papers being moved about. He did not enter the building but instead crept to the front where he could look through a partially open blind. It looked as though his suspects were rifling the files. He called for backup then went back around to his patrol car and kept an eye on the rear exit.

It was really hard to work on the files with rubber gloves on, opening and closing the drawers with pliers. Marie was nearly through the "K-L" drawer and Tony was working on the "T-U" drawer when the front door opened with a terrible crash. Screaming terrorists charged in both the front and rear doors. The two in the rear saw Marie holding a file and screamed something unintelligible at her. Charging forward, they fell into the big hole in the floor.

The second man in the front door saw the pliers in Tony's hand. He had been trained to respond, not to think. He did not see pliers but thought he saw a gun. He fired one shot into Tony's chest and a second one into his arm. Tony was able to scream, "Run, Marie, run! Call Emil!"

Marie ran in the only direction in which there were no screaming terrorists in her way. She ran into the back room. For some reason she could never explain, she ran to the laboratory bench and jumped up onto it to avoid the big crater in the middle of the floor. Two of their assailants lay at the bottom, injured and confused. Halfway across the bench, she saw a piece of paper and an envelope. Without stopping, she picked them up and kept running to the end of the bench. She jumped down and carefully made her way along the north wall to the corridor then through the back door to the outside.

She removed her rubber gloves and opened the Volkswagen door to retrieve her cell phone. While running down the alley, she dialed the number of the Kilabrew Testing Laboratory in Chicago. While the connection was being made, she glanced at the paper she had picked up. It appeared to be the object of her search! It described a sample of a boy's toe that was to be examined by the electron microscope. The phone in Chicago rang many times before a tired-sounding Emil finally picked it up.

"Emil, it's Marie! Tony has been shot! I think I have the letter! I escaped from some terrorists, but I have to find a place to hide!" *Huh, huh, huh.* "I can't get the car out! There is a police car blocking the way." *Huh, huh.* "Maybe I can hide among these piles of concrete blocks." *Huh, huh.*

"What did you say about Tony?" a now alert Emil asked her.

"Tony has been shot! We were in the lab searching for the letter when these beasts smashed in the front door, screaming something at us. They shot Tony! Two of them came in the back door, but they fell into the basement, so I was able to escape. I found the letter you want on the lab bench. I picked it up on my way out."

"*Ach du lieben*, Marie. Those beasts, as you call them, are probably policemen. Are you hiding now? Wait just a minute while I tell Hans what has happened."

Emil quickly explained the situation to Hans. Hans did not get excited or turn pale as Emil had. He picked up another phone on another line and placed a call to Darmstadt, Germany. Then a call was made from Darmstadt to Bonn. The next call in the series was from Bonn to Washington, DC—to the White House! From there a call was made to the Federal Bureau of Investigation and on to the field office in Binghamton, New York.

Each of these calls required several minutes because each caller had to convince the receiver of the gravity of the situation. There was much time used by the German government convincing the president of the United States that this was not just a local problem. It was a worldwide threat to our existence.

Emil continued to talk to Marie and calm her down. She finally was able to read the letter to Emil. He wrote down the name of the doctor who had written the letter and his phone number and address. This was done in case the police confiscated the letter when they caught Marie.

After she was calmed down somewhat, Emil told Marie to walk back to the lab and give herself up. Marie refused to do that. "Emil, those men are beasts! They shoot first then ask questions. I am afraid they will shoot me too!" She said this as she was looking out through holes in the piles of concrete blocks, and she could see several black cars passing by.

Marie had found the concrete yard only a block away from the laboratory and could hear shouting coming from the lab. Then there was silence. After a while, her curiosity got the best of her, and she crept out from her hiding place and went out to the alley. She saw the black cars, along with the police car, that were blocking the lab's driveway. She also saw an ambulance with its back door open. She ventured closer and saw an injured SWAT team member, a young girl, being loaded into the ambulance.

The other SWAT team members were getting out of their body armor and other hardware, and they looked a lot less threatening. In fact, they appeared to be very docile and embarrassed. Marie hid the letter in her bodice, even though Emil already had all the information he needed, and slowly made her way back to the lab. She approached a man in a suit and tie and told him who she was.

To her surprise, he treated her with great respect. Marie asked about Tony, and the FBI man said that he was on the way to the hospital. He was still alive. The agent then asked Marie what all this was about, but Marie never heard him. She fainted and fell at his feet.

Marie quickly recovered but realized that she had to protect all the people there. They were going in and out of the lab. Marie told the FBI agent to get everyone out of the lab, and to board it up—to treat the building like a hazardous waste site.

"Is it really all that dangerous?" the man asked.

"It is far worse than that, I think. Far worse!" Marie replied. Again the FBI man surprised her by not questioning her opinion. He immediately ordered everyone out of the building.

Marie began to enjoy the feeling of power. "Sir, all of those people who have been in the building should be quarantined until more is known about this strange phenomenon. That's why Tony and I are wearing these poorly fitting clothes and rubber gloves. We were supposed to change back into our own clothes and throw these away, after we found the address we were looking for. Our regular clothes are in that Volkswagen. May I get them out of there?"

"Yes, of course. You can change clothes in your car. I'll keep everyone away. If you bag up the ones you have on, I'll have our hazardous waste people dispose of them. We can get Tony's at the hospital too. I'll take you to him as soon as I get things in order here."

Actually, only the two officers who fell into the basement through the big hole were in danger. Those two were in grave danger until Emil and Hans or other scientists could figure out what was happening.

Tony went into surgery immediately upon reaching the hospital. The bullet was removed from his chest and the damage repaired, then his arm wound was stitched up. The surgeon remarked that this ruffian was young and tough and would recover quickly enough to stand trial. He changed his opinion of Tony when he saw the FBI people treating him with great respect after he woke up in recovery. The doctor was even more surprised when informed that he and everyone who had had contact with Tony and his clothes were now under quarantine!

MAGNETISM

As soon as Emil knew that Marie was safe with the FBI, he ended their phone call and placed a call to the doctor who had sent the toe sample to the electron microscope lab.

"Dr. Staneck, I am Emil Finkenbinder. I operate a small testing laboratory in Chicago. We received a sample of a circuit board from an electron microscope. That scope has been disappearing without any sign of heat or light or any debris at all. It had been exposed to a sample you sent to the laboratory. Can you tell me where that sample came from?"

Dr. Staneck said, "Yes, sir, I think I can. That had to have been the sample from Aaron Fisher 's disappearing toe. He is a nine-year-old boy who kicked a rock in a forest south of here. His toe has been slowly getting shorter and shorter. It is now just a stub, about half the size of his other big toe.

"I ordered an MRI, but it failed to show any part of his toes or even much of his foot. I then ordered another MRI, and it showed the same thing. There was just a white spot where his toes and part of his foot should have been. I did notice that the toe stopped getting smaller after each MRI, so I put a magnet on his stub of toe. That stopped the disintegration of his foot.

"That changed Aaron's life a bit because he always went barefoot before. Now he has to wear shoes to keep the magnet in place. Other than that, he is the same little boy he always was, full of fun and mischief.

"I suppose that magnet saved his foot and maybe his life, but I still wanted to know what is happening to his toe. I sent samples to two different laboratories for analysis, but I have never heard from either one."

"Dr. Staneck, are you still seeing the boy? Can you get in touch with his parents at any time?" Emil asked.

"Yes, I do follow-up checks often, and I can call the boy's mother anytime. She is a housewife and at home most of the time," the doctor said.

"Doctor," Emil said, "that small sample you sent to the lab in Binghamton completely destroyed a very expensive electron microscope and even the building that housed it. The sample of the circuit board from that scope completely disappeared. Every tool and measuring device that touched it are also disappearing. My friend Hans and I have nearly one hundred years between us of studying all kinds of science. Never have either of us seen anything like this! We are completely bewildered by this strange thing. We want to keep in touch with you and perhaps even meet this little boy and talk to him too. Thank you for the information."

Dr. Staneck had one more bit of information to pass along. "I had looked at that sample on my microscope before I packed it up and sent it to the electron microscope lab. My microscope is fine. It was not affected at all."

Now Emil was even more confused as he hung up the phone and turned to Hans. His friend was still on the other phone making calls to Germany, Switzerland, Israel, and several universities in the United States.

Emil and Hans looked at each other and, without a word being spoken, considered with awe the enormity of that which they had just set in motion. What was this strange new anomaly that made such a huge step necessary?

Finally, Emil laughed and said, "We will be the laughingstock of the world scientific community if this turns out to be something simple that we both overlooked!"

Hans smiled and said, "I wish that it were so, but I am afraid it is not. Frankly, I am frightened of this thing!"

Emil said, "I just spoke with Dr. Joseph Staneck, who sent a sample of a boy's toe to that electron microscope. He said the toe was disappearing from thc tip all the way back to the first joint. He said he stopped it by putting a magnet around it. But he also said his microscope was not affected at all."

"Ach, Emil," said Hans. "That sounds like voodoo science to me. But at one time, the earth being round sounded like voodoo to the great thinkers of the world. Let's get to work on this new bit of information."

The two scientists went back to work with renewed fervor and a new direction for their research. Tony had a big radio in the office that usually drove Hans crazy playing country Western music. Hans remembered there were big speakers attached to the boom box, as Tony called it. Each speaker had a powerful magnet. Both speakers were sacrificed to yield the magnets for research.

Emil winced when he tore apart Tony's speakers.

"I guess I owe Tony big time for this," he said.

"I wish Marie were here," Hans said. "I have to arrange hotel rooms and meals and meeting space for scientists from all over the world."

"She will be back here, as soon as Tony is released from the hospital," Emil said. "She insisted upon staying with him."

Hans sank into a soft chair and asked, "How can their love bloom so brightly amid their terrible experience and this strange, strange thing that neither of us can understand or know the extent of?"

"Love will always prevail," replied Emil. "After all, it was love that created this whole universe."

"This is the one thing that has always come between you and me," Hans stated. "Love is merely an emotion. An arrangement of brain cells brought about by sexual passion, an emotion that causes turmoil, confusion, and even war among nations. But love creates nothing, except maybe children. The universe was created by a balance of forces and a coincidence of events and arrangement of mass."

"But what are the forces?" asked Emil. "Were the forces not amplified or multiplied whenever two units of mass were brought into close proximity, just as the magnetic field in a coil of wire is magnified many times over that of a straight piece of wire? Was it merely a big coincidence that the first two units of mass met in the infinity of space? I find it much easier to understand all phases of science when I acknowledge the fact that the rules were all written by God, which is the love that created us. Is evolution the way he did it? I don't know. I wasn't there then. We are among the most enlightened people on earth, but as long as our scientific power is used to find new ways to kill more people, we have not advanced beyond the Neanderthal man. We have learned nothing useful to promote harmony among all people of all nations. How can our little minds hope to comprehend anything as big as the origin of the universe or of man? I think we had better just accept the time line presented in the Bible and not worry about the way God created us. When he wants us to know, then we will know."

"Ach, I don't understand you, Emil," Hans retorted. "But I do understand that we have only a week to work with this new bit of information about magnetism before the rest of the world descends upon us. Let's get to work. We can measure the length of that forceps now. We know it has been getting shorter all the time. We will have to get several new measuring tools, calipers, and rulers since everything that contacts a shrinking tool or device also shrinks and disappears. Oh, where is Marie? She could be going to the supplier for us!"

Emil simply called the supplier and asked that his purchases be delivered. It was then that he realized his bank account was also shrinking, like everything else they were working on. He had closed the lab. It produced no more income, and he didn't know how much money Tony and Marie were spending. He told Hans about his lack of funds, and the old scientist simply made another call to Germany. He asked Emil for his bank account number. Two days later, Emil's bank called and informed Emil he could not keep so much money in one checking account.

Emil didn't know where the money had come from, but he knew he did not have a finance problem anymore. Actually, donations were arriving from organizations all over the world! Emil was awestruck by the power Hans had at his command! Emil told the banker to open any accounts necessary but to make sure that he had unlimited access to funds with no delay.

"When Marie comes back, she will come to your office to do any necessary paperwork," Emil said. "Marie will have power of attorney." His voice was so imperative that the banker did not question Emil at all.

Hans, meanwhile, mounted an already-diminished forceps in a vice and measured its length. Then he simply stuck one of the speaker magnets to the protruding end of the tool. It would be measured again in several one-hour intervals. Then Hans and Emil commenced to read everything they could find in their science journals about magnetism and how it aligns atoms and molecules. They both knew, of course, that only the valance electrons, those in the outer ring of the atom, were active in electricity. These electrons, when moving through the space between the electron gun of a cathode ray tube and the face of the tube, could be deflected by magnetic energy.

They knew that electrons moving through a copper wire did not alter the wire's composition. It was still copper. They knew that electrons could be forced onto the plate of a capacitor to give it a negative charge, and electrons could be pulled from the opposing plate to give it a positive charge. The molecules of the electrolyte between the plates could be warped by the charge but not chemically altered. They had to remind themselves that they were studying an abnormal change, not a familiar one. Hans also noted that this aberration was first observed in an organism: the boy's toe. So what should they be looking for? Is it physics? Is it chemistry? Is it biochemistry? Both of the scientists were convinced that this problem was not anything anyone had ever seen before. Emil suggested they measure the forceps just to give their brains a rest. The forceps was the same length it was when the magnet was placed on it.

Now both men were bewildered! Hans said, "Scientists all over the world are concerned about global warming brought about by our pollution and removal of forests. We know for a fact that this is happening, but is there another form of destruction of the earth going on? The earth is a huge magnet. Is every motor or relay, or anything else that becomes an electromagnet, adding to or detracting from this great magnetic field we live in? Is every power-generating plant in the world decreasing the strength of gravity or adding to it? Will the damage at some point be enough to change, or even destroy, the delicate balance between centrifugal force and the magnetic attraction between earth and the sun? Could it pull the earth closer to the sun? Has this already happened? Is this the real cause of global warming? Perhaps random alignment of the power generators will prevent such a thing. Could this be what is affecting that boy's toe?

"Until about one hundred fifty years ago, nothing went around and around fast, except maybe oxen turning a big round rock to grind grain. Now there are billions of motors and engines with rotating parts. Could this affect the centrifugal force that keeps the world or even the universe in balance? There are still so many mysteries!"

Then switching to more practical matters, Hans said, "Ach, my mind jumps around so. How did Dr. Staneck know that magnetism would stop the deterioration of that boy's toe?" Hans wondered, *Is it possibly the Staneck I knew fifty years ago?*

Emil noticed the deep frown but said nothing.

RECUPERATION

Meanwhile back in Binghamton, the surgery department of the hospital had become a place of joy and laughter. A young gunshot victim from Chicago turned the department upside down. Even before Tony was fully over the anesthesia, he had the nurses believing he was a rough, tough grandson of Al Capone. The FBI men, the chief of Binghamton police, and a very meek and frightened young officer watching over him made the picture complete.

For Tony, all that remained of the raid at the microscope lab was some pain. Once he thought of his gangster role, he played it to the hilt. He snapped his fingers and demanded Cuban cigars. After a while, he began calling Marie his "gun moll." Marie was laughing so hard she had tears in her eyes.

Finally, Tony began to wonder why none of the officials in the room questioned him or Marie about their mission. They all seemed to enjoy his joking and readily moved out of the room whenever his nurse wanted to do something like check his dressings.

Pulling Marie close, he asked, "Are these guys waiting to take us to jail? They haven't even asked us any questions. I am not even shackled to the bed. What is going on?"

"Tony, I'm not sure myself," Marie said. "I guess we just have to ask them. I only know that I called Emil, and when they finally found out what we were doing, they were very nice to me. They even apologized for terrorizing us. I think that young officer is the one who shot you. He seems really scared. Emil must have told them about our mission, but no one is saying anything yet." Then she asked, "Tony, how do you really feel now? Do you hurt much? Do you feel sick at all? Oh, Tony, you will never know how scared I was for you. I know this thing at the lab is really important and dangerous and all, but I don't care about that. I just know that I love you, Tony, and somehow Emil will solve that problem, and you and I will get married and have kids and—"

"Whoa, girl! *Wow!* I sure do love you too, but I hadn't thought that far ahead yet!"

"Well, I guess I'll have the doctor put a ring in your nose so I can lead you to the altar!"

Tony just looked into Marie's eyes then finally whispered, "I guess I have to talk to Emil about a raise. Cribs and diapers and stuff cost money!"

"Oh, Tony, I love—" The *you* was not spoken because Tony's good arm pulled Marie to him, and he covered her mouth with his.

The officers heard all this even though Tony tried to whisper quietly. One of the FBI men who seemed to be senior in command smiled and said, "I guess it is time for some explaining. I'm the agent in charge of the local FBI office. I got a call from my superior in Washington, who got a call from the president himself telling us to treat you folks with great respect. We know you are not criminals and, in fact, were on a dangerous mission involving public safety or something. Can you give us any information about that?"

"Wow! Marie, did you hear that?" Tony asked. "I thought Emil was working on something big, but I didn't know it was that big. When you and I could find nothing we understood on that circuit board, I thought it was just because we didn't know enough. If Emil told the president about it, it must really be something!

"No, sir, we can't tell you anything about that yet because we don't know. We only know that our boss took over what we thought was just another job that Marie and I didn't understand. Then a couple days later, some old guy from Germany showed up, and he and Emil would not let us in the lab anymore, except to deliver food and tools and stuff."

The agent said, "That old guy from Germany must be a well-known scientist. He is the one that rescued you kids from us terrorists. He called the German government, and they called our president."

"Wow, this is getting really scary," said Tony. "What is going on?"

There was silence for a minute or so, then the young officer stepped up to Tony's bed. He said, "Sir, I am the officer that shot you, and I would like to apologize."

Tony hesitated for a second then slipped back into his gangster act. "Young man, do you have a will made out? My boys in Chicago, the new ones from Sicily, will hunt you down like a dog and grind you into the dirt! Your days are numbered!"

Then Tony laughed, and the young officer grinned. He and Tony shook hands, awkwardly, because Tony had to use his left hand. Tony said, "I guess we were both just doing our duty."

Just then the bedside phone rang, and Marie answered it. The caller was Emil. He asked how Tony was, but Marie could tell that Emil had more on his mind than just Tony's welfare. She told him that Tony was just fine.

"Do you know when he can come home?" Emil asked.

"Not yet," Marie replied, "but he is in great spirits and not much pain. He just woke up about an hour ago." She turned around and pressed Tony's call button. A nurse responded immediately, and Marie asked her for Tony's doctor. To Marie's surprise, the doctor responded immediately also.

Marie asked, "Doctor, how soon can we expect Tony to be well enough to go home?"

"Well, that depends on Tony, I think. The bullet just missed his lung. If he doesn't do anything strenuous, I could release him tomorrow morning. Let me have a look-see here," he said as he turned to Tony and applied his stethoscope.

Listening to several places on Tony's chest and pushing and prodding until Tony yelped once, the doctor exclaimed, "Holy cow! I'll never get over how tough these young men are. Do you intend to drive back to Chicago as soon as I release you, Tony?"

Emil, who was listening through the phone, spoke to Marie, "Tell him *no*! Is there a helicopter pad at that hospital?"

Marie relayed that question to the doctor, who nodded his head as he was checking Tony's dressing.

"Yes," Marie answered Emil.

"Then leave the Volkswagen there. Tomorrow morning there will be a helicopter there to bring you and Tony back here. Hans and I need you two."

Marie said, "Okay, Emil. We will see you tomorrow."

Marie finally answered the doctor's question of Tony. "No, we will not be driving back. We will be picked up here by a helicopter tomorrow morning."

This was too much for the young officer. He looked from Marie to Tony and back to Marie and asked, "Who are you people? What is going on? Do you work for the president?"

Marie replied, "We are no one special. We are just Tony and Marie. We work in a testing lab in Chicago. I don't think our boss even knows what is going on for sure, and we are just his assistants."

"We are just Emil's assistants," Tony filled in. "He is the scientist. We thought we knew our boss pretty well, but we didn't know he has so many connections to governments. Emil and Hans, a scientist from Germany, are working on something really strange that apparently started here in Binghamton. They would not let us in the lab after Hans showed up. Emil sent us here to get information from that lab where you found us. He told us to buy all new clothes and shoes and rubber gloves and tools. Then after we had the information, we were supposed to throw away the new stuff."

To Marie, Tony lamented, "I guess we failed our mission here. But now that the police know who are, we can go back to the lab and search some more."

"There is no need to, Tony," Marie answered brightly. "We didn't fail! I found the letter that Emil wanted. I read the letter to him over the phone while I was hiding in the brick yard, or whatever that place was."

"Oh, good for you, Marie," Tony cheered. "Hot dog! I guess we still have our jobs. Where did you find it?"

"When you were shot and told me to run, I was so scared I ran without thinking and jumped up onto that lab bench beside that big hole in the floor. As I ran to the other end, I scooped up a piece of paper that looked like a letter. Just by dumb luck, it was the one we were looking for."

The police detective saw the look of love and admiration on Tony's face. Looking at the folks with him—the FBI man, the young officer who had shot Tony, and a newspaper reporter—he suggested they all leave and give Tony and Marie some private time. The reporter, who had been constantly writing in a small notepad, asked Marie for the name and phone number of the lab in Chicago.

Marie started to answer her, but then a picture of a furious Emil tearing the phone wires from the wall came into her head. She said, "I think phone calls with a lot of questions would really disturb my boss, but I promise that I will call you as soon as Emil and Hans say we can release the story. I'll call you only, and the story will be yours to break."

The reporter gave Marie her card and then left the hospital room hastily to catch up with the departed police and FBI people. If she couldn't get the really big story, at least she wanted to write something about the break-in to the laboratory! She could hardly conceal the excitement she felt about Marie's promise. She had a feeling this was to be a really big scoop! And she trusted Marie.

After the reporter left, Marie and the nurse helped Tony to the bathroom and back. Then he said he was tired and needed to rest awhile. The nurse checked the dressings and IV line then left Tony and Marie alone.

Marie sat with Tony and held his hand until he was asleep. And so they stayed for two hours until it was time to check dressings, IV line, and instruments again. Marie never left Tony's side from the time they arrived in the hospital, except when he was in the operating room.

Tony's brain wasn't totally at rest though. He dreamed of an ivy-covered cottage in a wooded area with a small steam running through. There was Marie, quite pregnant, putting cherry pies in the kitchen window to cool. There were about thirty children between the ages of one year and ten years. Suddenly, the children were screaming and fleeing from a monster. Tony could not see the monster, but two old men were chasing it with microscopes, which they carried as clubs. One by one the children simply disappeared until there were no children left.

Next, Tony and Marie went to a church to get married. But they were turned away by a cleric who said, "We consider your proposal disgusting. This church marries only men to men."

Tony and Marie could see at least two hundred men inside the church, and all of them were laughing and pointing at Tony and his would-be bride.

They fled that church, Marie crying and Tony shaking his head. They made their way across the street to another church. This one was filled with women. The woman who met them at the door said, "I am sorry. No woman should marry a man. That is disgusting! This church marries only women to women."

All the women in the church were laughing at Tony and Marie. They fled. This time Tony cried too as his body thrashed around on the hospital bed. He was drenched in sweat and wailing, "It won't work! It won't work! It won't work!"

Marie was shaking him, crying, and begging him to wake up. She pushed the call button, and when the nurse arrived, Tony awakened. He saw the two women standing side by side looking solemnly at him. He screamed!

Marie was instantly on the bed, hugging Tony and telling him everything was all right. Her kiss settled him down somewhat, but he was still upset and trembling.

"That must have been a horrible nightmare," the nurse said. "I am going to get you a sedative."

"No!" Tony said. "No more drugs. They are making me crazy!"

"Tony, what did you dream about?" Marie asked gently.

"It must have been caused by all the drugs. It was really weird," Tony replied before he gave a description of his dream.

Marie was in no way a student of dream interpretation. She asked, "Tony, did I tell you any of the contents of the letter I found at the lab?"

Tony thought for a second then said, "No, not really. Only that you found the name and phone number of the doctor who sent the sample to be examined by the electron microscope."

Marie said, "That sample came from a little boy's toe. The doctor said the toe was just disappearing with no visible reason. Are you sure I didn't tell you that?"

"Not a word of it," Tony replied. "But you know how we often are thinking the same thing. Maybe our brains are on the same frequency or something."

They were both quiet for many seconds. Then Tony asked, "What about the other part of the dream?"

"I don't have a clue," Marie said. "I sure hope it doesn't mean we should not get married."

"Banish the thought, woman! We shall overcome any obstacle to accomplish our union," Tony replied imperiously.

That made Marie and the nurse both laugh. Then Marie said, "If Emil knew we were trying to interpret a dream, he would assign us to wash glasses, beakers, and tubing for a month!"

Tony went back to sleep and slept peacefully the rest of the night. Marie slept too, in a chair by the bedside.

DR. STANECK

The next morning the doctor arrived at seven sharp and took another look at Tony's wounds. Then he signed the release forms. The day nurse and Marie helped Tony to get dressed.

When an orderly showed up with a wheelchair, Tony objected. Pointing at his chest, he said, "Hey, I was shot up here. I can walk just fine."

"Sorry," said the nurse. "This is hospital policy."

So after getting a hug from all the nurses on the floor, Tony was wheeled down the hall to an elevator that took him and Marie to the roof of the hospital. There, with its engine idling, was a Bell Long Ranger helicopter.

"Wow! Are we going all the way to Chicago in this thing?" Tony asked.

"No, sir. We could, but this flight is just to the airport," answered the pilot, who met his passengers at the elevator. He put Tony in the front seat and Marie behind Tony in a rear seat. He strapped them both in securely and told them to don the headsets so they all could hear each other. After the pilot was seated, Tony could see him speaking but could hear only Marie. Then he realized the pilot was talking to an air controller.

All of a sudden, he heard the pilot say, "Here we go."

The helicopter rose straight up then started moving forward and up higher and higher. Tony was awestruck.

Marie exclaimed, "Look how small the cars are! Oh, look, Tony! Look at the swimming pools! Those cul-de-sacs look like rose petals or something!"

Tony watched the pilot as he maneuvered the helicopter in a circle then straight toward the airport. He asked, "How are you controlling this thing? I can hardly see you move at all."

Dave the pilot said, "This machine requires a very light touch on the stick. If I were to move it too much, we would be upside down or straight up or down, but definitely out of control."

"Wow! That is like the joystick on my computer game," Tony exclaimed. As they flew over a patch of thick woods, Dave asked Tony if he could see the deer in the woods below.

Tony replied, "There are deer down there? No, I can't see them." Then they flew over a meadow and another patch of thick woods.

Again the pilot asked, "Do you see the deer down in that patch of woods?"

Again Tony said, "No, I can't see them, Dave." There were several hunters in blaze orange coveralls, and Tony could see them well, but not the deer. Suddenly, the helicopter was heading straight down with its nose down, all the way to the treetops.

"Now do you see the darn deer?" Dave asked.

"Yeah! Yeah! I see them now. They 're running away from us and look like the spokes of a wheel, and we are the hub!" Tony was hoping that none of the hunters would get angry and shoot at them, but Dave just took the chopper up and away. Marie did not say a thing. Her heart was still in her throat from the fast descent.

It was a short flight to the airport. The helicopter did not approach the tower but instead landed alongside of a taxiway, where a small jet airplane was waiting. Marie and Tony were both very excited!

Marie said, "Boy, oh boy, Tony. We get a helicopter ride and a jet-plane ride too!"

Tony thought to himself, *The pilot must think we are like a couple of little kids.*

Actually, Dave was a bit awestruck himself. He had been scheduled to take an investor to some Pennsylvania coal mine locations, but that flight was superseded by this short ride to the airport. The pilot was ordered to wait as long as necessary for his two passengers. *These kids must be really important,* he thought.

Tony and Marie were ushered from the helicopter to the small jet plane. Tony wanted to walk around a bit and look at both aircrafts but didn't ask for the delay. He didn't feel that he had the right to ask for time to examine them.

He could have asked for almost anything, and either pilot, Dave or George, would have gotten it for him. Once seated in the plane beside Tony, Marie put her arms around him and gave him a big kiss. Then she said, "Isn't this exciting? What a story—"

"Ouch!" Tony yelped when she squeezed too hard.

Marie suddenly felt embarrassed and said, "Oh! Tony, I am so sorry. I wonder if I broke anything."

"I don't think so," Tony replied. "It hurt only when you squeezed me. I'm sorry I hollered. I love it when you—"

Just then the little plane began to accelerate, and the next words were "H-u-u-u-g m-e-e-e" as they felt the G forces push them back into their seats. Very shortly they were above Lake Erie where they could see ships and barges making their way to and from various ports on the lake.

"Oh, Tony, those boats look like the little plastic ones in your Battleship game," Marie said.

Tony thought about correcting Marie, that they were ships she was seeing, not boats. But a little voice in his head told him, *This is the woman you love, dummy. Don't expect her to be perfect.* A feeling of warmth and passion enveloped Tony as he gently squeezed her hand.

"What was that about?" Marie asked shyly.

"Oh, nothing. Just I love you," Tony said.

Marie returned the gesture with a kiss and a gentle hug, which led to the rustling of clothing. They were interrupted by a clearing of the throat and a gentle laugh from the seat just behind them.

Tony and Marie both turned around and saw an elderly man and woman sitting there. Neither of the youngsters had seen the older couple when they boarded the plane. Two faces turned beet red, and Marie mumbled an apology. The old man just smiled and introduced himself.

"I am Dr. Joseph Staneck, and this is my wife, Sophie. I am the man who wrote the letter that you risked your lives to find. Your boss asked me to accompany you to Chicago so I can relate my knowledge of this strange phenomenon."

Forgetting his embarrassment, Tony asked the doctor, "What is going on? Marie and I are Emil's assistants, and we do most of the preliminary testing of samples sent to our lab. We did tests on an electronic circuit board that was part of an electron microscope. None of the tests worked. Emil called an old friend of his from Germany to help solve this, and now they won't allow me or Marie to go into the lab at all."

"For a scientist, your Emil is a very emotional man," the doctor replied. "He told me over the phone that he loves you kids and does not want this weird thing to hurt you. He couldn't get any work done all day after Marie told him you had been shot. Nobody knows what is going on yet, and now scientists from all over the world are converging in Chicago to help your boss."

The airplane left Lake Erie and flew over a big city, lots of farmland, some smaller cities, and another lake. Soon Marie noticed her ears began to pop a little. The ground seemed to be coming up to their level, and then they were landing in Chicago.

The plane stopped on a taxiway far from the terminal and was met by a police cruiser.

Oh no, Tony thought. *Not again*. A very pretty and young female officer got out of the car and met them at the plane's door.

"I am supposed to take you folks directly to the laboratory," she said as she and the pilot loaded the doctor's suitcases in the trunk. Tony, Marie, and Sophie were crammed into the backseat while the doctor rode in front all the way back to the lab.

Emil was wearing a pair of rubber gloves and coveralls, as was Hans. Neither scientist would shake hands with Tony or Marie or touch them in any way when they arrived at the lab office. In fact, neither of the scientists would actually leave the lab. There were empty pizza boxes and fried chicken and Chinese food containers strewn about. There were empty beer and soft drink cans all over the floor inside the lab.

Marie clucked her tongue and said, "What a mess you left for me to clean up!"

"*Nein*, Marie," Hans declared. "Don't you touch anything in this lab. You and Tony stay in the office. You can tell us about your adventures later, but now we need you to arrange about seventy or eighty hotel rooms and meals for about one hundred people or more. They will start to arrive tomorrow."

Emil asked, "How do both of you feel? Are you both well? Do you have any strange feeling in your fingers or faces or anything?"

Marie replied, "I feel fine. I am just hungry and tired."

Tony laughed and said, "I am starved. I haven't had a decent meal in nearly a week, and I seem to have holes in my chest and arm!"

"That is good," Emil said. "You have not been contaminated by that Binghamton lab."

Just then Dr. Staneck stepped into the office, followed by Sophie. Hans, upon seeing them, turned white. Emil could see an emotional change come over Dr. Staneck as well. He turned to Hans for an explanation.

"Vas ist unrecht? [What is wrong?]" he asked.

Hans could not reply. He was so upset he could not speak or move. He just stared at Joseph and Sophie.

Emil was dumbfounded too. He thought Hans was not capable of any emotion at all, but the old scientist was so disturbed he was shaking.

Both Tony and Marie felt that the tension in the air was thick enough to cut with a knife, but it was Sophie who finally broke the spell. "Hans, we thought the American soldiers had killed you."

"I, I, I escaped through a tunnel," stammered Hans. "I thought both of you had gone to the gas chamber."

"We were in the killing box, along with fifty others," declared Joseph. "The Americans rescued us. Sophie nearly died. Ten people did die."

"I am so sorry!" said Hans. "I have lived with the horrible things I did for sixty years. I thought I was doing a good thing then, but nothing I discovered there at Dachau is even important now. I don't expect you or anyone else to ever forgive me. If you report me to the Israelis, I cannot blame you."

"Hans, that was a long time ago. Besides, if it had not been for you, I never would have met Sophie," Joseph said, defusing the situation. "Now, let us fight on the same side against a very strange enemy."

These exchanges were all in German, and Marie had not learned that language. She did not know what had caused this emotionally charged exchange. Later, Tony would explain why it was extremely intense, that Joseph had saved the day—and maybe the whole project—by being so conciliatory.

Emil took another look at the travelers then asked Marie if he and Hans still had spare clothing in the closet in the restroom.

"Yes," Marie answered. "Your wife brought clean clothes just before Tony and I left for Binghamton. Hans has still not unpacked his suitcase."

"Good! I haven't been infected by this devil we are fighting. Have you, Hans?" Emil asked in English.

"Huh? What?" answered Hans, still recovering from shock.

"Have you been infected at all by this strange thing we are fighting?"

"No, I don't think so. I feel good, and I am careful to wear gloves and an apron," Hans replied. "Why do you ask?"

"Because I don't think I will get any work out of my two assistants until I feed them. I am sick and tired of pizza. Let's all go out to a good restaurant and get a good meal."

Emil thought to himself that he would find an opportunity to speak to Tony and Marie alone. He needed to explain Hans's strange reaction to Joseph and Sophie and to explain the visions of utopia brought about by an insane but charismatic dictator. Those visions had swept up Hans and himself and carried them, along with millions of other young Germans, into a world war and holocaust.

"That's a really good idea, Emil!" Marie shouted.

Tony said, "Hot dog" and tried to raise his arms in the air, but the sling and the pain in his right arm made him look awkward. Marie was immediately concerned that Tony may have done some damage to himself, but he said, "I'm fine. I'm fine. Let's go eat!"

Hans finally was able to laugh, and Emil said, "We will all go as soon as Hans and I get into clothing that wasn't in the lab."

While Emil and Hans changed clothing, Marie called Martha, Emil's wife. It was arranged for her to meet the work crew at a fine local restaurant that featured European food.

At the restaurant, seated and having ordered, Tony tried asking Emil if he and Hans knew any more about the weird thing in the lab that had brought them all together. Neither Emil nor Hans cared to discuss that subject in a public place. Hans glanced at Emil then asked Tony and Marie to relate their adventurous trip to Binghamton.

Tony began the narrative by saying, "I was a little worried about driving Emil's Volkswagen all the way to Binghamton, but that little car just hummed along all the way. We drove straight through, stopping only for gas and the restroom. When we ate, it was just burgers from the drive-up window."

Marie continued the story. "When we got there, we found a secondhand store where we bought clothes that looked like they might fit. We also bought burglar tools there. You should have seen the clerk look at us when we paid for it all. She looked like she expected us to rob the nearest bank, but Tony didn't crack a smile. He looked so serious!"

Then Tony said, "When we drove away from that store, I thought I saw a policeman stop and go in. Then I saw him again before we got to the lab. Our next encounter with the police was—"

"Oh, Tony, don't tell that part yet," Marie interrupted. She wasn't ready to relive the shooting. "We found the lab on a side street, with houses alongside and some businesses too. There was an alley behind the lab, so we drove down that to the parking lot. Between the parking lot and the alley was a fence covered with ivy. That is where we parked to change into work clothes."

Tony took up the story again. "If you ever change clothes in a Volkswagen, you will find it seems to take forever and you bang elbows and knees often and—"

"Oh, Tony, it would not have been so bad if you had kept your hands to yourself."

"But you asked for help with your straps and stuff!"

Laughter and table pounding interrupted the saga again, not only from their table, but also from the surrounding tables and the waiter who arrived with their food.

After the food had been served, Marie took up the story again. "You should have seen Tony in his temporary clothes. His pants were too short but too big around the waist. The shirt was much too big, and his shoes were so big he looked like a circus clown!"

"Now wait a minute, lady. You didn't look much like a movie star yourself, unless it's in a scene that follows a tornado. That shirt you had on was so big, it made you appear pregnant whenever you bent over a file. It didn't hide anything at the top either."

"No wonder we couldn't find that letter from Joseph," Marie interrupted again. "You were looking at me instead of the files."

"Now, Marie, you know we didn't find it in the office because it wasn't there. You found it in the lab, but I sure did enjoy the view of a beautiful angel in rags!"

"Oh, Tony," was all Marie could manage.

"Your dinner is getting cold," Hans prompted, "and we will never hear the rest of the story as long as you two are looking into each other's eyes."

There was no laughter from the older folks. Warm smiles greeted Tony and Marie when their reverie was broken. Perhaps each one was remembering their first love, but the general feeling was one of reverence.

Marie continued the story. "Oh! Well, we searched those files for an hour or two or three. I really don't know how long. Then there was a huge crash, and three terrorists came charging into the office through the front door. Two more came through the back door, and they were all yelling and screaming like a bunch of drunk idiots. Emil, you told us not to touch anything, so we were opening drawers with a pair of pliers. Tony had the pliers in his hand. One of the idiots thought it was a gun, and he shot Tony. Tony yelled at me to run, and I did. I ran into the lab and jumped up onto the lab bench to get to the back door because that electron microscope had eaten a big hole in the floor. There on the bench near a Bunsen burner, I found your letter, Joseph. I wasn't sure what I had picked up, but I just kept running. I jumped off the bench at the back wall then ran out the door."

"Marie, why didn't the two terrorists who came in the back door stop you?" Emil asked.

"Those two were so wild eyed and determined to catch America's most wanted that they fell right into the basement through that big hole. I think one of them got hurt. It was a woman, and she was crying out in pain. They fell on top of a pile of junk that must be the remains of the electron microscope. Oh, I wonder if 'the thing' got them? Anyway, I kept running until I found a place to hide in a brick yard. That is where I was when I called you, Emil. After I talked to you, I finally found enough courage to come out of the brick yard. I talked to someone I thought was a plainclothes policeman, but he turned out to be an FBI man."

"Marie, those people who smashed their way into the lab were policemen too," Emil reminded her.

"I know, they said they were afterward, but I will never think of them as policemen. They were all dressed in black, and their faces were covered with something, and they couldn't talk. They only screamed and smashed and shot Tony. Oh migosh! They were everywhere in that lab, touching everything. I'll bet 'the thing' got all of them. Someone will have to check them out. They should be in quarantine." Marie rushed on, "I'll never think of those monsters as men, but I guess they are. The one that shot Tony seemed to be human when he came to the hospital. He was wearing plastic booties on his feet and kept his hands at his sides, except when he shook hands with Tony. He had on gloves. Was he in quarantine already?"

"Yes," answered Emil. "The FBI men who arrived next informed them of their quarantine status and the danger they were in from touching things. Unfortunately, it took time for you to get to a safe place and call me. Then it took more time for Hans to make his call and even more time for the message to be relayed back to Binghamton FBI, through the German and American governments. I'm afraid all those officers are doomed unless we can find a way to stop 'the thing,' as you call it."

Hans was silent and hung his head. Marie's reaction to the raid made the old scientist reflect on the horrible things he had done more than fifty years ago. He thought that if Marie knew of them, she would hate him too.

He was brought back to the present with a shock when Dr. Staneck replied to Emil, "Perhaps there is a way to protect those people. The tissue sample I sent to the electron microscope came from a little boy's—"

Emil interrupted Joseph, "I am extremely interested in what you have to say, Doctor, but I think we should keep technical details in the lab." There were people at nearby tables who were very interested in the conversation at Emil's table. The two scientists did not want the world to know of "the thing," as Marie named it. If the news media got involved, there could be mass panic. Also, it could be nothing. They could be overlooking something very simple and would look really silly, if that were the case.

Marie understood immediately and turned to Tony. "You are having a terrible time trying to dig out that lobster meat with one hand. Let me help you."

"Aw, Marie, you make me feel like a little boy," Tony whined.

"Shut up and eat this," she said as she forked a generous chunk of lobster into his mouth. "You would starve to death without my help." Then she picked up his wineglass and lifted it to his mouth.

"Wait a minute." Tony gulped. "Gimme a minute to eat this. Do I have a choice between starving and choking? Boy, the lobster is good!"

"Don't talk with your mouth full. My goodness, if we have little boys, I will know just how to care for them. I'm getting my experience from raising you!" Marie declared.

By now "the thing" was forgotten, and all the older people, even Hans, were laughing at the youngsters. Finally, Joseph asked both kids how they enjoyed the helicopter ride.

"It was great," replied Tony. At the same time, Marie said, "It was fun. We passed over several patches of woods where there were deer. The pilot asked Tony several times if he could see the deer down below, and Tony always said no. Finally, just before we got to the airport, the helicopter went straight down, nose first, almost all the way to the treetops. Then we could see deer running in every direction away from the helicopter. I was scared to death.

"The pilot asked Tony again if he could see the darn deer, and Tony said, 'Yeah! Yeah! I see them now!' I was so frightened I couldn't say anything until we went back up and were flying straight again."

Tony said between mouthfuls of food, "That patch of woods looked like a big wheel, and the running deer were the spokes."

"It was funny flying over backyards that were fenced in and people thought they had privacy. They went swimming without bathing suits," Marie added.

By now everyone at their table and at the surrounding tables was laughing so hard they couldn't eat.

Tony looked around and said, "Marie, we are in the wrong business. We should be in show biz. I'll be the straight man. You kill 'em with one-liners."

"Okay, Tony, let's do it," Marie agreed. "I'll start calling agents when we get back to the lab."

"Oh no, you won't," Emil said. "We have only two phone lines, and besides, you kids have not been home for days. Your folks must be worried about you. I want you both to take a day off and just rest. I will write down the names of all the people who are coming to help us, and you can call the hotels and arrange rooms Monday morning."

"But, Emil," Marie objected.

"No buts," Emil said.

"Today is Monday, *mein liebchen*," interjected Martha.

"Oh? It is?" a confused Emil answered. "We have been working day and night. I guess I lost track of time. But that is okay. Take tomorrow off and relax. I'll handle the phones for a day."

Tony and Marie did take the next day off, and each went to their own home. Tony went to his lonely apartment and alternately paced back and forth, slept, and wished he were with Marie.

Marie went to her home where she lived with her mother and father. She didn't tell her folks about all the adventures she had just experienced. She said only that she and Tony had gone to Binghamton, New York, to get something for Emil. Marie knew that her mother, and father too probably, would have a fit and ask a million questions if they knew the kids had been shot at and possibly poisoned by "the thing."

Her mother reacted in a typical mother's way. "You went there alone with that boy? Where did you sleep? Did you sleep with him? If you got pregnant, don't expect your parents to raise another kid. Did you use protection? Doesn't that crazy German you work for have any sense at all, sending you kids off together like that? What is going on that you are at that lab day and night? Or are you not at the lab? Are you two using drugs? Well, what do you have to say for yourself?"

"Mom! Mom! Relax," Marie replied. "You should be glad that Tony loves me. I am too fat to be every man's choice for a bride. If it were not for Tony, you and Dad would have to provide for me until I am old and gray." She said the last, even though she was paying most of the household bills.

Her father asked, "You say he loves you?"

"Yes. I think he is crazy about me."

"Well, maybe I don't have to clean the shotgun. Did you two set a date?" he asked.

Marie said, "No, the date hasn't been set yet." She thought about telling them how busy they were at the lab but didn't. It would have opened up another can of worms and invited another torrent of questions.

Like Tony, Marie spent the day pacing the floor, sleeping, and wishing she were with Tony. Both were up early on Wednesday morning, and Tony arrived at 6:45 a.m. to pick Marie up to go to work.

Marie's mother insisted they stay for breakfast. Marie looked at Tony, and he said, "Okay, we will stay. We probably won't get anything else to eat all day, unless it would be delivered pizza again."

They had a really good breakfast, but Marie had a difficult time deflecting questions. She elbowed Tony when he acted like he was going to answer them. Marie definitely didn't want to reveal "the thing." They never would get to work if that came up. Instead, she shocked and confused Tony by trying to discuss things like a wedding date, how many babies she wanted, and how big a house they would need.

Tony had been thinking about all those things too. But he was not ready to set anything in concrete yet by discussing it in front of "judge and jury": Marie's mom!

Finally their plates were empty, and the kids escaped to Tony's car. They drove straight to the lab where they found Emil on one phone and his wife on the other. Both of the older folks looked like they had had no sleep for two days.

Tony and Marie took over the phones. Martha went to the grocery store then home to prepare a good meal that she could take to the lab. Sophie went along to help with the preparations and transportation.

Tony and Marie worked out a system. Tony, who knew French, German, and Spanish, received the incoming calls. He wrote down the names of the visiting scientists and how many beds and rooms each party required. Then he passed the paper to Marie, who called hotels and motels and eventually even bed-and-breakfast establishments. She wrote the reservations on the same paper that Tony handed her. They even recorded special diet needs. By the end of that day, which ended at 2:00 a.m., they had registered one hundred scientists and their support people. Most of the scientists would be bringing their wives, husbands, or other family members.

When they finally quit for the day, both Tony and Marie were exhausted. But the two old scientists and the doctor were still hard at work discussing and experimenting on the one very important fact they had learned about "the thing." A strong magnetic field can abort the deterioration of effected mass. Even these unemotional old men of science were using Marie's term for the strange phenomenon: the thing.

Tony invited Marie to his apartment for the rest of the night, but she demurred. "Oh, Tony, I love you and would love to go home with you. But I was home only a few hours yesterday and not at all for nearly a week. Mom would have a fit."

"Yeah, you're probably right, moll. I sure don't want to upset your ma. She makes the best cherry pie I ever ate. I'd sure hate to lose my weekly fix of pie and ice cream," Tony answered in his tough-guy role.

"Oh, Tony, I'm sorry," Marie said as they embraced and kissed good night. Tony dropped off Marie at her mother's home then went to his apartment.

At home, Marie cautiously opened the front door and entered as quietly as possible. She closed the door very carefully then removed her shoes before ascending the stairs. Marie was somewhat overweight, and total silence was not possible for her. Nearly every step creaked and groaned as she went up the stairs.

Marie was near the top of the stairs when she was dismayed to hear her mother's voice. "Marie? Is that you? Where have you been? It is nearly three in the morning! Were you at that Tony's house? You should be ashamed!"

"No, Mom. I was at work, but I am very tired. Tony and I have been on the phones all day and night. We talked to people from all over the world—or rather Tony did. I called every hotel, motel, and bed-and-breakfast in Chicago. I had to find rooms for about five hundred people. Tomorrow I will have to find more."

"What do you want with that many rooms? The only thing that brings people to town like that is a wedding or funeral! Good grief, girl, what are you mixed up in? That old geezer isn't selling dope, is he? Are you and Tony finding dealers for him?

Come in here, and turn on the light. I want to see what you look like. Look at you! You're a mess. Sex is the only thing that can mess up a girl's hair like that! Have you been lying to me about all that work? You need to get away from that boy. Woolworth is looking for a clerk—"

"Mom! Mom! Mom, I love my job, and I love Tony, and he loves me. You should be happy for me. Just look at me. I am way overweight. Heck! I am fat! Who else would want me? Tony does, and yes, we are going to get married. We don't know when yet because we are so darned involved with 'the thing.' Mom, I love you too. I won't hurt you by having a shotgun wedding, but I just can't tell you exactly what is going on at work. I simply do not know.

"I was the first one at the lab to look at a sample to be analyzed, and then Tony. Neither of us could make sense of it, so we gave it to Emil. He couldn't figure it out either. He called another scientist, and even that scientist can't tell what is going on. When they get it all figured out, I'll tell you about it. Now I really need to sleep. I love you, Ma. Good night."

Marie was undressed and asleep within two minutes. Her mother lay awake a long time.

When Tony got to his apartment, he managed to kick off his shoes. Then he fell onto his bed. His last thought was that he was glad Marie had not come home with him. He would have just made a fool of himself trying to make love tonight.

POISON?

At Kilabrew Laboratory, the two scientists and the doctor continued to work, trying to understand the thing. Emil's second wife loved him probably as much as Krystal had, but she had no interest in Emil's work. She knew that Emil often worked long into the night whenever he had an interesting problem to solve. Martha and Sophie became good friends and went to shows, shopped, or just talked for hours. It was good for Emil and Joseph to know that both women were enjoying each other's company and were not bored or restless.

Emil and Hans were very aware that they might have overlooked something really simple. They had alerted the world scientific community, and hundreds of their colleagues would be arriving soon. They would really be embarrassed if a simple enzyme or fungus was the cause of Aaron's problem.

Hans asked, "Joseph, do you know what kinds of plants are growing around that rock the boy kicked?"

"Aaron said there are none. The rock is in the middle of a big bare spot, with no vegetation at all, in an area as big as his school playground. He said the soil is like sand, but softer," Joseph remembered.

"Well, that kills the poison theory," Emil said.

"Not necessarily," said Hans. "What if the skin was broken when he kicked that rock, and then it came into contact with a poisonous plant later? Joseph, do you know if there are any poisonous plants anywhere in that area?"

After thinking a bit, Joseph answered, "Yes, I think there are one or two, but I have never heard of symptoms like little Aaron has."

"What made you think of using a magnet to stop this thing?" Hans asked.

"I ordered an MRI on Aaron, and everything looked normal except the affected area of his foot. It simply did not appear at all on the picture. I ordered a second MRI and got the same result. When I saw Aaron after each test, there was no further deterioration for several days. Sometimes my grandson visits me at the office, and he likes to play with magnets. I keep several in my desk drawer.

"I tried taping one of those magnets to Aaron's toe, or what was left of it. I measured the toe every three days, and there was no more loss of toe. Aaron complained of the bulk, so I ordered a special magnet to fit the stub of toe. Aaron has had no more loss of toe or foot. However, that has not restored the part of the toe that was lost."

"Was that a strong magnet?" Hans asked.

"Yes. When I ordered it, I asked for the strongest possible, with the poles closest to the toe."

"When you examine the boy again, would you measure and record the gauss level of the magnet? I am curious to know if the thing is absorbing high levels of energy."

"Where can I purchase a meter to measure gauss?" Dr. Staneck asked.

Emil replied, "We can get one for you here in Chicago. We use a dealer that supplies every kind of scientific instrument. Because of the odd shape of the boy's magnet, your reading will not be precise, but that doesn't matter. We just need a rough estimate of the strength. What is really important is the rate of change in the decay. Ask Marie to order the instrument for you."

"Just what is the magnet affecting in the toe and in our tools that are being consumed by the thing?" Hans wondered. "What has been added to the toe and tools? If it were a virus or bacteria, we should be able to see them somehow, but we see nothing. Is it a chemical that has eluded discovery until now? Perhaps the atoms are oscillating at a heretofore unheard of frequency."

"We have a spectrum analyzer that will measure radio frequencies up to thirty gigahertz. But I believe you are thinking of frequencies beyond light, aren't you?" Emil asked.

"I really don't know. Get that instrument you have, and let's look at the forceps. We can put a loop of wire around the effected end."

Hans and Emil scanned the forceps from the lowest frequency the spectrum analyzer would cover to the highest. At 87.8 megahertz, they could see a weak signal, but it was just the local oscillator in Tony's FM radio. Joseph stuck his head out the door and asked Tony to turn his radio off for three seconds then turn it back on again. Tony did so, and the signal disappeared for a few seconds. At 10.7 megahertz above that, there was a much bigger signal that appeared to be modulated. That probably would be the radio station that Tony was listening to. Emil asked Marie to call the station and find out the location of their transmitter. It turned out to be fairly close to the laboratory.

Tony said, "I could have told you that. This old radio won't play any station that isn't close. That's why I listen to hillbillies, as you call them, all the time. It sounds even worse with these funky speakers I have to use since you guys wrecked my good ones."

Everyone had a big laugh about that. Emil had been trying to influence Tony to listen to classical music for a long time. That afternoon, among the many boxes of scientific instruments, samples, and glassware that Marie and Tony were unpacking and cataloging, was a brand-new high-power, highly sensitive radio.

When Tony asked Emil how to classify that device, the old scientist replied, "Don't classify it. Put it on the shelf where that old piece of junk is and tune in some decent music." Soon an overture was heard throughout the laboratory.

"Sounds like I found 'Beet-hoven, Batch, and the Boys'" Tony said.

"Oh, Tony, you should be more respectful," Marie said.

"Actually, I am. That country music is not country at all. It is just about broken hearts and cheating lovers. It is depressing! I don't know anything about this music, but at least it is much more cheerful. If we get tired of Bach, we can tune in some rock," Tony said.

"Oh, that would get all three of those guys out here in a hurry, and they would all be carrying some kind of club or something." Marie laughed.

Tony laughed too. Both youngsters then went back to the phones, answering a multitude of questions about hotel accommodations, golf courses, soccer fields, food availability, and even some technical questions about the thing.

There wasn't much the kids could tell about that, only that it is making things disappear with no trace of heat, smoke, smell, or anything. One of the more arrogant scientists insisted that Emil had to know more than that.

Tony replied, "We only know what it is not. That is why Emil called this conference. You are supposed to find out what the thing is."

"Grouchy old Frenchman," Tony muttered after hanging up.

The wife of a scientist from India called and asked Tony if there was a woman she could talk to. Tony turned the call over to Marie. After the call, Marie said, "She has some kind of female problem and wanted to know if we have any good doctors here in Chicago. I swear the rest of the world still thinks we are colonists and everyone in Chicago is a gangster!"

"Yeah, I know what you mean." Tony laughed. "One guy from Austria insisted that all meetings be terminated before sunset. Everybody could be safe in their hotel rooms before Al Capone starts to shoot up the town. He was serious too!"

Marie said, "Oh, this is going to be fun, Tony! We have to get you a gangster outfit and clothes from the twenties. You will need a tommy gun, one that is big and impressive, and a pack of cigarettes. You can hang one out the side of your mouth." She laughed at the mental picture she had drawn.

Back in the lab, the testing, experimenting, and discussion went on and on. Only food deliveries and relief breaks could interrupt the work. Hans and Emil were desperate to discover what the thing was. They were so afraid that some young scientist would break up laughing at them and tell everyone the thing is just a common occurrence that they had overlooked. But at this point, no one at Kilabrew had a clue.

Dr. Staneck was fully aware of the enormity of the problem that Hans and Emil were working on, but he had a personal problem that was foremost in his own mind. His life was that of a country doctor. He was more interested in family problems that his patients experienced. This might be anything from mumps to stress caused by a man's job-security problems. He was very happy that Aaron's problem was held in remission by a simple magnet, but he knew that he needed to find a permanent solution. He wished that he could restore the lost toe. During a coffee break, he asked if Hans or Emil knew anything about regeneration of appendages.

Emil replied, "I have never studied much about that subject. I do know that some reptiles and lower forms of life can regenerate parts of their bodies. Even human livers can regenerate themselves if damaged. I read in a medical journal that two scientists at the University of New Mexico were studying that subject until their funds dried up. Maybe we can get some information from them. I'll have Marie try to find them and give them a call."

Marie tried for three days to contact the two professors at the University in New Mexico but was diverted to other offices. One secretary told her to forget her pursuit of these two men. One girl did happen to mention the name of one of the men. She quickly realized her mistake and tried to cover it up by saying that she was mistaken and that man had been fired.

At home, Marie's persistence paid off. She went on an Internet search and came up with the professor's home phone number. She was going to put off calling him until the next evening because of the late hour but then remembered the time difference between Illinois and New Mexico.

The professor's teenaged daughter answered the phone and said, "It's for you, Pops."

"Who is it?"

"I don't know. Some girl, I think. Maybe one of your favorite students."

During the transfer of the phone, Marie could hear an old rerun of *M.A.S.H.* until she heard, "This is Ben Lingle. How did you get this number? What is your name, young lady?"

Marie could hear a giggle in the background and then, "Uh-oh, Dad's going into his tough act again."

Marie gave her name and apologized for bothering the professor at home. She told him of the problem she was having in trying to contact him at the university. Then before he could cut her off or berate her, she said, "I am calling for Dr. Hans Gossl of the University of Darmstadt." Marie didn't even know for sure if Hans was still affiliated with that university, but she hoped that Ben Lingle would recognize the name.

He did recognize the University of Darmstadt and also Hans Gossl. He nearly dropped the phone. He asked Marie to hold a few seconds while he went to his home office phone. Then he asked his daughter to hang up the living room phone. She did just that, but she did not bother to wait until her father picked up the other phone. The call was abruptly cut off.

By the time Marie called back, Ben was in great distress and stumbled all over his own words when he answered the second call. He apologized profusely for the dropped call and for being so hard to access. He explained that he and his partner had been working very hard to find out how lizards can regenerate body parts until the funds for the study had been suddenly cut off. The philanthropist who had been financing the study had learned of the new work being done in genetics, and he insisted that the two professors switch their study to this new science.

"Mr. Lingle, Doctor Gossl is extremely interested in your study of regeneration and would like to discuss it with you. He and my employer are deeply involved in a related subject and would like to collaborate with you," Marie replied.

"I am more than sure my partner, Sam Jack, would be eager to work with a famous scientist like Hans Gossl. But I will have to talk with him about it before I commit us to a collaboration," Ben said.

They exchanged office phone numbers, and Ben promised to call Hans in the morning.

When she reported to work in the morning, Marie surprised everyone when she bowed deeply to Hans and then even kissed his hand. "I am so honored to work with you, Your Majesty," she said.

Hans replied, "What is this? Have you lost your mind or something? Vass ist?"

Marie laughed and then related the story of her difficulty in contacting the two professors in New Mexico. She told about the sudden humility of Professor Ben Lingle when she dropped Hans's name and the name of Darmstadt University.

It was two hours later when Ben made the call to Kilabrew Labs. He and his partner, Sam Jack, were both on the phone. At the lab, Hans, Emil, and Dr. Staneck were all on phones at that end. A long discussion of regeneration, genetics, and finance problems tied up all the phones for several hours. Finally, they all agreed to keep in touch.

HELP ARRIVES

Still confined to the office, Tony and Marie were bored silly and started to act like it. They threw erasers at each other and paper airplanes and told dumb jokes and chased each other around the furniture like two children. They were scientists trained in physics and biochemistry and definitely not accustomed to idleness. Their boredom and silliness covered an undercurrent of fear. They were aware of something very dangerous going on in the lab. They continued their ribaldry until there was a knock at the door.

"Did someone order pizza?" Tony asked.

"I sure didn't. I was too busy," Marie said with a giggle.

When Tony opened the door, he met a beautiful blond woman who appeared to be about fifty-five. She had a puzzled look on her face.

"Sind sie Emil Finkenbinder? [Are you Emil Finkenbinder?]" she asked.

"Nein, ich bin Tony. Bitte eintreten. [No, I am Tony. Please come in.]"

As she entered, Tony called out to Marie, asking her to call Emil out to the office.

"Ich bin Annamarie Lowenstein. Sint sie Deutsch, Tony? [I am Annamarie Lowenstein. Are you German, Tony?]"

"Nein, ich bin Americanish [No, I am American]," replied Tony. He was not sure of his heritage. He thought perhaps he might be descended from an Italian and maybe an Englishman far back in his lineage, but he just accepted being American, nothing else.

Just then Emil emerged from the laboratory and greeted the visitor. "Good evening. You must be the first of my rescuers from the thing."

As Emil shook hands with her, she said, "Ich bin Annamarie Lowenstein, aus Dusseldorf [I am Annamarie Lowenstein from Dusseldorf]."

"Gut abend [Good evening]," Emil greeted her. "Do you speak English?"

"Yes, but not as well as *Deutsch oder Französisch* [German or French]," she replied.

"We have people coming from many countries," Emil advised. "We will need to use English to communicate since most of us can speak that language. When we have technical problems, we can revert to German or whatever we need. Sometimes getting thoughts across may be slow, but we will get this done somehow."

"Yes, I start now to speak your English," Annamarie said. "And who is this young lady?" she asked as Marie came out from the kitchenette.

Marie extended her hand and said, "Hi! I'm Marie. I am Emil's assistant. But on this project, I am just a secretary and gofer."

"What is gofer ?" Annamarie asked. "In my studies of America, I learned of a small rodent called a gopher, but you are not rodent."

Marie laughed and said, "It means that I am the one who goes after anything that is needed here. I go for it."

Emil grinned and said, "Yes, you certainly went for it today. Didn't you?"

Marie turned beet red and looked at Tony, who was also turning red and grinning sheepishly. They had forgotten the intercom that monitors the office.

Annamarie had no idea what this bit of private conversation was about. She just looked from Tony to Marie to Emil but could not understand what was going on. She asked, "Where is this project I have been summoned here to work on? Can you American scientists not solve your own problems?"

Hans heard a familiar voice and came from the lab to the small lobby. He had heard Annamarie's question, and he answered it. "No, not this one, and neither can I. I have never seen anything like this before."

"Uncle Hans, I know not you here! Is good you here. These other people be too much like childs. They look at each other and laugh when no one says anything. They are silly!"

"No, no, Annamarie," Hans corrected his niece. "They are all good scientists who have been working much too hard for a long time. We all need a day of rest, and we didn't expect you for three more days. Emil and I will explain our problem after we have all eaten a good meal and have had some rest. Marie, call the hideout and tell them we are coming. After the work you and Tony just did, you must be hungry too!"

Again Marie turned beet red and hastily escaped to the office. She called their favorite restaurant and asked for a private table for eight.

Annamarie looked at Hans and Emil and proclaimed, "I cannot go to a restaurant with two men dressed in paper!"

The two old scientists pretended to be offended. Hans told her that if she is to work on the project, she must wear paper too. Emil had asked Marie to order the paper lab suits for all the scientists to limit outside exposure to the thing. It seemed to spread very easily. Marie had ordered two thousand of them. After use, the suits were considered to be hazardous waste.

"What iss dis zing?" Annamarie asked.

Hans looked at Emil, who said, "We do not know. Whatever it is, it makes things disappear. It was first seen in a boy's toe. He kicked a rock in a forest in New York, and soon afterward, his toe began to disintegrate. When Dr. Staneck examined the toe, the toenail and tip of the toe were completely gone, right to the hyponychium. It too was gone when he examined the toe again three days later."

Just then, Dr. Staneck came into the office and took up the account. "I ordered an MRI, and after that was done, the disintegration stopped for a few days. However, the MRI showed nothing at all! I had a second MRI done, and again the thing stopped eating Aaron's toe. I tied a magnet to the toe, and there hasn't been any more disintegration."

"If that solved the problem, why am I here in this heathen land?" asked Annamarie.

Dr. Staneck continued, "I sent a sample of Aaron's toe to a lab that had an electron microscope. The thing infected that sample, and it infected the electron microscope. It destroyed an older but very expensive scope."

"We received a sample of the scope, a circuit board. After we tried to identify the thing, we noticed that anything that touched that circuit board began to disintegrate," Emil continued. "That is why we wear rubber gloves and paper suits. I don't know how to dispose of them properly. I hope to find that out, when we identify the thing."

"Why you call it zuh zing?" Annamarie asked.

"We have no knowledge of what it is, and Marie called it that once. The name just stuck. It is as good a name as any other until we identify it," Emil explained. "We here at Kilabrew Lab tried every test we could think of—chemical, physical, optical, electrical—but we could not figure it out. That's when I called Hans for help."

"Yes, and I repeated every test and did many that Emil had not thought of. I got the same results—none," Hans added. "That is why I called everyone I could think of to come here and help. Surely someone will recognize the thing."

"It is important that we keep this project a secret from the public. If the television or newspaper people got a piece of this story, there would be mass panic. When we leave this building, we do not mention the thing or talk about it at all," Emil said.

The three old men changed into their street clothes, and the six of them joined Sophie and Martha at the hideout.

Since Annamarie was new to the group, most of the conversation centered on her and her trip to America. Annamarie said, "I grew up in a village of dimwitted, slow-to-learn people. I started school at age four and quickly advanced far ahead of my classmates. Their heads were made of stones. I was put into a class several grades above my age group, and I quickly advanced to the top of that class. I finished primary education and enrolled in a university. I studied biochemistry and nuclear physics. After university, I worked for several different arbeit geberin—uh, werks, or how do you say uh, jobs. The people I had to work with were *dummkopfen* [dumb heads]. I could not stand to work with them. I had to teach them everything! Finally I opened my own testing laboratory where I do mostly forensic science for police departments. Even dealing with them is very difficult for me."

"I do not understand why people are in a hurry all the time," Annamarie continued. "They drop off tissue samples to be examined and leave a note rather than tell me what to look for. Do they think I am too forgetful to remember? I am not! I am perfect! I remember every detail. I do not make mistakes like some other lab people where the police go with their forensic work."

When Annamarie excused herself to go to the ladies' room, Hans apologized for her. "She was not allowed to grow up with her own age group. She never learned how to interact with people. She grew up in East Germany and was not allowed to play or read anything that wasn't part of her lessons. She is like a walking computer."

Nothing was said for a few minutes. Everyone became engrossed in eating. When Annamarie returned, Emil looked across the table at Tony and Marie, declaring, "You two are much too quiet this evening. What are you up to now?"

Tony looked at Marie, and both of them turned beet red again.

Hans said, "Ach du lieben, kinder [Oh, you lovers, children]! Stop worrying about that. You know we all love you both very much. What you did was good, not bad. This world needs much more of love. You two kids have taught me, in just the short time I have known you, what sixty-two years of science failed to teach me. I have never in my life been so happy as I am now, and your unabashed love is what has changed my life. Tony, eat your carrots!"

"Why do I need carrots? My eyesight is perfect. I found Marie, didn't I?"

"Yes. I have to concede that you found perfection," Hans answered.

"Oh, knock it off, you guys! My head is getting so big, I'm afraid it will fall off my neck," Marie said as she cut off a piece of her meat. "I am perfect only for Tony, and he is perfect for me. We already have our family planned. We will have two boys, two girls, and we will live in an old farmhouse in the country. We will have a cow for milk, horses to ride, chickens, and a field of corn and potatoes."

"Wow!" Martha exclaimed. "And how are you going to make sure each child is a boy or girl?"

"We haven't figured that out yet," Marie said. "Maybe Annamarie can help us there."

"Yes. That is all determined by the father. Perhaps if I had a sample of Tony's sperm, I could isolate the X or Y chromosomes then use them to impregnate Marie," Annamarie began. Then she continued to elaborate on the procedure, the necessary timing, and temperature. For this austere scientist, this was merely a clinical procedure. There could be no love or passion involved. Such emotion would only contaminate the results.

"Well, that certainly is interesting," Sophie said. "But I always preferred the old way—just love each other and see what happens."

"Have you two set a wedding date yet?" Martha asked.

"Not yet," Tony replied. "It all depends on, on you know, on our work."

"Yes, dear," Emil said. "Our work will keep us even more busy until we solve this big problem. I'll tell you now that just as soon as we do solve it, Tony and Marie will have the biggest and best wedding ever!"

Just then the waitress arrived to take dessert orders. When it was Marie's turn to order, Tony had to poke her. Marie was lost in flowers, photos, a wedding dress, and the wedding party. Everyone laughed. Marie just ordered chocolate cake and ice cream.

Hans declared the next day a holiday. They all went home or to their hotels, and Kilabrew was quiet for a day. Quiet, but not completely inactive as samples, tools, testing devices, paper clothes, and even trash cans continued to disintegrate.

THE BIG LABORATORY

When the working group convened at Kilabrew, they were all in the kitchenette having coffee. Hans proceeded to describe the thing to his niece. He asked Joseph to begin by telling Aaron's case.

When Dr. Staneck told how he stopped the disintegration by placing a magnet around the boy's toe, Annamarie declared, "You have made a mistake. That is voodoo medicine."

"No, no," interjected Hans. "We tried that here. It works. A strong magnetic field stops the growth of whatever this thing is."

Joseph went on, "I found a solution for Aaron, but I knew something very strange was going on. I sent samples of the infected area of his toe to a testing laboratory and also to a lab that I knew had an electron microscope. I never got an answer from either lab."

Nobody ever knew that one of the small packages had fallen off the back of a truck and onto the ground at the dock of the finest mail facility in the world. That facility uses the most modern electronic and mechanical methods of routing millions of packages every day to their destinations. Many trucks arrive at that dock every day. Nobody ever noticed that the small package slowly just disappeared from under the loading ramp. The building maintenance people noticed that they had to add new asphalt ever so often where a hole appeared under the dock. If it wasn't filled up with new asphalt at least once a month, the hole got bigger in diameter and depth.

The other package did arrive at the lab with the electron microscope. At this point, Emil continued the story. "The thing destroyed the electron microscope slowly, circuit board by circuit board, and eventually the entire scope disintegrated. One of those circuit boards was sent to me to analyze. Tony and Marie do all my preliminary work and actually most of the testing of everything we receive here. They could find nothing at all. The affected parts of that circuit board simply did not respond to any test at all. They tried acids, alkali, enzymes, heat, light, and everything they could think of, but there was no response at all."

"But they are childs, not scientists," Annamarie blurted. "Surely they made mistakes."

"These two are no longer children," said Emil as he put his arms around Tony and Marie. "They are the best assistants I have ever had, and I have complete confidence in them. When they could not get any response from the circuit board, they asked me to analyze it. I got the same result—none. Then I called Hans, and so far we still have no answer, but piece by piece, our lab is disintegrating. Every forceps or clip that touched that board began to disappear. Even the paper clothes we wear are disintegrating. That is why there are so many boxes of them here. You will have to wear paper too. Every few hours we change paper. Modesty cannot be predominant here until we know what the thing is."

"Annamarie, I am getting old," Hans said. "Perhaps there is something simple I have overlooked. That is why I called you, and many more scientists from all around the world, to convene here in Chicago. Surely someone will find the answer! The thing has already done harm to a boy in New York, and it has also gotten Tony shot and nearly killed. We have to stop this thing! We have to!"

"How did Tony get shot?" Annamarie asked. "He looks healthy to me."

Tony and Marie answered her question by telling of their adventurous trip to Binghamton. Annamarie almost smiled when Marie described their changing clothes in the Volkswagen.

"It must have been like this place will be when hundreds of scientists are taking off their clothes together in this little laboratory," Annamarie predicted.

"No, that will not happen here," Hans said. "We have rented a warehouse and have had a special facility built there for our work. Emil, I think we should go there today to check on the progress of the work there. We have only a few days to correct mistakes and finish up."

Annamarie was amazed when she saw the huge building. "This is as big as the hangar that once housed the Hindenburg!"

Hans smiled as he remembered that huge hangar. Then he began a description of the laboratory that he and Emil had built inside this warehouse. "Only these two doors open from the outside. All the other doors will be kept locked. Come on into this auditorium. I'm not sure exactly how many people will be working in here since some of the scientists I invited to help me will be bringing assistants with them. We have two hundred seats here. I hope that is enough. I guess we can rent more folding chairs if we have to.

"Those tables along the sides will be set up for the noon meal, which will be served by a catering company. We will be using this room quite often because I want full disclosure of everything each scientist discovers. Each of us can relate that bit of data to whatever we are working on individually."

Dr. Staneck said, "I have never seen an auditorium built of plywood before. It sure isn't the lobby of the Biltmore."

Hans explained, "Besides contacting the best scientists around the world, we also contacted governments and investors. Each scientist also contacted friends with money to donate to our cause. However, it is really hard to ask for money and not explain exactly what it is for. Therefore, we do not have unlimited funds.

If we had revealed what we know, there would be mass panic around the whole earth. Besides, we built this place to work in, not to enjoy like some kind of resort. Everything here is very spartan but very functional."

The group walked through the small auditorium to the stage in front. There Tony explained, "This stage is not only the stage. It is actually the floor of the laboratory itself. Everything is built on this platform. We wanted to keep it lower and just use two-by-eights. I could not find a conveyor belt system to fit in such a small space, so the floor of the laboratory is twenty-four inches above the warehouse floor. The conveyor belts carry away any trash to a big Dumpster, which is at the back of the laboratory but still inside the warehouse. It too is raised above the floor. All of this is to prevent contamination of the building or the city. Under the workbench, each lab has a hole in the floor right above a conveyor belt."

Dr. Staneck asked, "Is that what I hear running below us?"

"Yes, the contractor must be testing it," Tony said. "It is a bit noisy, so I guess we will just run it after quitting time. I could not find a silent one. I know some of the scientists will complain about the noise, but we are not looking for sound waves or music, so it should work.

"The whole thing will just be thrown away after we solve this mess, so I kept the conveyor system within a small budget."

"Are these the restrooms? Annamarie asked. "What are these other two doors for?"

"No, these are locker rooms where we will change into work clothes, which are those paper clothes you saw Emil and me wearing at Kilabrew," Hans explained. "We will put our clothes in here. Then we will take them back out the other side of the locker, when we come back out of the lab area. These shelves will be kept supplied with paper clothes and paper booties. Tony, have you found a supply room clerk yet?"

"No, sir," Tony answered. "I have not had a bite, or even a nibble, from my newspaper ads."

"Not a bite or nibble?" Hans asked. "Do you want people to eat their newspaper?"

While Tony and Marie were laughing, Emil explained, "Tony was comparing his effort to catch a person to run the supply room to throwing out a line and hook to catch fish."

"Ach so!" Hans said then went on to further describe the project. "The exit room has a shower that I hope will carry away any contamination our bodies might have picked up from the thing. To protect Chicago, the laboratory is not connected directly to the water supply. Instead, the water runs out of the end of a pipe then drops into the top of that big tank you can see up there."

Tony continued the description of the special facilities that were installed to prevent contamination. "The waste water does not go into the Chicago sewer system either. It will be pumped into a big tanker truck. I hope we find a way to cure the thing before that tank is full. If not, we will have to buy another tanker truck."

Annamarie looked around in the locker room and said, "There is no toilet in here, but we are still human beings. We can't work all day without relief."

Marie laughed and said, "Oh, we thought about that too. Each lab within this big laboratory has its own toilet and a wash basin. They are really plain, and there is just a plywood panel for privacy. This keeps us from wasting time decontaminating every time we have to pee. What good is modesty if we don't find a solution to this thing that will eat our bodies and the whole earth anyway?"

Then as she thought about that, Marie began to cry. Tony took her in his arms and held her, but soon he was crying too. Before long there was not a dry eye in the group. One of the workmen who was building the big project stopped hammering and just stared at the whole crying group. He had heard the rumors going around that this bunch of scientists was planning to ship babies to Mars or someplace by osmosis or something. Their crying frightened him even more than the rumors had.

Emil opened the back door of the locker room, and the six of them entered a long corridor that had rooms on each side. Emil explained to Dr. Staneck and Annamarie that the first two rooms were an office on one side and a small meeting room on the other side of the corridor. "These meeting rooms are for sharing information among small groups of scientists who will be working on similar problems. We want to keep this a completely open group with no secrets at all. Any small detail could be the answer to eliminating or controlling the thing."

Tony added, "We are leaving the rooms on all four corners of this complex to be meeting rooms. Each of all the other rooms is a complete laboratory. Each room will be supplied with scientific equipment. There will be microscopes, spectrographs, centrifuges, balances, Bunsen burners, and racks of glassware and tubing. Every electronic testing device—like voltmeters, oscilloscopes, spectrum analyzers and frequency counters, Geiger counters, radio frequency detectors and whatever other devices a particular branch of science needs—will be supplied here. We are going all out to catch this wild turkey. Like Mom used to say, 'If we don't come home with a bird, there ain't gunna be no Thanksgiving!'"

Marie laughed and said, "Oh, Tony. Your mother doesn't talk like that."

"Well, you know what I mean. If we don't stop the thing, our goose is cooked—or rather we are."

Hans said, "We grouped the labs around similar sciences. This first group of rooms is for chemistry. As you can see, it is being stocked with glass and Bunsen burners, at least one centrifuge, and some other special instruments. The next group of labs is for biochemistry. Other groups are for physics and electricity. We had to rearrange some of the labs after we found out that magnetism stopped the growth of the thing on that little boy's toe. We made a whole group of labs just to study that energy."

Annamarie looked around inside one of the labs, and sure enough, she saw a toilet with just a single sheet of plywood put up for privacy. Each time the group walked past one or several workmen who were putting finishing touches in the strange thing they were building, the hammering stopped. The workmen just stared at the strange group of foreign-sounding scientists.

Tony could not help himself. He looked up at one man and said, "Boo!"

The poor man dropped his hammer and had to climb back down the ladder to retrieve it. Tony laughed, and Hans gave him a dirty look. They were all having a hard time with the city officials, contractors, and the building owner because they were afraid to reveal the real function of the laboratories. Tony should have known better because it was he who had the most direct contact with all the city officials the scientists had to deal with.

Hans, Emil, Tony, and Marie examined each of the twenty-four labs on the north side of the temporary building then crossed another corridor that led to the south side. Two carpenters were installing shelves in the first two rooms there at the rear of the labs. There was a door at the rear of the building that was open, and another man was unloading supplies from Emil's favorite scientific supply company. He was filling shelves in the two supply rooms almost as fast as the carpenters were building them.

When Sam saw Emil, Tony, and Marie, he stopped work for a minute to talk to them. "I always thought that Kilabrew is the best testing laboratory in Chicago, and now I know it is. You folks really stop at nothing to solve a problem. I still don't know what it is you are working on this time, but you should hear some of the stories going around in here and even all around Chicago. I heard that you will be reducing children to their atoms and then laser-beaming them to some planet across the galaxy. Of course, by the time they get there, they will be adults. I nearly died laughing when I heard that one. The guy telling that story was pointing to the big machine I was carrying in on a handcart. It was just a centrifuge."

Everybody laughed about that. When the group had moved on to the labs on the south side of the site, Hans said, "Well, as long as the people believe those stories, their children will be well-supervised and safe. If they knew the truth, they would all be much more frightened. We would have complete panic and chaos."

Sam overheard Hans, but he knew Tony, Marie, and Emil well. He just stared at the receding people and said nothing. He was sure curious though. The rumors gave Tony a problem that he had not yet solved. He had to find someone to work the storage rooms and take supplies to the laboratories. So far he had no response to the want ads he had posted in the newspaper.

Emil and Hans examined every one of the labs but spent the most time in the one closest to the supply room. This was to be the one they would share for their own experiments.

Emil explained, "This is our project, and we do not want to have to wait for anything. Besides, we are too old to be running back and forth very far."

When the group reached the front of the building, they followed the front corridor to two doors that led out of the complex. One door was at the end of the south corridor and bore the international symbol for men. The other door was at the end of the north corridor and bore the sign for women. Passing through those doors, the group entered other rooms that had showers on the outside walls and lockers on the inside. This was the other side of the same lockers, which they had seen when they first entered the laboratory.

Memories linger for a lifetime. Dr. Staneck was glad when Emil checked each of the showers. It was water that came out, not gas. He kept that observation to himself and said, "You two have taken great pains to protect this building and the city of Chicago. I can't think of anything you might have missed."

Emil and Hans knew their precautions were not foolproof, but at least they would slow down contamination of the city by the thing.

Joseph and Annamarie were both awed by the size of the facilities and the extent of the precautions that the two old scientists had taken.

All six of the scientists were amused when they overheard some of the workers who were still constructing the labs. The workmen had been told that the two crazy old Germans who were building the project wanted to find a way to travel through space by osmosis or something.

Emil found the project foreman, made some suggestions, and asked if the project was on schedule. It was indeed on schedule. Emil thanked the foreman for that. He mentally thanked Marie and Tony for the tremendous amount of work they had done to oversee and complete this project. He loved those youngsters more and more every day.

LIFE AND WORK

Two days after Emil and Hans inspected the construction of the labs, the scientists began to arrive. Marie chartered a shuttle bus to take them to their hotels. Most of the scientists were quite content with their accommodations, but there were about fifty or sixty complaints about food, location, bed size, and hotel personnel. Marie handled all she could, but many complaints required Tony's knowledge of other languages. Both of the lab assistants were kept quite busy for two days.

Most of the complaints stopped when all the scientists convened in the auditorium at the warehouse. A few problems persisted because spouses stayed behind in the hotels or ventured forth, in spite of gangsters, and got lost in Chicago. They would call the only number they had, which was Kilabrew, and Marie would send a cab or give directions.

After two more days, Tony and Marie shut down Kilabrew and reported to the warehouse office. There they joined in the morning and evening meetings with the scientists. Emil still would not allow his assistants to work in the lab. His reason was that he needed them by the phones and to pick up whatever was needed.

"At least we don't have to eat pizza every day," Tony commented. At lunch and dinner, meals were catered in the auditorium. The chairs were moved, and tables were added. After about two weeks, Emil noticed the food was not as good as it had been earlier, and the service seemed really hurried.

When Marie called the catering company, the owner told her that the catering staff was frightened of the scientists. The rumor was that they were experimenting with ways to combine osmosis and genetics to teleport people great distances. If anyone got too close to the scientists, they could pick up something that would cause babies to be born without arms, legs, or heads.

Marie reassured the caterer that the rumors were not true. There was no danger. Emil and Tony addressed the catering staff that evening, and Tony assured the people that the scientists were equally afraid of them. In his best gangster mode, Tony said that the men of science were no match for Chicago gangsters. Any street urchin with a tommy gun could blow away any scientist who tried to mutate the babies and teleport them to Mars!

He had everyone in stitches, except two of the scientists. One was Annamarie, who failed to see the humor. The other was an elderly atomic scientist from Uzbekistan. This man had lived most of his life under Soviet Union rule. The poor fellow actually believed Tony and tried to escape through a locked door. Another scientist from Uzbekistan, a young woman, stopped him and explained that Tony was only joking. Jokes were foreign to this fellow from Tashkent. It took quite a bit of talking to calm his fear.

Marie also addressed everyone and assured the catering people that if they quit, Emil would make her do all the cooking. Then the scientists would be in grave danger. This produced more laughter, and from then on, the meals were great and on time.

There were problems among the scientists themselves. There were fifty-two labs altogether with two or three scientists in each lab. Problems arose from simple personality clashes, as in any group of people suddenly thrown together. Men from eastern European countries didn't trust any of the Russians. The three Israeli scientists didn't trust anyone. In one lab where three American scientists were working, a strange chart soon appeared on the blackboard. When Emil and Hans visited there, they asked about it.

"Oh, that has nothing to do with science," a man from Denver said. "It is our football pool."

Neither Emil nor Hans knew what that was until the three Americans explained it. Hans was still confused. Football was soccer to him. Emil laughed and said that after this was all over, they would go to a Chicago Bears game. The American scientists were advised to keep their minds on the thing and to erase the football pool. This they did, right after they copied it onto paper and hid it in a drawer.

There was one team that consisted of a French scientist and his wife, a really gifted and well-known geneticist. The third member was a young woman from Switzerland who was an expert in inherited diseases and conditions.

Every time Emil visited that lab, he could feel tension in the air so thick he thought he could cut it with a knife. The French couple was near fifty in age, and the Swiss girl was young and very pretty indeed. The Frenchman was constantly stressing the "fact" that different ways of doing sexual intercourse affected the genetic outcome of offspring. Also, he often found it necessary to adjust the paper clothing of the Swiss girl.

On Emil's third visit there, he could tell that the wife was very angry. She actually had her fist wrapped around a microscope base, and not in any position usually used to adjust it, but rather in a grip to use it as a club.

He solved that problem by moving the Swiss girl to the lab with the two from Uzbekistan. There the two young girls got along well together and with the older man.

Other adjustments were made too. Hans and Emil decided that the ability to work together was more productive than restricting each lab to experts in just one branch of science. Some of the labs where adjustments were made became very productive indeed. Discoveries were made that could later be used in industry. None of the labs, however, even came close to solving the thing.

This work went on for months. Babies were born back home. Grandparents died. Young men went off to war. Sometimes the children or grandchildren of two scientists who were working together went to war against each other. None of this stopped the relentless pursuit of the thing. Scientists would fly home to attend a funeral or, in democratic countries, to vote. All who took leave returned and resumed the work.

Robin, the reporter Marie had met in Binghamton, called Marie at home three times. Each time she begged to be called first whenever the story was ready to go to press.

The Chicago media was buzzing with curiosity about the warehouse that could not be rented. Something really strange was going on there. Rumors were rampant, but no reporter got any information at all from the young couple that manned the small office.

Inside the labs, every cycle of the frequency spectrum was being studied, from very, very low audio frequencies to cosmic rays. Ever more powerful generators of these frequencies were being employed. More and more powerful magnetic energy was also being studied. Emil and Hans had not invested much money in magnetic, electrostatic, or electromagnetic shielding. All this energy leaking out of the warehouse caused weird anomalies in electronic equipment passing by on the street. Taxicab radios would sometimes play music. GPS equipment would give erroneous directions or locations. Even coffeemakers in nearby buildings did not work right. Every night the evening news told of strange things happening around that warehouse building. Even the national news media mentioned the weird happenings.

One such report prompted Robin to call from Binghamton and pump Marie for any news she could release. All Marie would concede was that the strange happenings were indeed related to Marie's visit to New York State.

"How is your friend?" Robin asked.

"Oh, Tony is fine. He can't lift his arm as high as before yet, and it is not as strong as before. But it is healing and improving steadily," Marie replied.

"Well, take good care of him. He is quite a man. And please don't forget me when this story breaks," Robin pleaded.

"I'll keep my promise," Marie said. "At this time, I just don't know enough yet."

ANNAMARIE

Month after month, the work went on relentlessly, but not twenty-four hours a day. People needed to rest. Even Annamarie, as dedicated as she was, had to have some kind of life besides work and sleep. Marie committed herself to the task of introducing the austere German scientist to American culture. She and Tony took her to movies, pizza shops, department stores, roller-skating, bowling, and baseball games. For a long time, Annamarie felt that her companions were frivolous childish fools. After months of observing their antics and seeing the amount of work they accomplished successfully, however, her point of view began to change.

One payday, when Tony was making the rounds of all the labs to deliver checks, Annamarie was peering into her microscope. She was comparing the effects of photosynthesis on samples of plants that had been exposed to disintegrating material and similar plants that had not been exposed. Tony greeted her cheerfully and tossed her paycheck onto her workbench. A new growth began in Annamarie.

Annamarie was born a Nazi in a country that was determined to rise from defeat in World War I to world dominance. Perfection was demanded of her right from birth. Her father was a local official in the Nazi party. He expected nothing but the best from his children. She learned to work hard. Play was discouraged, silliness was forbidden, and personal feelings were suppressed.

Then came another defeat for this great nation. Food became scarce. To live, one had to be wily and crafty. Annamarie had to steal, cheat, or do anything to survive.

Then along came Communism. This "ism" promised food for everyone and a life of idealism. The government owned everything in Annamarie's part of divided Germany. Private initiative was discouraged. Absolute devotion and loyalty was demanded of everyone by the new regime. Reporting of any disloyalty to Communism, past or present, was encouraged and rewarded.

Annamarie's father had been an important Nazi party member, but under Communism, he was working at collecting goose fat in a soap factory. Three days after Annamarie reported his former Nazi status, her father was marched out of the soap factory and hanged in the nearby woods. Annamarie was rewarded with an extra ten marks, about $2.50 in her next paycheck.

Within this ten-year-old girl, fear, hate, loneliness, and sorrow created a thick defensive wall of suppressed feelings. Crushed under heavy layers of desolation was a tiny, almost nonexistent germ of normal life—of love. Marie's abundance of love for people and life put fertilizer and water on that small germ. It began to grow. It pierced the thick layers of oppression, suppression, and toughness and sent tentacles forth to probe the area beyond Annamarie's own sphere. After fifty years of dormancy, they finally attached themselves to another human being—Tony.

Annamarie had had a few relationships with men before, but they involved little besides sex. There was never any feeling of love or trust, and now she was a newborn baby in this department.

She looked away from her microscope and gave Tony a big smile and said, "Hi, Tony."

This was the beginning of a really big problem for Marie. For Tony, it was the beginning of a source of amusement. He was totally dedicated to Marie, but he was also aware of Annamarie's delicate and fragile mental condition. He didn't quite know how to respond to her beaming smile.

He simply replied with a smile and a, "Hey, what's happening, babe?" and continued on his rounds

He was thinking, *Did I see what I thought I saw? Is that old gal hitting on me? Oh my! Should I tell Marie? No, I better not—not yet anyway.*

In the days and weeks that followed, Annamarie found every excuse she could think of to be near Tony. She even found every excuse to send Marie away on wild-goose chases and consulted with Tony as much as possible.

Of course, this attempt to steal her man had an impact on Marie. Annamarie was much older than Marie, but she was still a beautiful woman. She had no scruples about hurting someone else who got in her way. Survival techniques learned during the war made Annamarie vicious and determined to succeed.

It didn't help when Tony teased Marie, telling her how beautiful, talented, and debonair Annamarie was. Marie began to feel very self-conscious of her being somewhat overweight. She began to try diets and even skip meals altogether. She did lose some weight, but she also lost much of her vitality. She began to make mistakes and arrive late for work. Sometimes she cried for no obvious reason.

Tony had no intention of ending their relationship. He was totally dedicated to Marie but was enjoying the fight over him. However, he felt that Annamarie was mentally unstable. He actually feared that she would do something radical to herself, or to him, if he told her he had no interest in her at all. He simply didn't know how to end her infatuation.

He did know how to handle Marie, however. He finally returned to the office after an errand, took her by the hand, and led her outside to his car. They went to a nearby park, and there Tony repeated his vows of love for her. He assured Marie that he had no interest in anyone but her. He told her he was worried about her losing weight and, most of all, her loss of vitality and spontaneity. Over and over, he told her of his love for her.

He talked and talked. Marie finally laughed and asked, "Okay, Romeo, what are you going to do about this mess?"

"I really don't know, Marie. I feel like I am in the middle of a mine field, that any wrong step will be my last. Annamarie is so unstable, I'm afraid to hurt her. I wish I had just ignored her at the beginning of this whole thing. I'm so sorry I hurt you. I just don't know what to do," Tony answered.

They discussed ways of getting out of the predicament all through dinner and most of the night, which they spent at Tony's apartment.

All of this did not go unnoticed by Emil and Hans. At first, they too were amused by Annamarie's attempt to steal Tony's affections. They discussed the situation and how it affected the search for the solution of their big problem. When Tony and Marie left work with no explanation or without even saying good-bye, the two old scientists decided to intervene.

Both men had survived the war and near starvation, just as Annamarie had. Both had had their hearts broken, at one time or another, and they survived that too. They decided to be blunt and tough with Annamarie, but also to employ a distraction technique.

The next morning, Tony and Marie arrived for work on time, and both were smiling and happy again. Hans called them and Annamarie into the office. He surprised all three by telling Annamarie to end her pursuit of Tony. It was hurting the mission they were all on. They reassigned her to a different laboratory in the complex. They said they needed her talent to be put to better use, studying the molecular structure of soil that had been exposed to disappearing stuff.

Their real reason to reassign her was that the lab they sent her to was manned by two men about her own age. The single men were not accomplishing much anyway, and perhaps Annamarie's ardor could be redirected.

Marie could only guess what was going on because the whole conversation was conducted in German. Tony told her later what had been said. Annamarie moved to the other lab, and immediately, life returned to normal in the complex.

Annamarie did, indeed, become interested in the two scientists in the new assignment. Not only did she get along well with them, but also that lab became very productive.

WHAT'S MISSING

Day after day, the work in the warehouse laboratory continued. Nearly every day, a truck from a scientific supply company delivered huge cartons of hands-free devices, beakers, tubing, electronic testing equipment, microscope parts, forceps, rubber gloves, and paper clothing. All of this equipment was needed to replace whatever the thing was destroying. It was just as relentless as the scientists.

At the end of each day, or more precisely at 5:00 p.m., each of the labs delivered, via computer, their daily report to a master computer. It was Marie and Tony who edited, printed out copies of each report, and made notations of any relationships between reports. One day Marie was taking a break with Tony. Marie had a strange look on her face, and she was deep in thought.

"What's on your mind, honey?" Tony asked.

"Tony, day after day we read those reports from the scientists," Marie said. "Every day they report on what they found. They never report on what they didn't find."

"Why should they report that they didn't find anything?" Tony laughed. "Day after day you would see the same words."

"That's not what I mean, Tony. They keep looking for something that is there. What if the thing is something that should be there and isn't?"

"Good grief, Marie, I think you're right! Conduction through a semiconductor is done by electrons, which are there, or by holes, which are the lack of electrons. Are electrons missing? And if so, why?" Tony asked. "Where is Emil?"

At the next general meeting of all the scientists, Emil asked Marie and Tony to come to the stage. Emil asked them to relate their observations to the entire assembly. Marie's message was greeted with complete silence. No one spoke.

Finally, Emil said simply, "Think about it."

Most of the scientists retired for the night. A few of them went back to their labs. The next day the quest for the thing took on a whole new approach. People who were discouraged or bored worked with renewed vigor.

REGENERATION

Dr. Staneck, a man of medicine, not pure science, went home to Binghamton and resumed his practice. Emil and Hans left one lab empty for quite a long while. They remembered the two professors from the University of New Mexico and called them several times about coming to work at the big Chicago lab. Ben and Sam wanted to leave right away, but they had a contract they had to honor at the college. They continued to work there and to coordinate their work with Hans's and Emil's. But they were hampered by the separation and by an interfering benefactor who insisted on controlling their research. They finally went to court to get out of the contract. The trial lasted several months. During that time, there was no effective work done on regeneration or genetics.

Finally, Hans contacted several of his colleagues from around the world who all testified that the court case was hampering scientific research rather than helping. The suit was dropped, and the benefactor released the two scientists.

The move to the Chicago lab was further delayed by problems that Ben had. His wife was an archaeologist working on ancient ruins in New Mexico and did not wish to interrupt her work there. His children did not want to change schools and especially did not want to move to a big city. Ben finally found a way to commute that would not put him into the poorhouse.

When these two scientists finally did begin to work in the big laboratory, they soon became very popular with all the other researchers. The two men were not any more friendly or handsome than anybody else there, but they did many experiments on all kinds of small animals. The little critters captured hearts with their antics.

All but one of the women loved the furry little critters. The mathematician from Ohio was afraid of snakes, mice, and just about anything with four legs.

Ben and Sam kept very strict records of their work. They were almost paranoid about their critters getting into any situation that might corrupt their data.

Of course, sometimes it is just too much temptation for a young woman to resist picking up and petting a furry little critter. Neither Ben nor Sam had eyes in the back of his head and could not always see what was going on in their lab. Sam turned around one time and saw a young girl from another lab with one of his latest projects in her hands. He lost it and yelled at her, frightening both her and the little guinea pig. The girl screamed and jumped back, and the guinea pig fell to the floor. It hit the floor running. It ran across the corridor and right into the mathematics lab and sought refuge behind the legs of the math specialist from Ohio.

The second scream was a scream of pure terror. It resounded throughout the laboratory and startled a chemist, who then spilled some sulfuric acid into a beaker of some kind of alkali. The reaction there was loud, smelly, and created smoke. It activated the sprinkler system, set off the audio alarm, and pandemonium broke. At least sixty people were shouting and cursing in about thirty different languages. The laboratory was flooded, and the liquid storage tank soon became nearly full before Emil got the water turned off. Suddenly the Klaxon went silent, and the deluge stopped. All that could be heard was the crying of one scientist.

After a few minutes of silence, Hans pressed the public address button and asked each group of scientists to clean up their own laboratory. An hour before the normal closing time,

Hans got on the public address again and said, "It is Friday afternoon. If your lab is cleaned up, go home. We will see you all on Monday morning."

It took Hans, Emil, Tony, and Marie all weekend to clean up the mess and remove the contents of the big liquid storage tank. It got pumped into another big tank on a truck. They did not know how to properly dispose of it, so they had it trucked to a different warehouse for storage until they knew more about the thing.

Hans installed a door with lock and key on the regeneration laboratory and put a No Trespassing sign on it. Marie found the terrified little guinea pig hiding under a desk and returned it to its cage. On Monday morning, Sam found it dead. The poor thing had died of a heart attack. Ben and Sam were set back in their work about eight weeks. They were brilliant scientists though, and their work was very fruitful indeed. In fact, Hans thought that their work would be of great benefit to the whole world, even if it did not identify the thing.

PERSONAL PROBLEMS

Every one of the scientists that Hans had invited to help him with this great problem of things disappearing was someone he knew personally or who was known around the world scientific circles as an expert in his or her field. They were all brilliant scientists, but they were all human beings too. Many had families. Some of them brought their families to Chicago. Sometimes that caused the scientist no end of problems. Everyone thought that Emil's great problem would be solved in a month or so.

The trip to America was expected to be an educational experience. Wives and children were eager to see Disney World and the Grand Canyon. They wanted to ski in Colorado and visit Philadelphia, where this great nation began. Hans and Emil both kept meticulous records, and each scientist had a file in the office that kept track of their accomplishments and expenses. Each scientist was free to review his or her own file, and it soon became evident that hotel expenses were way out of line.

As the weeks became months, the expenses mounted so high that some of the scientists began looking for homes to buy. They did buy many homes, and each family settled in to a new kind of life. Children went to school and began to speak English as well as their native tongues. Men who were the spouse of a female scientist found jobs. One man even purchased a restaurant and then expanded it to a chain of popular restaurants that soon outgrew Chicago.

The wife of one scientist from a South American country became part of a protest group that fought for immigration rights. She was a very intelligent woman, and her knowledge soon put her in the leadership of that group. She addressed Congress, attempting to cut through red tape. She herself did not expect to become a citizen, but she fought for those who did. As the time went on, she realized that only in America could a foreigner stand before the greatest and most powerful group of people in the world and state her cause.

Her husband was so engrossed in his work that he was completely unaware that his wife was even in the protest group. He was only dimly aware that she had been gone for a couple days when she went to Washington. He did not even know where she went. He did not know that his seventeen-year-old daughter had won a science scholarship and was accepted by MIT.

This South American scientist was studying subatomic changes occurring in organic substances that had been exposed to the thing. He was thoroughly enjoying the freedom to study and to obtain materials he needed. He was free from having to bribe officials, free from endless red tape, and free to just study and learn as he had never been before. He was so engrossed in his studies that he would sometimes get up in the middle of the night and go to the lab to confirm a theory that had entered his mind.

He was unaware of problems at home or that his sixteen-year-old son was also a gifted student and at the top of his class at school. The son complained that he had to do all the chores at home. Finally, one day, his wife hid the coffeemaker and the coffee. This guy drank coffee all the time, and this was the only way to interrupt his thoughts. It worked. The poor guy went bananas trying to find some coffee.

His daughter just happened to let it slip—uh-huh—that the coffee was hidden in the bathroom. While he was looking for it there, the other three pushed him into the shower and turned on the water. Then they proceeded to undress him and gave him a bath with hot water and then a cold rinse. This guy had even forgotten to wash or shave or brush his teeth. Only the pressures of metabolism got him into the bathroom.

This unexpected bath got his attention, and his wife informed him that he would not be going to work the next day. She informed him that his wife and children were becoming American citizens that day and that he would be required to attend the ceremony. She had already cleared this with Emil. After the ceremony and during dinner at a fine restaurant, she informed the foreigner that she lived with that he had six months to study things like the Constitution and Declaration of Independence and to become a citizen himself. He complied.

He was not the only one. One country had several scientists at that project, and all of them became American citizens. This almost caused an international incident. Their country had a dictator who made it nearly impossible to express any kind of individuality in science, art, economics, or business. These scientists often socialized together in Chicago, and then they learned of our South American scientist. They convinced him to join them in learning English better and studying to become Americans. They all attended the next naturalization ceremony.

At the United Nations, there were several countries complaining about the brain drain. They demanded an investigation. Three of those countries voided visas and completely restricted travel outside their countries. That divided families, of course, and it gave Hans and Emil the biggest problem they had besides identifying the thing. They worked hard to support their scientists, but it was very difficult to do this without revealing the thing to the general population. The resulting terror and panic would be almost as bad as the great tragedy that would result if they did not find a solution to the disintegration.

There were unmarried scientists in Chicago too. These men and women were brilliant people, but outside of work at the labs, loneliness was their only companion. Thrown together by their common interest in biochemistry and, specifically, the chemistry involved in the beginning and end of life, were a young girl from a small far east nation and a young man from Latvia. Neither of them could speak English very well, but their common interest and their intelligence made it possible to communicate.

Ming Su checked her personal file every day. She soon came to the conclusion that she could not stay in the bed-and-breakfast establishment that Marie had found for her and remain cost-effective. She befriended a young Chinese American girl and two other American girls, and they discussed everything from boys to expenses. Finally they rented a small house together and shared expenses.

Loneliness was never again a problem for any of them. Many an evening was filled with pillow fights, hilarious laughter, and stories of relationships with boys and even their parents. Ming Su had a difficult time relating her stories to the other girls because her English was not very good at all. It required a lot of word searching, gesticulation, and help from the Chinese American girl, who spoke only a little of Ming Su's dialect. Ming Su finally made the others understand her story of the obvious physical effect that very scientific discussion of copulation had on Valdi, her Latvian partner. The girls' laughter could be heard a half block away and long into the night as Ming Su tried to duplicate Valdi's various contortions when trying to hide his obvious reaction.

The next morning, Ming Su had a very hard time keeping from laughing whenever she looked at Valdi or talked to him. Valdi was very confused by Ming Su's demeanor that day, but they shared lunch together. There they decided to attend classes where they could learn English together. Marie got them both signed up at a local community college.

Ming Su's loneliness problem was solved, but Valdi still had lonely evenings. He filled many of his by looking for a cheaper apartment. He was the only Latvian working in the labs, and relating to the other men was not easy for him. The classes in English with Ming Su helped fill his evenings.

Most of Valdi's money was sent home to help support his parents. The fifty or so years of Communism had left them in poverty, and Valdi's help was much appreciated. He got a part-time job washing dishes in a restaurant and many mornings came to work tired and sleepy.

Tony knew none of the Latvian language, but they both knew German, so a friendship developed. Often Tony invited Valdi to share dinner with him and Marie. Valdi did accept once but felt like a third wheel all evening. He demurred after that one time. Besides that, he had to wash dishes in the very restaurant where they had eaten that evening. When Tony learned of Valdi's part-time job, he related that bit of news to Emil and to Hans, who hit the ceiling. He immediately called Valdi to the office for a meeting. Poor Valdi thought he was in deep trouble.

After discussing Valdi's financial problems back home, Hans ordered him to quit the job and just concentrate on solving problems in the lab. Hans believed that Valdi and Ming Su were at the very heart of the whole problem. He did not want anything to interfere with their work, especially fatigue. Hans then set up a special account for Valdi's parents and even boosted Valdi's salary.

The hours spent with Ming Su affected Valdi greatly. English is a very hard language to learn, and the two found that it required many hours of study outside the classroom. They tried studying at Ming Su's house, but Valdi's problem with "th" and Ming Su's with the letter *L* usually caused so much laughter that the other girls were no help at all.

They met in Valdi's tiny apartment. They were both young and healthy and soon learned that their knowledge of biochemistry did not protect them from its affecting them. Within two months, they were looking for a bigger apartment. Soon they began to double date with Tony and Marie. The four of them went to restaurants, theaters, ball games, and even stores. Within six months, Valdi and Ming Su were both speaking English with a Chicago accent. Also within six months, Marie had Valdi, an atheist, and Ming Su, a Buddhist, attending church with her and Tony.

Ming Su soon became engrossed in learning of the life of Jesus Christ and his teachings. Valdi found it hard to believe that his own intelligence was not superior to that of a fictional character who lived two thousand years ago. A dead man coming back to life was only a dream of illiterate fishermen and shepherds. Many hours with Tony and Marie and much discussion turned his thinking completely around. It was actually Valdi who first stated that the existence of God explained many mysteries of science.

This new knowledge was a great comfort to Ming Su when she learned that her mother had died. Her government had pulled her visa, and Ming Su knew that if she went home for the funeral, she could never leave there again. She agonized over that for two days but chose freedom and stayed in America. She knew that her father's heart was twice broken, but he was a strict government official in his country and did not even respond to Ming Su's letters.

Ming Su was not the only scientist who suffered from insecure governments that used dictatorial powers to protect their policies and right to exist. One plant biologist was from an African country that was run by a general whose power was maintained by clubbing to death anyone who did not agree with him. He even killed his own brother. His main interest in life was finding better weapons to protect himself and to solidify his control of his country.

This tinhorn dictator learned that Sati had taken a leave from his job, that of trying to find a poison that would kill many people very quickly. He sent an urgent message to the lab in Chicago telling Sati that if he did not return in five days, his family would be killed.

Sati took the next flight out. When he arrived two days later, he learned that his family had already been clubbed to death. Sati was chained to his lab bench and forced to continue his research on poisons. Sati committed suicide.

DISASTER

When the big laboratory was built within the warehouse building, the floor was made of heavy sheets of plywood nailed down onto two-by-eights. The whole floor was laid. Then when the walls were put up, the walls did not always stand at the end of a four-by-eight sheet of plywood flooring. It was not the best or strongest way to erect walls, but this was a temporary building not meant to last very long.

At every meeting, Hans and Emil stressed the need for infinite care in handling corrosive materials, especially those that had been effected by the thing. It had been learned that a single grain of any effected material, which had been ground up for analysis, would in turn affect anything that it touched. The thing seemed to have infinite power and was extremely dangerous.

Chicago had been Krystal's hometown. She was born and raised there. Her whole family was living in the area, and she was happy living there. She did not marry a hometown boy though. After high school, she went to nursing school, and then she joined the army to help out in the war effort, as so many people did in that great generation of Americans. She did not end up caring for wounded boys from Washington, Pennsylvania, or Florida, but instead she cared for wounded enemy soldiers from Germany.

Some of those young men were very bitter. They had been caught by their enemy and could no longer dream of special blessings from Der Fuhrer when he had finally conquered all of Europe. Their dreams were shattered.

Most of the soldiers, however, were like any other boys. They were just glad to be alive and out of the fighting. They were all fearful and homesick. Many of them had personal problems that the terrors of war had intensified. The American nurses did all they could to alleviate the fears, but the language barrier made that difficult.

Some of the prisoners did speak some English, and these men were able to converse with their nurses. Some even flirted with them. Krystal was often reprimanded for spending too much time at the bedside of one German soldier who seemed to have quite a good sense of humor. He had some infection problems that justified extra attention, and Krystal spent more and more time with him. Within a month, they were discussing his future, her future, and soon, their future.

Soon, Krystal was showing up in the ward when she was off duty. She would wheel Emil out to a grassy area outside where they would talk for hours. Emil's wounds finally healed, and he was put to work in the butcher shop. Krystal continued to visit with Emil, using the excuse that his wounds needed to be monitored.

By the time Emil returned to his home in Germany, he was totally in love with his American nurse. He became a student in a university in Darmstadt where he studied under a young scientist named Hans Gossl. He continued to correspond with Krystal. Three years after the end of the war, it was plain to see that, with help from their former enemy's Marshall Plan, Germany was recovering and fast becoming a major industrial power in the world. Volkswagens were being loaded onto ships at Bremerhaven by the thousands and then the millions. The future looked bright for a young budding scientist in this great land.

Emil was blinded to that great recovery and future. He was blinded by love. That love became the most powerful force in

Emil's life. He too boarded a ship at Bremerhaven. After a stop at Southampton, England, it sailed to America. After several days at the foot of the Statue of Liberty, Emil boarded a train for Chicago. There he was received not only by Krystal's open arms but also Chicago's. He began a new married life and also a new business that soon flourished. Emil was a happy young man, and he loved his new city. Emil spent most of his life in Chicago and raised his children there. His beloved Krystal died of cancer in his latter years, but he stayed in Chicago and kept his laboratory business going.

Emil was not about to allow the thing to injure his adopted city. He was extremely careful of anything that showed the effect of whatever it was. Over and over he stressed the danger to personnel, to the building, and even Chicago itself. He put "BE CAREFUL" signs in every lab.

Hans had invited only the very best of all the scientists in the world to help with this strange and dangerous project. He and Emil knew that they had the most experienced men and women in every field of science, but they also knew that these were still human beings. They were still prone to mistakes, even though some of them, like Annamarie, denied any such weakness.

Accidents did happen though. One scientist spilled some liquid that had possibly been affected by the thing. Emil had a square meter of wood removed and replaced around the spill, even though it was only a spot about six centimeters in diameter on the floor. Then Emil made a mistake. He publicly reprimanded the man at the next general meeting. When there was another spill in another lab, that scientist cleaned up the spot as well as he could. He sandpapered the spot, collected the dust, and disposed of it properly.

His effort to avoid a problem was not good enough, however. This happened on a Friday afternoon, and nobody was in that lab all weekend. By Monday morning, there was a huge hole in the floor. Two of the two-by-eights that supported the floor were eaten about halfway through.

The scientist who made the spill and then covered it up had been making great progress in his study of the glue that holds everything together at the atomic level. However, Emil was so upset that he sent that man home. The whole project was put on hold until the damage could be repaired. That particular lab was dismantled, and all the wood was carefully put into the disposal Dumpster. The spill was directly over the conveyor belt that carried waste to the Dumpster, so none of the effected material actually touched the warehouse floor. Emil did have the conveyor belt replaced though.

The cleanup and repairs took a whole week. Emil had a trapdoor put in the new lab so he could get down under to check for any damage to the building. He found that he was too old to crawl around there though, so Tony did all the testing on the warehouse floor. Years later, janitors were still trying to clean up the spots that Tony made with his testing chemicals.

All of the scientists were really concerned about the loss of work time because they were all conscious of the desperate need to solve this great problem. To relieve their stress and fill their idle time, many of them ventured out to explore Chicago. Many of them got lost or lost family members and had to find them.

One young man got in a fight in a sports bar over a soccer game. This man's English wasn't very good, and the policeman who showed up to stop the fight could get no information from him. He was afraid to reveal his reason for being in Chicago. Tony had to bail him out of jail.

Annamarie explored Chicago with one of her partners in the laboratory. They spent much time together, and she, who made no mistakes at all, made a big one that week. She got pregnant!

THE MIDDLE EAST LAB

When Hans had enlisted the help of scientists from all over the earth, he called a man from Iraq. This man asked if he could bring two of his assistants. They were young men that he was mentoring, and both of them showed great potential as scientists. One of them was becoming an expert in finding safe containers for various chemicals, and when he heard of the thing, he became very animated and insisted that he be included in the adventure.

Hans thought that any material from the labs that was contaminated could be disposed of at some remote site in Colorado or New Mexico, so he didn't consider any other means of disposal but was pleased that the young man was investigating alternatives. The senior scientist in that lab was assigned to study the molecular changes in liquids, so the study of containers was a handy by-product of the partnership. The liquids had to be stored in something!

The other young man assisted the scientist and became very interested in the study of molecular changes. Together, those two repeated every test that Hans and Emil had conducted on shrinking and disappearing tools. Day after day they repeated test after test and monitored them in many different ways, but like Hans and Emil and Tony and Marie, they could not record any changes of any kind. The stuff just seemed to cease to exist with no sign of residue or energy change.

One anomaly that they all noticed was that anything that touched the samples slowly disappeared. Solids, liquids, and gas all disappeared. The older scientist was slower to notice this anomaly, and all three of the Iraqi scientists agreed that his failing eyesight was the cause. None of them was aware that the brighter light he used to illuminate his work was the real cause of slower depreciation of materials.

Other labs within the laboratory were studying the same thing and reaching the very same conclusions, so the Iraqi scientists concentrated on their assigned study of molecular changes in liquids. Some of their experiments became explosive and some caught fire and some were so caustic that sealed containers were used, but every one of the experiments produced expected or at least explainable results. There were always changes in heat, light, odor, energy, and state—that is solid, liquid or gas—that could be expected and measured.

Once a liquid was impregnated with some thing they knew to be contaminated by the thing for a few minutes and then drained off, that liquid failed to respond to any substance that had previously reacted with it. Some of the reactions had been quite violent before the liquid was exposed, but afterward, there was no reaction at all. The liquid did, however, disappear slowly.

These two Iraqi scientists that were studying liquids were both Shi'a, and the other junior scientist was Sunni. In their home country this would have been a big impediment to their working together, but here in Chicago, they seemed to get along well. Even though they were studying different subjects, the differences were complementary. The two young men got along especially well and would sometimes come up with stories or comments at meetings that would make everyone laugh. Almost everyone anyway.

Tony and Marie enjoyed visiting this lab whenever they had mail to deliver or special information bulletins pertaining to related discoveries made in other labs. Tony did notice that Mufid's laptop was always snapped shut whenever he went into the lab. Also, when he surprised Mufid one time, Tony noticed that the computer was codeword protected. This was not in the spirit of the project since Hans insisted in completely open exchange of information in case someone would notice a change or anomaly that had been missed.

Marie always enjoyed her visits there and enjoyed joking and sparring with the two young men until one day Mufid informed her that she was to be his wife! She was to return to Iraq with him after the project ended. He did not ask her to be his wife. He informed her that she was being ordered to. He was dead serious and made sure Marie knew it!

That evening, Marie informed Tony of Mufid's order. She asked if she could get out of any visits to the Iraqi laboratory. They were still in the office, and Hans and Emil were both there also. None of them had ever seen Tony get so angry. His face was beet red and contorted.

"Where does that camel jockey Arab think he is? What does he think he is? Does that prehistoric rutting billy goat think he can just run off with any other man's wife? Maybe I'll invite him out to a biker bar or introduce him to some of my stevedore friends down at the docks. Those tribesmen have been fighting among themselves for seven thousand years! Isn't that enough for them? Must they come over here and try to take anything they want? Emil, I think we should deport that creep right now! Honey, don't you even go near that lab anymore until we get rid of all three of them Arabs."

"Now, Tony, just settle down a bit. We can't just throw them out. We can't afford an international incident that would bring publicity upon us. News of the thing would get out, and then we would have mass panic all over the earth," Hans pleaded.

In his best mentor mode, Emil put his arm around Tony and pleaded with him to settle down. "We will handle this somehow. Nobody is going to mess with Marie. Nobody! You two collect all the data from that lab. How much good information have we harvested there?"

"Those rutting billy goats have not produced anything as far as I can tell! *Der Hund ist los, die katz ist in die keller und jetzt der bürgermeister* thinks he can play with my wife [The dog is loose, The cat is in the cellar, and now the mayor thinks he can play with my wife]!" Tony fumed.

Marie was more in control of her emotions. "I get regular reports from the two Arabs, uh, scientists working on liquids but never anything from the other guy who is supposed to be studying containers."

"Tony, please give me and Emil a chance to deal with this mess. Maybe a simple reminder that our customs are different here will be enough to solve the problem," Hans pleaded. Then he and Emil ushered Tony and Marie out the front of the complex and suggested they go to a movie or a good meal.

Tony was still in no condition to enjoy a meal or a movie, so the two of them walked for several hours around the streets of Chicago and through a park and then returned to the lab to pick up Tony's car, and then they went to his apartment.

The next morning, they were in the office early and dug into the files. They found no information at all from Mufid. When Tony tried to hack into his computer, he found it so protected that he could not get into it at all.

Marie checked the files and found that his computer was not even connected to the LAN at all. She then checked the telephone records and found invoices for a phone line that was used for only one number. All the calls were very short, which suggested very short data bursts or code words.

Tony located that phone line on the terminal board and connected a high-impedance data-recording device. The high impedance would protect the tap from detection. For several weeks they monitored that line and found that it was encoded and in a Sunni dialect.

Marie located a college professor who was able to decipher the code, and he was invited to the lab by Hans. In the office, that professor was told about the function of the laboratories and the necessity for secrecy. Hans held nothing back and even demonstrated the strange anomaly by showing him equipment that was slowly disappearing.

The professor turned white with fear. The enormity of the destruction that was suddenly revealed to him was almost too much to deal with. But when he started to decode the data that was coming from the recorder, it was Hans's and Emil's turn to turn white.

Mufid was the ringmaster in a plot to eliminate both Shi'a and Kurds from Iraq by having young girls carry either dust or water contaminated by the thing into neighborhoods occupied by the other two groups. It was Mufid's task to develop an innocent-looking jar made of such material that would slow down the activity of disintegration. It didn't have to eliminate it altogether, just slow it down. It didn't even matter if some of the girls became infected. After all, they were just girls.

Hans, Tony, and Emil watched Mufid's activities for several days. Sure enough, after about a week, pottery-making equipment was ordered for Mufid. Also, a motorized grinder and an order for magnets appeared on Marie's list of supplies needed. Tony saw Mufid grinding magnets into very small pieces that were mixed into his pottery mud. He made several water jars like ones seen in Iraq, and each one had different amounts of ground magnets mixed into it. Mufid filled each one with contaminated water or dirt. Each day he measured the thickness of the jar walls and the level of the liquid remaining. He was making meticulous records in his protected computer.

When Hans and Emil thought they had enough information collected, they made a phone call, and one hour later, four men in black suits and dark glasses appeared and escorted Mufid to the shower. At gunpoint, he was made to shower three times. Then he was wrapped in a large towel and escorted out of the laboratory complex. Nobody at the labs knew where he was taken. They never did find out what happened to him.

The other two scientists in that lab were informed of Mufid's plans, and Hans even showed them the recorded data. The elder scientist confirmed the professor's revelation. Both of the men asked for time off, and Hans agreed that it was a good idea. He didn't blame them if they wanted to go home. Neither of them did go home though. Both of them felt it was absolutely necessary to solve the great problem of the thing and to keep other insane people from using it to kill.

The two Shi'a scientists continued Mufid's experiments and measurements and indeed found that the jars greatly extended the life of the material inside. Then Hans had them empty a jar and place it on scales and monitor its weight and thickness. Its disintegration was extremely slow.

A BARE SPOT IN THE WOODS

Dr. Staneck continued to monitor the condition of Aaron's toe, and on one of Aaron's visits, the boy mentioned the big bare spot in the forest that kept getting bigger. He aroused Joseph's curiosity.

"Aaron, what do you know about that spot? Isn't that where you stubbed your toe on a rock?"

"Yeah, that's the place all right, but guess what! That rock is gone. There ain 't nuthin' there now 'cept a hole in the ground, and the hole is gettin' bigger!"

"Aaron, you aren't going near that place, are you?"

"Yeah, but I won't get off the grass. I climbed a tree and went out a limb with binoculars to look at it. My mom told me about a place in the forest where there was a big pile of bones and dirt where some kinda weird people were buried. Mom told me to stay away from there. I never found a big pile of bones and dirt, but Lorraine's great-grandma told her about a big pile like that and said it was haunted. She told her where it was. Lorraine and I figured out that big pile was where the bare spot is now."

"Could you lead me to that spot, Aaron?"

"Sure, but we will have to go the long way. The shortcut goes through some thick mountain laurel. You are too big and old to crawl through the tunnel I made in it. Do you want to go right now?"

"No, I can't go today. There are two men in Chicago I want to take along to show them that spot. Besides, I have other patients coming today. Aaron, I have a weird feeling in my gut about that place. I want you to promise me that you will never go near there again except to lead me there."

"Okay, I'll stay away. I have already told Lorraine to stay away too. Do you believe those old tales about that place?"

"I only know for sure that there are more than a hundred scientists trying to figure out what happened to your toe, and no one knows yet."

"Wow! A hunnert! What's a scientist? I didn't know my toe was so important."

"Scientists are people who try to figure out how things work."

"Oh, you mean like old Harv Mullins who's always trying to figure out how to fix people 's cars?"

"No, not like Harv. Old Harv knows how a car works. The scientists study things like rocks, trees, critters, and all the stuff those things are made of."

Aaron's eyes got big, and he exclaimed, "That's what I do! I like to pick up stuff and write what I know about it and where I find it."

Dr. Staneck looked really surprised. "Do you still have some of the stuff and whatever you wrote about it?"

"I have it all. Dad lets me use the old chicken house for my collection. Mom was really happy when I moved it out of my bedroom. She can clean my room again."

As soon as Aaron left his office, Joseph placed a call to Chicago. He called Emil's home and spoke to Martha because he didn't think he would find the scientist at Kilabrew. He didn't know the number at the warehouse laboratory.

"Please have Emil call me at my office as soon as possible," he requested.

"I sure will," Martha assured him. "How are you and Sophie?"

"We are both well. I have resumed my practice, and Sophie is busy at the senior center where she is senior coordinator and at school where she reads to children. We have a happy life!" Joseph said.

"That's wonderful!" Martha said. "My life is a little lonely now, but I guess that will change whenever Emil finds whatever he is looking for."

"Be encouraged, Martha. That is a noble quest your husband is on, probably the most important quest man has ever made," Joseph said to comfort her.

"Well, I knew it was something important, but I didn't know it was that important. I'll get off the line now so I can try to find Emil for you," Martha declared.

Joseph was surprised to hear Emil's voice only five minutes later.

"Hello, Joseph! It is good to hear from you. What's on your mind?"

"Emil, have you found the thing yet?"

"No, we haven't," Emil answered. "But Marie just turned us all upside down and shook us a bit. She told us to quit looking for whatever is there and to look for whatever is missing. Everyone is now working much harder than before. I think that girl has more common sense than two hundred scientists and certainly more than I have."

"I know what you mean," Joseph replied. "Tony is one very lucky young man. He is very smart to choose brains over good looks, although that slightly chubby girl looks more and more beautiful to me every day. Pretty is one thing, but Marie is beautiful.

"Emil, perhaps you should come here to Binghamton and bring Hans too. The thing first appeared in the forest south of town a few miles. Aaron told me more about the spot where he stubbed his toe and started all this. Emil, I know we are men of science, but I have a strange feeling about that place. And, and, Emil, there is a local legend about it," Joseph stuttered.

"You don't need to stutter, Joseph," Emil said. "I have seen more strange happenings in the last eight months than in the whole rest of my life before this. Hans and I will be in Binghamton tomorrow morning."

AARON

Emil and Hans left Tony and Marie in charge and took the little private jet plane to Binghamton. They didn't want to waste time waiting for a commercial flight.

Joseph picked up the two scientists and immediately launched into a description of the boy who would lead them to the bare spot in the woods.

"He seems to be a miniature Tony. He has very varied interests and, from what I understand, a big well-documented collection in his chicken house."

"He collects chickens?" Hans asked.

"No, no, not chickens. He collects anything he picks up, I guess," Joseph explained. The drive to Aaron's house took only half an hour, and when they arrived at the old farmhouse, Aaron greeted them on the porch steps.

"Hi! Are you guys real scientists? I wondered what a scientist looks like," Aaron said.

Hans answered, "Yes, we are real scientists. We want to see your chicken house."

Just then, Aaron's mother came out onto the porch and introduced herself. "Good morning, gentlemen. I see Aaron has already captured you. I'm Donna, his mother. Have you had breakfast?" She was relieved to find only the three men. Making breakfast would be easy for her.

Emil looked at Hans. They were on the most important project in their lives, but both of them were indeed hungry. The woman and boy seemed to be very interesting people. Neither had ever met a real-live American Indian before, and even though Donna was only part Indian, she presented an opportunity. In that one-second visual exchange between the two old scientists, all these thoughts were exchanged and a decision made between personal curiosity and haste to continue their quest. Breakfast won out.

Emil said, "We have had no breakfast. While you prepare it for us, we can inspect your chicken house. I understand it has been converted into a museum."

"Is that what you call it? I call it a junk shop because most of it is stuff my ancestors threw away because it was broken. When all that stuff was in Aaron's bedroom, there was no room to dress. I tried to get him to throw it all away, but he had a fit. His dad prevented a family feud by telling Aaron he could have the chicken house."

"Well, let 's have a look at your collection, young man," Hans proposed.

Aaron had a difficult time understanding Hans because of his accent, but after a few seconds, he figured out what had been said. "You talk funny, mister. Come with me."

"I talk funny because I came from Germany to help Emil," Hans explained.

"Germany? You mean the Germany across the ocean? I saw the ocean once, but I couldn't see no Germany, or England, or China, or nuttin ' but water," Aaron said.

"Yes, I came from that Germany," answered Hans.

By then the group had reached the chicken house. Aaron dug up a key from his pocket and opened the padlock on the door.

When they entered, the two old scientists were astonished. There were hundreds of items, from rusty gun parts to pottery shards. There were leaves, flowers, whole plants, insects galore, and even two kinds of salamanders. Every item had a label that was one of seven different colors, and each label had a number on it. The colors matched seven different areas on a large map of the forest that Aaron had so far explored. The map was hand-drawn, but the handwriting didn't match the labels.

When Hans asked about the different handwriting, Aaron said, "That's because Lorraine made the map."

There was a circle near the southwest corner of the map with a big *X* in the center of it. Aaron saw Emil looking at it and said, "That's where we are going today. We'll walk down this trail to about here, then we have to kinda bend over a bit to get through here 'cause the trees and vines hang low. Then over here is another trail that goes up this way then over to the big bare spot. This last trail here used to be a creek a long time ago."

"How do you know that, Aaron?"

"'Cause Lorraine's grandmom told her about it. This trail here used to be a creek too. There used to be a really big tree right here where the creeks came together. That's how come I know that big pile of bones used to be where the bare spot is now. That big tree fell down a long time ago, and now it just looks like a little hill that's covered with moss and vines. I know it used to be a tree 'cause I dug into it with my knife and found dead wood."

"How old are you, Aaron?" Emil asked.

"I'm almost nine and a half!" Aaron replied proudly.

Just then there was a loud clanging and banging coming from the back porch of the house. Hans and Emil both looked surprised, but Aaron said, "Aw, that's my mom calling us to breakfast."

"Does your mother know anything about the legend of the pile of bones?" Hans asked.

"She heard about it but forgot most of it," Aaron answered. "Let's go in and see what's cookin'."

All four washed up at the basin on the back porch then entered the kitchen. There they found bacon, eggs, fried potatoes, sausage, toast and jam, and even stewed crackers.

All five people ate heartily, but Emil could not believe the amount of food that Aaron ate.

"Does he always eat this much?" Emil asked.

"No," replied Aaron's father, who had just come in from doing morning chores. "He usually eats more, but I think he is excited about your visit today."

Hans asked Donna what she knew of the old legends of the area, but she said she didn't know very much.

"Most of them were forgotten, but if you really want to learn of them, go see Lorraine's great-grandmother in the nursing home," she advised.

She looked up the name and address of the home, wrote them on a piece of paper, and gave it to Hans.

The boy and his father and the scientists and the doctor then began their journey to the bare spot. In just a short time, Emil and Hans learned what Aaron did with all the food he ate. The trails were almost invisible. They were just deer trails, and most of the time an adult had to walk bent over. In several places, they actually had to crawl along.

Emil, between pants for breath, said he had never worked so hard in all his life. Even Aaron's father had to struggle along.

Three hours later, the party of explorers finally reached a big bare spot in the woods.

Hans opened the backpack the men had been taking turns carrying. First he took out the camera and took pictures from several angles and locations around the spot. He was careful to save five frames for later. Originally, he had intended to expose all twenty-four frames at this site. But as he was struggling through the forest, an idea began to grow in his mind about that chicken house display. As they walked and crawled, he asked Aaron many questions about the boy's observations and conclusions.

After taking pictures, Hans and Emil both donned rubber gloves and took up camp shovels to dig up soil samples. Because of the difficulty in transporting the soil through the forest, they took only four small samples. Each sample was divided up among four plastic sandwich bags. Each of those was put into a bigger plastic bag, which in turn was put into a bigger bag. It was put into a still bigger bag until finally there were sixteen sealed freezer bags.

Emil dug up another sample. Hans brought out a small chemistry set to do basic alkali, acid, and organic content tests on the soil. None of the tests worked! It was the same as the tests that a hundred scientists were trying to do in the lab in Chicago. There was nothing!

Hans dug up another soil sample several meters away from the bare spot and repeated the tests. All of those tests worked normally.

Aaron was watching very closely as each test was made, and Hans explained the results of each one.

"I dug up this sample to test my chemicals and to affirm my testing methods. Now we have just enough for one more test. We will dig up another sample from the spot and try this again," Hans explained.

Emil dug up another sample. The tests were repeated. Again there were no results. None!

Hans repacked his test tubes, litmus paper, cotton swabs, and little glass spoons into their small black case. Then he threw it as far as he could into the center of the spot. He then threw one of the camp shovels into the spot, but not as far as the chemistry case. He threw the other shovel also, but not as far as the first one. Everything was thrown into the spot except water canteens and the soil samples, which would be carried back to Chicago.

Aaron thought Hans was angry or else he had gone crazy. He asked, "Hey, why are you trashing up the place? Mom would thrash me for that!"

"This is just one more test, Aaron," Hans answered. "This test depends on you. I want you to come back here every Saturday and look at the stuff I threw in there. Don't go in there though. Stay out here on the good ground. I want you to write down what you see every time you come here, and each time I want the date and time on your report."

Dr. Staneck again reminded Aaron not to go onto the spot. "I know I told you never to go near this place again, but if you are a scientist, you have to take some risk to identify the unknown. Just be very careful, Aaron."

Aaron pointed to a big tree limb that hung over the spot. "See that big limb? That's where me 'n' Lorraine go sometimes and just look at the place to see how much bigger it is."

Hans was delighted with Aaron's report. "Aaron, just how fast is it growing?"

"Well, lemme think. It was on my eighth birthday when I found this place. I remember 'cause I was mad at Mom and Dad 'cause I didn't get the bicycle I wanted. I ran out of the house and just kept going all day. When I got here, I sat on this little hill here, which is really a big tree trunk that fell down years ago. I sat here and cried awhile, then got to wonderin' why that spot was bare. It was about as big around as the haystack behind Lorraine's barn."

Hans and Emil looked at each other. Without saying a word, each knew the other was frightened. They were both thinking that if it grew that much in just a year and a half, how big would it be in five years, or twenty, or one hundred?

"Let 's get out of here," Emil said. "I want to talk to that old lady at the home."

"She's not just an old lady. She is Lorraine's great-grandma," Aaron said indignantly. "Her name is Dancing Star."

The soil samples were divided up among the four men, and the return trek back to Aaron's house didn't seem so long as the trip to the spot. At the farm, Hans went right to the chicken house and took pictures of Aaron's museum. Then the travelers all went into the kitchen for a bit of refreshment.

As Emil was drinking a glass of good cold well water, he looked out of the window and noted that the ground sloped downward from the farmhouse toward the spot in the woods. It wasn't much of a slope, but it should be enough to keep the water in the aquifer under the bare spot in the woods from flowing to the house. Aaron's family should be safe for many, many years from contaminated water.

Hans and Emil advised Aaron and his parents not to tell anyone about the bare spot. They were not ready to deal with mass panic or even a mass of media people. Aaron's job was to keep an eye on the spot and monitor its growth.

The two scientists and the doctor then got in Joseph's car and headed for the nursing home.

DANCING STAR

The home had very strict rules about who could visit the residents. These three old men who had crawled through the woods sure looked suspicious to the receptionist. She refused them entry.

Back in the car, Joseph called Aaron on his car phone and asked if he could bring Lorraine and her parents to the home to vouch for the men.

Donna called Mary and arranged to pick up Lorraine and her parents. She explained that Aaron's doctor and his friends wanted to visit Dancing Star. This surprised Mary because Lorraine never told much about her exploring with Aaron. Donna didn't know how much to tell about the spot, so she just said that the old German guy was interested in ancient Indian lore. Mary agreed to meet at the home with Aaron's doctor and his friends, so it was a party of nine people that greeted Dancing Star.

"Oh my gosh! I never had so many visitors at one time in all my one hundred four years! Come here, Lorraine. Let me have a big hug. Oh, you're growing up too fast, but you look strong and healthy. I guess the white man's food isn't too bad. Oh, Joe, it is good to see you again. Who are these other people? Did they all come to see me?"

Joe began the introductions. "You remember my wife, Mary, don't you Grandma?"

"Oh yes, now I remember," Dancing Star said with a twinkle in her eye. "She's that white squaw you ran off with."

Actually, the old woman remembered Mary very well. The two ladies were very fond of one another and embraced warmly with a laugh.

Lorraine introduced Aaron. "Grandma, you remember my friend, Aaron, don't you?"

"Oh yes. He's been around a time or two. When are you two getting engaged?" the old lady asked.

"Hey! Wait a minute! I'm just a little boy," Aaron protested. "What does engaged mean? I like her a lot, but I don't wanna be a slave like Pop and have to go to work every day."

Everyone laughed, but Aaron hugged Dancing Star. He and Lorraine stopped to visit her often. They usually stayed and talked for a couple hours or until the staff suggested they leave so their patient could rest. Dancing Star loved both kids.

Aaron then introduced his parents. "This is my mom and pop, Donna and Henry."

"You're from the tribe, ain't cha?" Dancing Star asked when she held Donna's hand.

"Well, sorta," Donna answered. "My parents moved into town to work in the silk mill years ago."

"Who are these old guys?" Dancing Star asked.

"I am Joseph Staneck, Aaron's doctor, and this is Emil and Hans. Emil is from Chicago, and Hans is from Germany. They are both scientists."

Dancing Star looked suspiciously at Hans and asked, "You're not kin to the kaiser, are you?"

Hans smiled and said, "No, I didn't even know him at all. He was gone before I was born."

"Well, he wasn't gone before I was born. He got my brother and several other boys from the tribe killed," Dancing Star replied with a frown.

Hans thought, *How am I going to get any information from someone who already hates me?*

Dancing Star herself opened that door for Hans. "I know what a scientist is. Are you here to learn how someone can live to be one hundred four?"

"No, it's not your age we are interested in," Hans replied. "It is one of your legends we want to learn about."

"I remember most of the legends. There was one about how the Great Spirit gave our men the ability to run great distance without getting tired. Then there was another about how our tribe should have become a great nation but didn't. That wasn't just a legend though. We were a small part of the great Seneca nation, but we never became very big because so many of our people were confused," Dancing Star revealed. "That legend lives on today!"

Hans said gently, "I think that is the legend we want to know about. Did it have anything to do with a big pile of bones near here?"

"Yes, it did," The centenarian answered. "The legend was old when I was born. There were many in our small tribe so confused or stupid that they did not know if they were men or women. The men shared their tepee with other men. Some of the women shared their tepee with other women! This does not make babies. It just won't work! The elders knew that if there were no babies, the tribe could not exist. They tried to discourage such abominable behavior. When such people died, they had no ceremony. Their bodies were not even wrapped. They were thrown naked onto a pile. People would urinate on the pile and throw dirt onto it to keep the stench from being too bad.

"Children were told to stay away from there. Children don't always obey though. One boy dug up a bone from that pile, and soon his hand began to disappear, then his arm, then all of him. When his fingers began to go, the men drove him out of the tribe. We all knew where he ran to, and the girls and some women took food to him at night. He slowly just melted away. He died a horrible, painful death.

"There were many confused people born to our tribe, and they all ended up on that pile. There were other diseases that the white man brought to us, so our tribe slowly died out. I guess I am all that is left. Joe's parents died. Joe married a white woman because there was no women left in our tribe! The legend was old when I was a girl. By then the white man and his sickness, wars, and hate kept our tribe from growing."

The old woman began crying, but she managed to blubber out, "Two of my own children were confused and are in that pile! I don't know why they got that way. I always taught them that the Great Spirit made woman for man. That is what works, but those two would not listen to me. I had other children, but only Joe's grandmother lived to have children."

The room was quiet. Only the sobbing of the old woman could be heard. There was not a dry eye in the room. Everyone was shocked to learn that the legend actually lived on.

After a few minutes, Lorraine suggested, "Grandma, tell the story about that bear you caught."

"Oh, child, you sure do like that story, don't cha? My grandma teached me how to catch rabbits with a snare. I made the best snares. Not even the boys could make a snare like mine. I caught many rabbits. One real cold winter, we would have starved if we hadn't had my rabbits. Once I caught a skunk. It was so mad it pissed on everything near it. The whole village had to move away from there. The skunk finally got away by chewing through my snare, but the place stank for a long, long time.

"One morning there was such a thrashing around and roaring and growling coming from the creek that it woke everyone up. Father and my uncle went very carefully down to the creek, and there they found a black bear caught in my snare. Usually I would just pound a stake in the ground to tie my snare to, but this time I set it in the creek, and I tied it to a stick that I stuck between rocks.

"That bear was so mad and roaring and tearing up the ground and splashing in the creek that there wasn't another critter anywhere near. Even all the birds flew away. Everyone just stood there watching that bear, and that made him even madder. Finally, Running Deer had a plan. He was the fastest runner in the tribe. His brother Moon was the bravest or craziest. He ended up on that pile. He was brave, but he sure didn't want anything to do with us girls."

Dancing Star was quiet for about twenty seconds, and a tear slid down her cheek as she remembered her unrequited love from many years past. Finally she continued the saga. "Everyone else left, or at least went where the bear couldn't see them. Running Deer picked up a tree branch and shook it in the bear 's face. Old Rope was so mad at that branch that he didn't notice that Moon went into the creek and cut the rope where it came up out of the water. That old bear chased Running Deer all the way back to camp, where we all made enough noise and waved sticks at him until he finally gave up and ran away. He never was able to get that rope off his leg and carried it there for years. That is how he got the name Rope."

Hans was amused, but his mind was still on that pile of bones. "Dancing Star, can you tell me where that pile of bones is?"

"I think I can. I believe it is west of that town of Hawleyton and a little south. There are two creeks that join up near a giant oak tree. If you stand by that tree and look south about as far as a man can throw a stone, you can see the pile. I don't know why the people threw dead bodies so close to the creek. It was a long way from camp though. There was a much bigger creek there," the old woman remembered.

Hans and Emil exchanged glances that said she confirmed Aaron's observation. The old pile of bones was now the bare spot!

Why did the pile disappear? Why did the child that dug up the bone slowly just disappear? Why did Aaron's toe disappear?

Why did a simple magnet stop the disintegration of Aaron? What strange force is at work here?

Emil asked, "Dancing Star, was there anything else strange about your two children besides being…uh, uh…confused?"

Again tears flowed from the eyes of the old woman as she thought back eighty-five years. "They were both such bright children. They both learned fast and always knew things other children didn't know. The first one was a boy. He talked a little funny, but I can't think of anything else different about him. I had several other babies. About six of them died before they could walk. Then about fifteen winters later, I had the girl that got confused. She was very bright too, such a joy to have around until she got confused. The only thing I can remember that was different about her is that her right foot always turned to the left. She walked a little different."

Hans asked, "Was there anything else put on that pile besides dirt and urine?"

"No, nothing else. No one wanted to carry garbage or trash that far," Dancing Star answered. "I stayed away from there, except when the men threw my two children on the pile. I never heard of anything else being put there."

Emil laid his hand on the old woman's shoulder and said, "I know we hurt you today by making you remember bad times. But, you see, that pile of bones and dirt is still dangerous. It can still cause people to disappear like that little boy you told about. You have helped many people by telling what you know. If you think of anything else that could help us stop that pile from hurting children, just push this button on this recorder and talk. Do you understand that this little thing can save your words for me to hear later?"

"Oh, yes," she said. "I am old, but Lorraine and Aaron are often playing with white man's toys like that. I even watch TV a lot. I really like watching baseball games."

Emil and Hans thanked her and said it was time for them all to leave. Actually, the foot tapping and impatient looks from two of the staff of the home told them their visit was ended. Emil pressed the stop button on the second recorder that he carried. Hugs and kisses were exchanged, and then the whole party went to their cars. The two children and their parents and Dr. Staneck all agreed to keep their ears and eyes open for more information.

CONTEMPLATION

When they arrived back in Chicago, Hans and Emil went to Kilabrew Labs. They wanted to be left to themselves for a while. They played and replayed the recording of Dancing Star's memories.

"Emil, what do you think of her mental state?" Hans asked after several playbacks.

"I think it is perfectly sound," Emil replied. "Her memory is excellent. My own mind is not as good as hers is right now. What strange force is at work here, or as Marie said, 'What is missing?'"

After hearing the recording ten times, Hans reached for the recorder and turned it off. Each of the scientists became lost in his own memories.

In 1933, Adolf Hitler envisioned a pure and superior Germany. He would rid Deutschland of any imperfect people. Not only were Jews to be eliminated, but also insane people and homosexuals. At that time Hans was a young research scientist at Dachau, the infamous concentration camp. The thousands of people held there were at his disposal to experiment on as he saw fit. He made meticulous records of the results of his experiments, but all of his notes and files were lost or destroyed when the Americans invaded the camp. Hans escaped through a secret tunnel that surfaced in a wooded area outside the wire fences. He had only his clothes when he emerged from the tunnel.

Hans evaded the Americans and suffered months of hunger, fear, and fatigue. He grew a full beard and mustache. With the aid of sympathetic German families, he was dressed in new clothes. He eventually secured employment in a prestigious university as a professor and later as a research scientist. His reputation and skill both grew. He tried to get a grant to cover studies of homosexuality, but the university absolutely refused his study of that particular affliction.

Hans really wished he had had Internet access in 1945. He could have sent his notes to his home even as the fences fell at Dachau. Now he had only his memory to rely on. He still had a good memory, even though he was eighty-four years old, but all he could remember of his work on homosexuals was that most of them were quite intelligent and very creative. He could think of nothing in their physical makeup that would cause their bodies and burial place and anything that touched them to vanish without a trace.

There was a young Jewish girl whom Hans had forced to work with him at the time he was trying to learn what made homosexuals different, but he was afraid to try to find her. It was bad enough that Joseph and Sophie remembered him from Dachau. Unfortunately, neither of them had worked on that project in the camp.

Hans tried to remember details of his early research on homosexuals. It was only on this pile of dead bodies of homosexuals that this disintegration of mass occurred until he and Aaron and Emil disturbed and moved some of the mass that was there. Hans had killed about twenty of the homosexual persons who were at his disposal back in 1944. Then he dissected them to discover any differences between them and normal people. He especially examined their brains. He remembered that the camp population was aware of this and that the homosexuals tried to hide their affliction. They were unable to hide it completely, even though it meant their death.

Hans never found any difference. He didn't have an electron microscope or a genome map. *So what goes on in their bod-*

ies? Nothing physical, or at least nothing that I was able to see. There were no strange odors or colors or even texture of material. I could see nothing different in their brains. Could it be an external force of some kind? The earth's gravity affects the orientation of a tiny magnet in a compass. Could there be some force I don't know about affecting people? Could this be where the physical and spiritual meet? Is there really a spiritual god? I have never believed in spirits, and if there is one, why would it want to destroy itself by limiting birth?

We know there are protons, which are positive, and electrons, which are negative. Could there be spirits that are either positive or negative? If there are, what force do they control to make a person confused about their gender?

What force is between the spirits? Electromotive? Electromagnetic? Electrostatic or some force that is not electro anything? Is there some force that deletes mass? I have never believed in God or the devil, and I certainly never believed that this mysterious god created the universe just by speaking. But there is certainly something, something that I do not know about. A huge supercollider is being built in Europe to look inside the atom for a tiny particle called boson, and a huge telescope is in orbit around the earth looking for the origin of the universe, but what are we scientists really looking for? Are we looking for God, and are we too bullheaded to admit it? Maybe I'll start going to church with Tony and Marie. I guess we better get back to the lab. Maybe, just maybe, there is some connection between God and science.

EMIL

Emil's thoughts also went back to the war years. He had been a young medic in the infantry. He had been wounded several times in a battle and left for dead by his comrades. He was found by the invading Americans and was taken to an aid station then to a field hospital where surgeons removed bullets and a piece of shrapnel from him.

Emil had noticed that the farther the Americans got from the battleground, the friendlier they got. Emil was placed in the hold of the troop ship USS *Maurice Rose*. It had several thousand hammocks side by side and stacked six high. Because of his wounds, he got the bottom of his stack. He spent two weeks in that hammock while the ship carried him to America. He ended up in Valley Forge General Hospital at Phoenixville, Pennsylvania, where he made a complete recovery. He was then made to work in the butcher shop. Thousands of wounded and sick American soldiers and hundreds of German prisoners had to eat, so the meat department was always busy.

An American civilian ran the shop. Emil knew him only as Butch. He was a very friendly man with quite a sense of humor. After working together with him for about a year, Butch learned that it was Emil's birthday.

"Emil, what do you want for your birthday?" Butch asked.

"Ach, Butch, I sure would like to have a beer," Emil replied.

Butch put a sweater and a butcher 's smock on Emil to hide his prison garb. Then he and two of his American buddies took the young prisoner of war to a bar in Phoenixville and got him a beer. Emil never forgot that kindness.

There were six German prisoners working in that butcher shop, and all but one, a surly SS officer, became good friends with Butch and most of the Americans that worked there.

They learned the date of Butch's birthday and decided to bake a cake for him. Being prisoners, they had little access to ingredients, so they started months ahead to scrounge for everything they needed.

During Emil's recovery from surgery, a young nurse named Krystal had treated Emil. They fell in love, and she used the excuse that Emil's wounds needed to be monitored to visit him often. Krystal was able to supply some of the ingredients needed for the cake. It took several weeks to obtain everything for a cake and then to bake it. All this they did without Butch finding out about it. The cake was in three layers and in the shape of a ship. It was a real work of art. The cake was prepared several weeks ahead of Butch's birthday, so the German prisoners hid it in a big meat freezer far back in a dark corner. Finally, the cake was presented to Butch on his birthday.

After the war ended, Emil returned to Germany and became a research assistant to a scientist named Hans Gossl. He learned much from Hans and worked with him for three years. But during all that time, he was corresponding with Krystal back in America. After three years, love won out, and Emil came to America. He and Krystal married and moved to Chicago where they opened Kilabrew Laboratory.

Forty years they lived and worked together and shared a happy life until Krystal died of cancer. After a time of mourning, Emil began the long search for a new assistant. There was a long string of applicants for the job. Many of them never showed up for the interview. Some of them Emil hired, but they either quit soon or Emil had to fire them. Then he interviewed both Tony and Marie on the same day. He liked them both and hired them both. The three of them became good coworkers and close friends.

But none of this daydreaming did anything to solve the mystery of the thing. Or maybe it did! *What if the missing element was spiritual, not physical? How could that be? What is the difference between energy and love? Marie and Tony were both well endowed with both qualities. Does energy become love, or are they both simply an extension of the frequency spectrum? Why does magnetism stop the thing? Does it replace the energy that is missing from molecules, or even atoms, and why is that energy missing? It has to be missing because there is no reaction to stimuli.*

Marie kept creeping—no, not creeping—blasting back into Emil's thoughts. She always went to church every Sunday. Even now in the midst of this constant work, Marie went to her church, and lately, Tony had been going with her.

In spite of having the best brains in the world all working on one problem, it was Marie who took the helm and steered the ship of science in a whole new direction.

The Bible says that God is love. Is love also energy? Why would a pile of rotting bodies eliminate energy? True, the bodies were of people who chose not to procreate, but they did love and were loved. If love were energy, why would their rotting bodies be without the normal energy of decomposition? Heat and even gas, which is mass, is present. Why not in that place in the woods? Why did Marie think something is missing rather than something strange present? Why could a simple, uncomplicated person have an insight that genius had completely overlooked? I remember something about believing as a child. Have we been microresearching this thing? Has mankind been overinterpreting the Bible, the Talmud, the Koran, and any other books of religion? Have we been seeing the wrong messages all these years? Have we made a colossal mistake? Have we killed millions of people just to prove our vision of God is the only right one? At the same time, do we ignore the message he tried to give us? Whether it is written in

English, French, German, Arabic, Yiddish, or any other language, the message is "Love one another."

Should we believe in God? No, of course not! The word belief *implies a certain amount of doubt. God just is. Just like this chair I'm sitting on, God is! Is God withdrawing from us at that spot in the forest? Why there? How far would it go?*

The other day Marie was teasing Tony about being so skinny. She said that in Genesis, the first book of the Bible, it says something about God making us in his image. She said that when they finally meet God face-to-face, they would know that God is just as chubby as she is. Then she laughed and laughed.

Tony laughed too, but then he said that it is our soul that is made in the image of God. Every mammal on earth is built similar to our bodies. One head, two arms, two legs, two ears and eyes, one heart, one liver, and even the reproductive systems are alike. Does God look like a cow?

Of course not. It is our soul that is in the image of God. Can a horse or cow know the difference between right and wrong? Can they even think of abstract things like space or time, or even the makeup of the grass they eat? No! Only we humans can do that.

What then is thought? Is it merely the activation of millions of synapses in our brain, just like in a computer? A computer is controlled by a clock circuit, the inputs from the keyboard and mouse, and whatever else is plugged into it. However, ultimately, it is controlled by a human being.

What then controls our brain? Is it God that controls us? No, I don't think so. That is where we are in the image of God. He has given us the ability to control ourselves. He has, however, given us an instruction book on how to use our ability to think. This book teaches us how to keep our thoughts, and therefore our soul, synchronized with God. Those that are will live forever with God and complement him. Those that are not synchronized will live forever, but will be put where they cannot possibly reduce the power of God. I think the Bible says something about a lake of fire.

The Bible also tells of a time when so many people were out of sync with God that he wiped us out. He started over with one man he could trust—Noah.

No, Emil! Don't even think that! Don't think that this thing we are fighting is God starting over again. It can't be! Why would he start with such a great little boy who has no thoughts of malice or any other bad thoughts? He is such a lovable little boy. There has to be another explanation for the thing.

But then it didn't really start with Aaron, did it? It started with people so out of synchronization with God that they refused to reproduce, and therefore, they refused to produce souls for God. They were definitely a negative opposing his positive.

I am glad Hans can't read my mind. If this new thought of mine is true, how can we reverse the thing? I have heard the Bible described as basic instructions before leaving earth. Perhaps that is true, and we really should read it like a service manual. I do know that in just one part of the Bible, Proverbs, there are nearly a thousand simple little instructions that no one can deny are useful.

I guess I better bring Hans back to earth too and get back to the warehouse. This needs much more thought before I discuss it with him. He is looking at me like he is reading my mind. Perhaps thought is a form of energy like electromagnetic and electrostatic waves. Maybe he is thinking the same thing.

"Wake up, Emil! You are a man of science, not a preacher."

He looked over at Hans, who was also lost in thought. Their eyes met, and Hans suggested they check in with Tony and Marie.

"If no one at the labs has found anything, the world will think I have gone crazy. Old friend, I don't think this is of this world, and I don't think there is anything anyone can do. I fear that our creator has given up on us."

"You are a scientist, Hans. How can you believe there is a creator? Do you not believe that man evolved from the first creature that emerged from the primordial soup?" Emil asked.

"Believe! Believe! Believe! I don't believe anything!" Hans answered. "Of course God created us! Evolution is simply the way it was done. For centuries we have believed that God created everything in six days. *Ha!* It was created in six of God's days, maybe, if each day is equal to 144 billion years or centuries. God's very first instruction to us is to work six days then rest on the seventh. That's how our bodies work. It was a practical instruction, not a mysterious message to make us doubt the authenticity of the Bible in the very first few lines. Mankind cannot comprehend God's infinity or that of time. Besides, if that one sentence about creation in six days is so important, why is the main message in the Bible completely overlooked? Why is there hate? Why are there wars? Why is there so much divorce? Why don't we all love like Marie and Tony? Those two don't just love each other. They love everyone. Look how Tony forgave the young officer that shot him. We should all be like Tony and Marie. But we're not. When God created us in his image, it was the soul of us he created in his image, not our bodies. Bodies are merely containers. Only man loves. But our souls have been broken or corrupted and are no longer in God's image."

Hans knew he was rambling on, and he wondered if Emil thought he had lost his head. He was really surprised when Emil said, "Hans, old friend, we have known each other so long that our thoughts are the same. We men of science are supposed to be the smartest people on earth, but all we can do is figure out how God did things, built things, or created things. I think that you and I are both convinced that the thing is not some freak of nature but a deliberate act of God."

Hans nodded his head and said, "Let's get back to the ranch, partner."

"You have seen too many Western movies," Emil replied.

DISCOVERY

They left without picking up their briefcases full of notes. Emil did pick up his rental car keys on the way out of the deserted lab. They had not worked there in months, and now there were great holes in the benches and even in the floor. Most of the equipment had simply vanished.

It was two very heavyhearted, sad men who returned to the temporary laboratory complex in the warehouse. Hans had sent many people to their deaths, and that had troubled him most of his life. But even that was nothing compared to the message he carried to deliver to all the scientists who were trying to stop the thing and ultimately to the whole world.

It was a real shock to enter the front office and hear Marie 's and Tony's laughter. Marie was laughing so hard that tears were streaming from her eyes. Tony was rocking back and forth in his chair. They both tried to sober up and stop laughing, but their explanation was fragmentary and mixed with laughter.

That arrogant young electronics expert from India had been making life miserable for his two partners in the electronics lab. They finally got tired of his imperial attitude. When he took a day off, they hid a cotton-covered fine wire behind the faceplate of his workbench. One end of the wire was grounded, and the other end connected to his power supply. Also hidden was an electrolytic capacitor connected to the power supply backward.

When the arrogant young man returned and turned on his power supply, smoke started to float out from under the bench top. Then when the smoke was quite thick, there was a big bang from the exploding capacitor. The young man in his paper clothes ran out of the lab to the office and commandeered Marie's telephone to call the fire department. By the time the firemen arrived, the smoke had dissipated, and the perpetrators were cleaning up the bits of paper and foil from the capacitor.

The whole laboratory was in an uproar. Some of the scientists were angry about the interruption, but most were, like Tony and Marie, laughing.

Neither Hans nor Emil laughed or even smiled. The expression on their faces was so bleak that the youngsters ceased their merriment.

Marie explained that the whole lab seemed to be frustrated, and everyone's temper was boiling over. No one had discovered anything missing or present. There had been few residual discoveries, and nothing new was invented. All of the best brains in the world working together came up with nothing at all.

Hans was prepared to shut the whole thing down and dismantle the lab, but Emil suggested they wait a while longer and call a general meeting in the auditorium. He was not ready to give up the project or the world. There had to be something they could do. Something!

Marie knew nothing of what Hans and Emil had learned in Binghamton, but the look of fear and futility on both men 's faces prompted her to say, "Have we tried prayer?"

To her surprise, Hans answered, "That is the only thing that is going to work. Marie, once again you have known all along what all of the world's best scientists have been unable or unwilling to see. This thing, as you call it, is an act of God, an act that was done only once before, and it was done with water that time."

Marie knew exactly what Hans was referring to, and Tony was almost sure he knew too. He said, "Noah had over one hundred years to build the ark. Must we build an ark or a spaceship?"

"Only a spaceship will work this time, but it can't be built by any of us or any of the scientists out there." He pointed toward the lab area. "We may be contaminated by the thing, and we are doomed!"

There was silence for three whole minutes until Tony exclaimed, "Hey, wait a minute! Why can't we buy some time by building a big magnet around that place where all of this started? All this stuff here and at Kilabrew could be dumped there, so it doesn't contaminate the whole world! How big is that place? Could it be done? Would it work like it does on that boy's toe? Would it take a whole power plant to run it?"

Tony rambled on a bit more while Hans and Emil stood agape.

Emil finally said, "We have thirty of the best physicists in the world trying to figure out why magnetism stops the thing, but nobody even thought about using that knowledge. Tony, you just turned this whole endeavor in a new direction."

"Marie, do you have a list of the people working on this magnetism thing?" Hans asked.

"Yes, I do," Marie answered.

"Call all of them to a meeting in the auditorium," Hans ordered. "We will start immediately."

Twenty minutes later, all thirty of the magnetism experts convened, and Hans wasted no time in starting the meeting. He first reviewed the progress the whole team had made so far.

"There has been no progress at all from any of the departments! None! We are changing direction, and you folks will be the point. We need time. The thing has grown from an area as big around as a haystack to the size of two football fields. We know magnetism can stop it, so you are going to build a magnet big enough to stop it before New York and Pennsylvania disappear!"

Immediately, discussion and questions started. Everyone talked at once. "How many square meters is a haystack? Is that American football or soccer? Is this to be a permanent magnet or an electromagnet? Is there a power source nearby?"

Hans looked at Emil with a grin. "We should have measured it when we were there." Then he remembered Aaron. He got out his little notebook to find the phone number then remembered that he never asked the boy for exact measurements, only an approximate growth rate.

He called Aaron anyway, but his mother said he was at Hawleyton helping Lorraine catch chickens.

"That is one fine boy you have there. Now he is a chicken catcher too! I think Aaron can do anything. Will he be free to help me again tomorrow?" Hans asked.

"Yes, I'm sure he will. School doesn't start until next Monday," Donna said. "He has quite a logbook of that bare spot. He even made a map of it that shows where it is growing fastest."

"Someday Aaron will be a great scientist. We need precise measurements, and we are sending our two young assistants, Tony and Marie, this time. Emil and I are too old to crawl through the forest again," Hans said.

Donna laughed. "Aaron and Lorraine get laughing fits every time they think about you fellows crawling along through the laurel. One or two times Aaron led you through the thickest jungle just to watch you struggle."

"Oh he did, did he?" Hans laughed. "*Ach du lieben*, I'll get even with him someday for that! I love that boy more and more each day."

"He is a handful all right, but everyone who knows him loves him," said Donna. "We are real proud of our boy. His little girlfriend is a real doll too! Whatever mischief Aaron doesn't think of, she does. But they are both such happy and lovable kids and so helpful too. Today they are helping Joe catch and crate chickens to take to market up in Binghamton. They help with everything except milking. Aaron says he doesn't like cows, but I think he just doesn't like having to be at the barn every day at the same times, four in the morning and four in the afternoon."

"Ach so," replied Hans. "That is much too restrictive for an explorer and scientist. I'll have Tony and Marie there at eight tomorrow morning. You will like those two also. They are a happy couple and full of tricks too."

Meanwhile, Emil was also busy. He chartered the little jet and scheduled a very early flight to Binghamton then called the car rental agency and rented a car for Tony and Marie. Then he rounded up the kids, who had wandered off to the snack bar, and informed them of their morning trip.

"Oh no!" cried Tony. "Not that place again! Where can I get a bulletproof vest and a tommy gun on such short notice? I wonder if I'll meet that cute nurse again."

Marie looked hurt and butted Tony with her hip and said, "Forget it, buster!"

Emil laughed and said, "This whole big magnet thing is your idea, not mine. Just be at the airport at 5:00 a.m. tomorrow with a transit and big tape measure."

"Ooh, no," groaned Tony. "That is about the time we get home from our dates and go to bed."

"Not this time, Romeo. We need precise measurements and no mistakes. Get some good sleep tonight, and wear work clothes tomorrow. You will be crawling through jungle. You will be led by two seasoned explorers named Aaron and Lorraine who are much smaller and can run through the forest where you will have to crawl," Emil replied as he dug out his notebook.

He made a map of the route from the airport to Aaron's home. "Watch out for the holes and ruts in the driveway. I asked Henry why he doesn't fix the holes, and he said it slows people down so they don't run over kids and chickens."

"Well, Sadie Mae, better get out your old trusty clod hoppers. Reckon ' we're off to the farm," drawled Tony.

"Reckon' so, Bubba. Gotta get the milkin' done and make hay while the sun shines," Marie answered.

Emil laughed then told them to prepare for a huge breakfast at Aaron's house. "That Donna can really cook up a meal fit for a king!"

"Hey, things are looking up," Marie said with a big smile. "Maybe I can learn from her too!"

RETURN TO BINGHAMTON

The next morning Tony and Marie, dressed in old blue jeans and long-sleeved shirts, met their pilot, George, at the airport. He helped load a transit, a bundle of stakes, a big tape measure, laser-powered measuring equipment, but no luggage at all. George told Tony and Marie that he used to fly around that area west of Binghamton when he worked for a gas well-driller in Indiana, Pennsylvania. He said he used to fly to Jamaica sometimes too.

Tony was glad George liked to talk because he didn't want to talk about their mission much. He just told George that they had to measure and stake out a plot of ground for a building project.

The flight to Binghamton was fast and did not take much time, but getting to the car agency and driving to the farm took a while. Tony and Marie met Henry, Donna, and Aaron at the porch steps at eight sharp. They all introduced themselves then entered the house where Lorraine was setting the table.

They ate a huge breakfast, and then Tony said, "Oh, I ate too much. I won't be able to crawl through the jungle."

Aaron and Lorraine both laughed and laughed while Aaron told them, "You won't have to crawl much. I led those old geezers on a merry chase through the thickest laurel just to watch them and listen to their moans and groans. They were really funny. I sure do like them old guys though!"

Tony and Marie looked at each other and busted out laughing. They could see Emil and Hans crawling along, swatting flies and mosquitoes, and moaning and groaning.

After breakfast, they began their safari into the forest. They did indeed have to crawl through mountain laurel in two places. In the first entanglement, Tony and Marie took another laughing fit when they thought of the old scientists struggling along, carrying supplies and instruments. By the time the youngsters crawled through the second patch of the stuff, it wasn't quite so funny. The two children seemed to be having a good time though, and Tony wondered if that route was really necessary. Were he and Marie also the butt of Aaron's trick?

As they walked, crawled, stooped, and swatted their way through the forest, Tony noticed that, like himself and Marie, Aaron and Lorraine seemed to know what the other was thinking. They often answered one another with just a nod or a laugh without anything having been said. He said to Marie, "Those kids are in love and don't even know it."

Marie smiled and said, "I noticed that too. Aaron was so gentle when he helped Lorraine up after she fell."

The four kids traveled much faster than the previous group, and when they arrived at the big bare spot, they went right to work. The two little ones were a great help. Tony employed the transit constantly to avoid having to cross the spot with the tape measure. The shape was very irregular, so many measurements were required to map it out.

Tony was equipped with the latest laser devices, a fine transit, and tape measure. His map was marked every meter around the outer edge of the spot. He and Aaron even measured the depth of the crater now forming in the interior of the bare spot. They called out the numbers to Marie and Lorraine. Tony and Aaron forbade the girls to get too close to the spot.

After working several hours, they took a break for lunch. The map the girls were making from the numbers called out to them looked something like a pear with the smaller part not quite closed at the top.

Tony compared the drawing of the bare spot to the one that Aaron had been working on for Hans. When he converted the feet, inches, and angles to metric numbers, he found that Aaron's map was very accurate!

"How did you measure without walking across the spot?" Tony asked.

"We measured pieces of string then shot one end across with my slingshot. Then we measured from the ends to the edge of the spot," Aaron replied.

"For the real long sides, we stretched the string out on safe ground then put sticks down beside each end of the string. If it touched the bare spot at all, we threw it away into the spot," Lorraine added.

"That must have taken a long time. Did you do all this in one day?"

"No, we camped here for about a week. It's a good thing we got done 'cause we were out of food and toilet paper," Aaron said with a laugh.

"If Hans and Emil had known how accurate your map is, we could have saved a trip," Marie exclaimed.

"Yeah, but then we would not know you, and we like you guys a lot. You're real cool."

"Well, thank you, Lorraine, but how do you know that Aaron feels the same way?" Marie asked.

"I dunno. We usually know what the other is thinking most of the time. It drives our parents crazy sometimes. Like when we all went to the movies once. Mom asked me which movie Aaron would like to see, and I told her. She thought I was wrong, so she called him on the phone. He said the same movie I told her. When we were ready, we picked up Aaron and his folks, and that's the movie we went to," Lorraine answered.

"Yeah, and like the time we made up a story about the Bigfoot we saw in the woods," Aaron added. "Lorraine would tell part of the story, then I would tell part. Then Lorraine would tell some more, and we made it sound so real until we both took a laughing fit. Nobody knew how we knew what the other was going to say next. I don't know either. We just do."

"Yeah," Lorraine agreed.

"You two kids are fantastic!" Tony said. "I hope we see a lot of each other after this mess is over. We better hurry and finish this measuring job so I can go to Binghamton to fax it to the old guys."

"Oh, you don't have to go to town. Just because we live in the sticks, it don't mean we're old-fashioned. We both have faxes. Lorraine's house is closer though. We can be there in a couple hours," Aaron said proudly.

"I didn't even see a television set at your house," Tony proclaimed.

"Aw, we had one once, but it was a big waste of time. There wasn't nothing fit to look at, so when lightnin' burnt it out, we never bothered to get it fixed. Pop just threw it in the dump," Aaron explained. "The computer and fax and stuff are in the office. I don't think you looked in there at all."

"Aaron, I am so sorry. I thought your folks were not up-to-date, but I guess you are all far more sophisticated than I. I'm still trying to find something useful on TV," Tony apologized.

Marie was awestruck. "Tony, I think these kids are wise beyond their years—far beyond. I have never seen such understanding between two people in all my life. Not even my grandparents can read each other's minds. And just look at that map! All it needs is to be converted to metric, and it is the same as this fancy one we are making. Oh, I am so glad I met you two!"

Lorraine gave Marie a gentle push and said, "Don't say any more. Our moms will be mad if our hats don't fit anymore."

Everyone had a big laugh, then it was time to get back to work. As they made the last few measurements, Tony noticed several lumps of something out in the bare spot. He asked Aaron if he knew what they were.

"That is all the testing stuff the old guys used here. After they made all their tests, they just threw everything out there. They told me to keep an eye on them to see how fast they disappear," Aaron explained. "They are going fast!"

"Oh boy, they sure are," Tony replied.

Marie shivered and said, "This place is evil! Evil! Let's get out of here!"

Aaron and Tony packed up their transit and other gear that had no contact with the bare spot and threw away anything that did touch it. Then the party made their way to Lorraine's house.

Mary heard them coming before she saw them. By the time the laughing, chattering group came in the house, she had a meal on the table for them. Mary helped out at the school and taught Sunday school so she was accustomed to youthful exuberance, but these four were really excited about something. It took a while to figure out that Marie had ventured away from the others for a potty stop and found that she was between a small black bear cub and its mother. The forest erupted in a huge roar and a thrashing and crashing of trees and bushes as mama bear charged. Then came a piercing scream and more thrashing and crashing as Marie quickly pulled up her pants and ran back to the others. When all four people roared back at the bear, she backed off and ran to her cub.

When all this was told to Mary, Marie's face was red as a beet, and she said, "I finished what I started in my pants, and I am an awful mess. That bear scared me half to death!"

"Oh, you poor girl! Come with me," Mary said as she took Marie to the bathroom to clean up. Then Mary went to look for clean clothes that would fit Marie. When she returned, Marie was standing in the shower crying her heart out.

"Marie, what's the matter?" Mary asked.

"Tony will be so ashamed of me. He won't want to marry me now," sobbed Marie.

"I'll be right back," Mary said as she left the bathroom. She went to Tony and told him that Marie was crying and the reason why.

Tony put down his coffee and rushed into the bathroom, and even though the shower was still on, he stepped right in and hugged Marie. He kissed her and said, "You silly goose. I love you, I love you, I love you. This mess is nothing. Just enjoy your bath and keep making those wedding plans. Ain't no mama bear ever gunna keep you from me, gurl. Not even a whole herd of bears!"

"Oh, Tony, bears don't come in herds. Do they? I love you so much!"

When they were both clean and dry, they returned to the kitchen to finish the meal.

Mary and Marie would rather not talk about the attack, but the boys were still excited. Marie was still trembling, so Mary thought it might be better to talk this adventure out. Also she wanted to defend Marie's fear, so she told a story of two young men, her husband's cousin and a friend of his. They were exploring abandoned logging roads through the forest and got their old pickup truck stuck on a fallen tree. They were between a bear cub and its mother. The bear attacked the pickup and was further enraged by the roaring engine as the boys tried to get loose from the tree.

They were found three months later. All the windows in the pickup were broken, and the two bodies were so torn apart they were impossible to identify. Only the license plate and the fact that both boys had been missing told who they were. That happened about twenty years ago. Marie's life had indeed been in danger, and it was a miracle that their screaming frightened the bear away.

The conversation turned to women who had fought and killed animals or men to protect their children. There were other stories related, and eventually, life in the forest and then the forest itself was the topic of discussion.

"Say, Tony, what are the old geezers planning to do with the big bare spot?" Aaron asked.

Tony answered with another question, "How is your toe now?"

"It is fine now, what's left of it anyway. Why?" Aaron asked.

"That magnet on your toe keeps it from rotting away, so Hans and Emil are building a huge magnet to cover the bare spot to stop it from spreading to the whole earth," Tony explained.

"Oh!" Aaron replied. "How are they going to get such a big thing in there? Are they going to tear up the woods? There are no roads to that place."

"I don't know, Aaron, but if they don't do it, there will be no woods and eventually not even Hawleyton," Tony lamented.

"Oh yeah. I guess you're right about that. We could scout out the best place for a road for them, couldn't we, Lorraine?" Aaron asked.

"I'll ask Emil about that when we fax the map to him," Tony suggested.

Aaron grinned and said, "That's already been done. Lorraine and I sent it off while you two were blubberin' in the bathroom."

"You guys are something else!" Tony proclaimed. "I guess we will call them back when we finish eating. By the way, who owns the woods where the bare spot is?"

Aaron and Lorraine looked at each other, and both just shrugged their shoulders.

Mary, however, knew who owned the land around the bare spot. "That land is owned by Anna McGruder. She used to be our neighbor and went to church with us, but about five years ago she moved to Hawaii. I think she is in a retirement home there. I have her address here someplace. Joe wanted to buy all that land so the kids would have it to play in, but Anna would never sell. She told Joe to just let the kids enjoy the woods and don't worry about it, but just don't sue her if one of the kids gets hurt there."

Marie copied the address and phone number, and conversation around the table turned to the bare spot itself and speculation about what was happening there. By the time they were done eating and talking, Marie's clothing was washed and dried. After she changed back to her own clothes, hugs and kisses were exchanged among the new friends, and the two travelers turned toward the door. Then they stopped, looked at each other, and erupted in laughter. The car was at Aaron's house!

It took Aaron and Lorraine a few seconds to figure out what was so darn funny, but then they joined in the laughing fit too. Mary was completely perplexed. Lorraine finally explained the situation to her mother.

"Well, what is so funny about that?" Mary asked.

"I dunno," Lorraine answered. "We just think it's funny."

"Well, I can't drive over there right now. I have pies in the oven for the pot luck at church," Mary said. "Aaron can drive you over in the old Ford. Joe won't need it for a few days."

Tony's eyes got as big as saucers. "But he's only nine years old!"

"Nine and a half," Aaron corrected. "Besides, I have been driving for a couple years. Don't worry, you'll be safe."

So Tony, Marie, and Aaron got in the old car and drove to Aaron's house. Tony was surprised that there was no grinding of gears and that the car traveled smoothly down the lane.

Tony and Marie had another cup of coffee with Donna and briefly explained what they had done, that a huge magnet was to be built to stop the thing. Tony said, "It works on Aaron's toe. It should work out there too!"

"What's Pop doin' out at the shed?" Aaron asked.

"He's trying to get a skunk out from under. I sure hope he doesn't get himself sprayed again. The last time I wouldn't let him in the house for two weeks. He stank to high heaven!"

"Yeah, and I had to do all the milkin'. The cows just kicked Pop when he got near them," Aaron added.

Just then there was a loud boom from behind the shed, and Aaron said, "Pop's not takin' any chances this time. He's usin' Ol' Bess."

A minute later, Henry entered the kitchen, set the shotgun down in a corner, and proclaimed, "Got 'em." He then got himself a cup of coffee and sat down to join in the conversation.

"Did you get that hellhole mapped out, Tony?" he asked.

"We sure did, but it was a big waste of time and risk. Aaron's map was just as good as the one we made today," Tony answered.

"My boy doesn't play any sports at all, but I sure am proud of him. There ain't nothing he can't do if he sets his mind to do it. And he does everything well too," Henry said with pride. "Now don't get a swelled head, boy, or I'll make you muck out the steer barn!"

"I'm as humble as humble pie, Pop. I sure don't want that job again. Lorraine wouldn't let me near her house for three days after the last time I helped you with that stinkin' job," Aaron assured his father as everyone roared with laughter.

"Henry, did you see this letter from the bank?" Donna asked. "They say that someone from Chicago opened an account for Aaron's college expenses and tuition. There's ten thousand dollars in it. Ten thousand, Henry, can you believe that? Aaron has to keep his grades up to A's and B's, and he has to go to a good school for science."

Henry was speechless.

Aaron wasn't. "I can easily get good grades in everything but English. I swear that teacher wants me to be able to equitably distribute bovine excrement in fluent prose and iambic pentameter."

"Mind your mouth, boy," Donna said menacingly. "I don't know what all them big words mean, but they must be some kind of swear words!"

Her words were only partly heard. Everyone else was laughing.

Tony finally said, "That must have been Hans who opened that account. He sure is fond of Aaron. Language is extremely important. You have to know how to describe your discoveries in a way that others can understand. It has to be precise."

Marie looked out the window then said, "Tony, I think we better get going. I have never had so much fun, except for that bear, but we will need some light to get the old Volkswagen running."

Aaron and Tony erupted in laughter, but then Tony agreed with Marie, and the two of them got into the rental car and headed for Binghamton.

When they reached town, they drove the main streets until Marie remembered a landmark, and then they found the street that the laboratory was on. Tony almost drove past the building. The whole building was tilted. Windows were broken, and the front door stood ajar and had been smashed. Yellow tape surrounded the property, and there were danger signs posted.

Tony said, "That used to be a good-looking building, but look at it now." He drove around to the rear and stopped. There sat Emil's old Volkswagen. It looked normal except for a thick layer of dust and dirt.

Marie put a hand on Tony's arm and said, "Tony, I don't think we should touch the car. We know the thing is here, and it might have spread out past the building."

"Let 's find a drugstore and get some chemicals to make simple tests on the soil and the car. We should measure the perimeter of the affected area," Tony suggested. Then he thought of something else. "We are going to visit the police too before we do anything here. I don't want to get shot again. My right arm still hurts from the last time."

Marie picked up her cell phone and dialed 911. "My name is Marie, and my friend is Tony. Could you please have an officer meet us at the laboratory at 3410 Robinhood?"

The dispatcher immediately called. "Six-eleven, are you available for a call?"

Then Marie heard a faint, "Ten-four."

Then the dispatcher asked, "What is the nature of your problem?"

"We are scientists and need to make some tests and measurements on the property at 3410 Robinhood and maybe some of the surrounding buildings. We don't want to be suspected of burglary and get shot or something."

Five minutes later, three police cars arrived, and one of the officers recognized Tony. He greeted the couple cheerfully, "Hi, Tony! What brings you back to Binghamton?"

"See how fast that building is falling apart? There is something really strange going on there and at a spot in the woods south of town. We don't know what it is yet, but we found a way to stop it. We have to measure how far the thing has spread," Tony explained.

"So why did you call us?" the officer asked.

"Because I don't want you to shoot me again. People going by will think we are burglars or something. Those maniacs on the SWAT team shoot first and ask questions later."

"I remember that, Tony. You are safe now. I'll tell dispatch and all the other officers to leave you alone. Tell me about this strange thing going on though. Do you think this place is haunted or something?" the officer asked.

"I only know that in Chicago, there are more than one hundred of the world's best scientists trying to figure out what is happening. So far they haven't found anything except a way to stop the spread. One of your local doctors discovered that much," Tony explained.

"What happens if you don't stop it?"

"There will be no building there at all, and then no land at all. Then the nearby buildings and land will disappear, then all of Binghamton, then all of New York, Pennsylvania and then—"

The officer gulped then said, "You're not kidding, are you?"

"No," Tony answered. "But keep it quiet, or you will have mass panic to deal with."

To Marie, Tony said, "Let's get this place measured first while we still have some daylight."

They drew a rough sketch of the property then measured the height, width, and length of the building. Next they measured the land around the laboratory and its location on the land. The young officer was still there watching, so Tony asked him to accompany himself and Marie to the nearest drugstore. "I don't want to get reported for buying ingredients for a bomb or meth."

"I'll go you one better. I'll drive you to the drugstore," the officer volunteered.

So Tony and Marie once again found themselves riding in a police car in Binghamton. While riding, Tony called Emil and reviewed the day with him.

"I'm glad you thought of measuring that lab. What does it look like?"

"It is kaput, Emil. I think the whole building is leaning. We can't see inside yet because it is getting dark here. We are on our way to a drugstore to buy basic stuff to analyze the soil. We haven't touched your car yet. I want to know how close the thing is to it before I touch it.

"Aaron and Lorraine are really great kids! They are full of tricks though! They went out of their way to lead you and Hans through the thickest mountain laurel. I think they did the same thing to Marie and me. It sure is easy to love those kids!"

"Why those little rascals! Wait till I tell Hans!"

"Emil, you should see the map that the kids made of that spot in the woods. It is accurate and precise. All it needs is to be converted to metric, and it will be exactly like the one Marie and I made!"

Emil had an ominous thought. "Did the kids walk around on the bare spot to make such an accurate map?"

"No. Aaron said they didn't get within five feet of the spot. They measured out lengths of string much longer than the width or length of the spot, and Aaron shot one end across with his slingshot. Then they measured from the ends back to the edge of the spot. They made many measurements that way. He had a stick measured to exactly five feet so they would not get on the spot at all. That boy is a genius, I think!"

"Yes, I think you're right about that. Hans and I are going to make sure he gets the best education possible."

Tony asked, "How is the magnet-construction project progressing?"

"Not very well," Emil lamented. "It seems some of our scientists are more interested in the intrinsic value of the project. The French want to hire a French firm to build it. The Germans want a German firm. The Chinese insist that only their yin and yang can succeed. There is constant fighting and no engineering being done! I wish one of those *dumkauffen* would figure out what the thing is. We haven't even calculated the minimum gauss level needed to stop the deterioration."

"Emil, those are the best scientists in the world! Could the thing be affecting their thinking?"

"I don't know. I just don't know. Tony, are you thinking that it is making a conscious effort to protect itself? Is the thing alive? Is it a new life-form? I am a scientist. I make unknown realities known. I work with energy and mass, things I can see and feel. This thing seems to be a lack of energy—a total lack of anything to hold mass together. But why? And how? There isn't even a dust cloud above the disappearing forest or around our tools that are just disintegrating. Energy can neither be created nor destroyed, just changed. But with this thing there simply is no energy. None! No heat! No light! No radiation! Nothing!

"Hans is going crazy too. He keeps mumbling about horrible things he did back in 1933. The other day when I went into the office, he was sitting at the desk crying his heart out. He is fearful. It is almost like he knows something so horrible he can't even tell us about it. He has me fearful too. Tony, hurry up and finish there and get back here. I need to talk to you and Marie. You two seem to be so strong, happy, and content, and I know you are as aware as I am of this menace. I need your strength. I guess we shouldn't be talking about this on the phone anyway. The CIA or FBI or whoever monitors this call is probably going nuts too. Hurry home."

Tony pushed the end call button on the phone then asked Marie, "Can we work in the dark? Emil wants us back in Chicago."

Before she could answer, the policeman said, "We have plenty of lights that we use at crime scenes. We can light up that place like daylight."

Marie laughed and said, "Well, that fixes that problem!"

While Tony and Marie were in the drugstore, their driver called dispatch and arranged to have the crime scene truck with its generator and lights go to 3410 Robinhood and light up the area. The whole police force was aware that the two young scientists were working on a project important to the whole world. By the time the trio was headed back to the lab, there was a bright glow in the sky.

Tony and Marie worked quickly to determine the affected area. They tested neighboring buildings, the street in front, and the alley behind. Last of all, they tested the Volkswagen and found everything normal with no sign of the thing.

Tony put the key in the ignition and tried to start the car, but it just groaned a little bit. One of the policemen jump-started it from his cruiser, and it seemed to run well. Tony let it run awhile to recharge the battery while he and Marie packed up their testing equipment and threw all of it into the lab. The area they found affected was quite small. It was just a few inches around the perimeter of the building. On the building itself, the thing had only progressed vertically about thirty centimeters.

Marie told the officers that they planned to build a big magnet around the building to hopefully stop the spread of the thing. They needed to control it so the building would completely disappear.

An older sergeant asked, "Just what is this thing?"

Marie answered while Tony nodded in agreement, "We don't know. There are about one hundred scientists from around the world trying to figure that out. But I think we, all of us, should be praying to God to spare us. I think that is the only solution. This big magnet we are building is only a stopgap measure. Prayer is the only answer."

CHICAGO

Tony and Marie thanked the officers and were soon on their way to Chicago. The old Volkswagen still ran just as it had on the trip to Binghamton. The rattles and other noises were actually a comfort to the two travelers. They took turns driving, stopping only at rest stops and fast-food places, and arrived at the warehouse laboratory late in the afternoon. Tony turned over the drawings and measurements of both the lab in Binghamton and the bare spot south of town. Even though Aaron and Lorraine had faxed the information from the bare spot to Chicago, no work was being done on designing the big magnet.

If Emil seemed frustrated, Hans was completely bewildered, disgusted, discouraged, and ready to give up the whole effort. When Emil, Tony, and Marie entered his office, he was staring at the wall and muttering something about fighting the devil.

Marie broke his spell with a cheery "Good afternoon, Hans. We made it back in one piece. We even brought Emil's car back."

Tony proclaimed, "We brought a solution to our big problem too."

Emil, Hans, and Marie all looked askance at Tony, and Marie asked, "We did?"

"Yes, we did. It's your solution, Marie—prayer."

All four agreed that this was the only answer. Hans pointed at the makeshift laboratory full of scientists behind him and asked, "But how do we explain that to them? Scientists pray? *Es geht nicht* [It goes not]! To them there is no God. To me there was no

God until I met Marie. Now I know there is, but what is God? A spirit? A ghost? A man? Is God a wooden or stone statue? Is God a town, like Mecca? Is God wealth or a golden calf?

"I am a scientist. I measure things. I test things. I theorize about how events happen or happened then try to prove my theory. But God is like electricity. I can't see it. I can surely feel it and even measure it, but no one has ever seen an electron move along a wire. That is still a theory, even though we do miraculous things with electricity. What is life? Is God life? How does life begin from only two cells, an egg and a sperm? We can look at one or the other with our finest electron microscope and still not see life.

"Ach! *Ich bin verruckt*! [I'm going crazy!] Theories go round and round in my head. Sometimes I even get wild ideas like the thing is the lack of God. Like that pile of bones in the woods is so disgusting to God that he refuses to even be a part of it. That's why it simply ceased to exist. But if that is true, why does the spot grow? Why has it affected the toe of such a wonderful little boy? Why has God abandoned him, and why can a simple magnet save him?

"I listened to Dancing Star's recording about fifty more times. She thinks that pile of bones is still there in the woods. She did not mention anything about it disappearing. The pile was gone when Aaron found the bare spot, which was as big around as a haystack then, perhaps three or four meters. Now it is as big as several football fields. That means it is growing fast. I did some calculations and concluded that the disappearing must have started sometime during the second World War.

"We have had homosexual activity since the early years recorded by the Bible. In fact, the word *sodomy* came from the city name Sodom. If that is so abominable to God, why did he not make us all disappear then? Two big cities and several smaller ones around them were wiped out, but not all the earth.

"What have we done that is so horrible that we deserve extinction? Was it our total disregard for human feelings when we tried to wipe out the Jews? Dancing Star said that the bodies of dead homosexuals were thrown naked onto the pile, but she did not say how any of them died. Was AIDS prevalent then? I do not think so. I think that what caused God's fury and decision to end his project was the tribe's attempt to end the practice. I think it was euthanasia by tribal leaders that killed the people.

"Do you think God is happy when leaders of families, tribes, or nations sacrifice their children to appease a volcano god, a storm god, or something? Was he happy with me and Hitler and the rest of the bunch for what we did? God is love, and there was no love in the souls of any of us when we committed such atrocities. How can God live in us? I think he sees his creation completely out of control and has decided to end the project.

"Our science is useless. Our religion is useless. I think that you are right, Marie. Only constant and fervent prayer can save us. All we scientists can do is delay the total disintegration of our universe as long as possible and possibly predict how much time is left. To save us, do we need the whole world praying? How do we tell this to the rest of the world? Who would believe us? Ach! *Ich bin verruckt!* Tell me about your trip to Binghamton, kids."

Tony and Marie told Hans and Emil all about their trip. They told about Tony's contacting the police in advance of going to the laboratory so they wouldn't get shot again. They told about the precision of Aaron's map of the spot and the crude tools he and Lorraine used to make the map. They told that Lorraine seems to be just as inventive and creative as Aaron, and they told about the way the kids seem to communicate without talking.

They told about the good food and abundance of love in both Aaron's and Lorraine's homes. They told about being led through the thickest mountain laurel, just like Hans and Emil had been. This brought on knee-slapping laughter in the whole group.

When the laughter subsided, Hans said, "Well, we can still laugh. If we can still do that, maybe we can stop the thing. Emil, who built your big atom smashers?"

Emil thought for a moment then said, "I don't know. It was probably some private company like General Electric. I'll have to look it up."

Hans asked Tony, "What is your idea of how to build this magnet?"

"The thing is spreading fast. I think I would try simply scattering magnets over the surface, around the perimeter of it. That may slow it down some. We don't know the vertical penetration, so I don't know the strength of the magnetic field required. I guess we really need a core sample from the center of that bare spot. Maybe we could buy an old drilling rig then just leave it there to rot away after we have our core. We should be able to get a ten-meter-deep core in one day. The only problem I can see is safety of the operator."

"I really misjudged you, Tony," Hans teased. "I thought your mind was only on Marie, but your gears have really been turning. We are already shopping for a drill, but I really like your idea of scattering magnets around. I guess that's your next assignment. Find a source of about one hundred thousand small magnets then figure out how to get them to the spot."

"Okay, Hans. We'll get right on it," Tony said brightly.

"Not 'we,' just you. I have to split up the dynamic duo. I need you, Marie, to go to Hawaii. I want you to find Anna McGruder and explain what is happening on her property in New York. Get her permission to build a road to the spot. Aaron has already faxed me a route for the road. He is a bright child, and I can see no reason to question his judgment. You are the best candidate for the persuasion job."

Tony and Marie both hated to be separated, but they immediately went to the phones. Tony had to find an old drill rig, and Marie had to schedule her flight to Hawaii.

Tony found a man with a rig and was assured the rig was the best to be found. He would sell it for a mere ninety thousand.

Tony nearly choked when he heard that big number, so the bargaining began. The man really wanted to sell the old rig and kept expounding on its fine qualities. In the course of his speech, he told Tony it was the finest stomper in the county.

Tony had to disappoint the man because a stumper would produce a core that was compressed. It would not give an accurate depth of the contaminated earth. He spent two and a half hours on the phone and finally found an old rig that could produce a good core sample. This rig was just a few miles west of Binghamton. The owner promised Tony that about the time Hans and Emil had their road built, the rig would be fixed up and ready to produce a thirty-foot core sample.

It took Marie only a few minutes to book a flight to Hawaii, so she helped Tony record the location of the rig and make arrangements to have it delivered to the site. The man even agreed that he and his two sons would do the drilling, although Marie told him it was on very dangerous ground.

Emil and Hans saw the hurt in Tony's eyes and tears in Marie's, so they suggested the couple get out of there and spend time together until Marie's flight at 2:00 a.m.

When the couple came through the front doors heading to Tony's car, they did not immediately see the television station truck. Before they were ten feet from the building, a reporter and TV cameraman accosted them.

"Excuse me, folks, but do you work in there?"

"Yes, vee do," Tony answered in his best immigrant voice.

"Are you scientists?" asked the reporter.

"Ach na, vee are sanitation engineers. Vee clean the toilets unt floor unt messes everywhere," Tony answered as he winked at Marie.

"Can you tell our audience what is going on in there?"

"*Ach, nein. Ich mine arbeit liebe. Unt ich wissen nicht.* [No. I love my job. And I don't know.] Uh, I know not."

The reporter knew a phony when she saw one and said to her cameraman, "We're not going to get anything out of this clown. Let's wait for the next one to come out of there."

Tony and Marie smiled and walked down the street toward the parking lot. They walked and smiled for about ten paces, and Marie couldn't contain her laughter anymore. She broke up laughing, then Tony started laughing, then they were running and laughing all the way to Tony's car. Before both doors were closed, Marie said, "Your place."

"*Yes*, ma'am!" Tony said as he backed out of the parking space and turned toward home.

At Tony's they locked the door, took the phone off the hook, and undressed together, all without a word being spoken there. They made love, made plans, and made hamburgers for a quick lunch. By midnight they had made love several times.

"Oh, Tony! That was great!"

"Hmm."

"Tony?"

"*Hmm*?"

"Tony, we are not married. Do you think we are going to hell for making love before we get married?"

"No, honey. I guess God doesn't like it too much, but look at what King David did. He already had a wife or three, then he had his best buddy killed so he could take his wife. That little caper cost him dearly, but I don't think he went to hell for it. Of course, he was God's favorite, and he really was needed. He did a good job of running Israel."

"Tony, you do intend to marry me, don't you?"

"Of course I do! Whatever made you doubt that? I had already committed myself to you before we ever made love the first time. You knew that!"

"Oh, I don't know. I guess it was that thing with Annamarie. I just know I love you without any reservation at all, and I could not stand to lose you. Tony, what holds an atom together? I guess the electron theory is still just that, a theory, but it seems to work all the time. But what is the force that holds it together? And where does the electron get the energy to keep on spinning around the nucleus?"

"Holy cats! That is a switch! I don't know if I can change gears that fast. Wow! Let me think a minute. I guess it is magnetism that holds the electron to the nucleus, but where does the electron get the energy to keep going around? I just don't know. Every scientist I know believes the theory of evolution or at least professes to. If that theory is true, what were the first two bits of mass that found each other in the vastness of space? Were they an electron and a proton, or something else that is even smaller? Where did the energy come from to unite them? If that happened billions of years ago, how is it that that energy still exists? Atomic energy has a half-life of millions of years, I guess, but billions? I just don't know. How did we get into this discussion?"

"Tony, why can't anybody find any energy in all that stuff that is just disappearing?"

"How am I supposed to know? All those guys downtown are a lot smarter than I, and even they can't figure that out!"

"Why did God destroy Sodom and Gomorrah?"

"Holy cats! What is going on in that brain of yours? Does sex do things to you or something? I guess it was because all the people there were homosexuals and thieves and liars and just plain rotten."

"Genesis 19 says that God rained brimstone and fire down onto those two cities full of evil people. But, Tony, there was nothing in that forest south of Binghamton but one sweet little boy. He is not evil. He probably doesn't even know what sex is."

"Hey, don't underestimate him. He is a bright boy. I am sure he knows what sex is, but you are right about him. He sure has his head on right. The thing didn't start with Aaron though. It started hundreds of years before. Lorraine's great-grandmother did say that it started when all the members of her tribe became 'confused,' as she says. Good grief! Are you thinking what I think you're thinking? Are you thinking that God isn't even going to bother with fire and brimstone this time? That he has just walked away? Are we that bad?"

"Oh, Tony, that is exactly what I think. I think that whatever holds an atom together is God. God supplies the energy to keep the sun burning and the energy to keep that electron running around the atom. Nothing can exist without God. Almost every religion on earth believes in some kind of supreme being. Even the American Indians knew of the Great Spirit. Maybe at some time, Jesus talked to them too.

"But the point is that all the great scholars study all the books of religion, including the Bible, and can probably quote them all backward. But every one of them has missed the one great message that God tried to give us. That is to love him first then love each other! Tony, we do not do that! None of us does that! Can you look at another man and love him without wondering what he wants from you, if he wants to hurt you or take your job or something? Is that why so many people are on drugs? Are we looking for the joy that God wants us to have? The Bible says very plainly that 'God is love.' It does not use any adjectives or adverbs. It does not say that that statement is a parable. It says plainly that 'God is love.'

"Is love energy? That could easily explain how God created everything and also why he created us. I know I sure get energetic whenever I get near you or even think of you, and then look what happens! Oh, Tony, I meant that as a joke, but maybe it isn't such a funny thing. We need food to keep going, and maybe God's food is love from our souls. Tony, there isn't much of that going around anymore. Sex is supposed to create more souls to love God, and it does. Then we go astray and love the devil instead. We are far worse than the people in Sodom and Gomorrah because we try to prevent pregnancy and even murder our babies. Men can't make babies with other men, and women can't make babies with other women.

"Oh, Tony, I am afraid that God just walked away. He isn't even trying to teach us anymore. He is not even going to have the rapture. He just bypassed all that stuff in the Book of Revelation. He just left. We need to pray loud and earnestly before he gets so far away that he can't hear us. Even Hans is convinced of that now!"

"Oh, Marie, I love you dearly, but I have to think about this awhile. The school of mines taught me that we came from some slimy mass that crawled out of the primordial soup. I learned about magnetism, electromagnetic force, electrostatic force, and chemical bonding and—"

"Oh, Tony, all of that is just different kinds of energy. That is love, and that is God. If God did just leave us, then all those laws of physics will just go away too. This whole universe will just disappear like Aaron's toe. I am just Marie. I can't bring God back by myself. I first have to get your help and then that of Emil and Hans and the whole world. Where do I start? Jesus had to die on the cross to get our attention. What do I have to do? What is greater than dying?"

"I don't know, honey, but I do know that you did just start. Maybe we can turn back God. Maybe we can. I guess the first place to start is with Emil. I guess you still have to make this trip to Hawaii. As soon as you get back, we have to convince Emil and Hans that only prayer will save us. We can start praying right now."

MARIE'S ADVENTURE

At the airport, Tony and Marie kissed good-bye at the security gate. Marie cleared security then proceeded to her gate. Hundreds of people passed by in both directions, and slowly the area around Marie's gate filled up with passengers for the same flight. Most of them were in a festive mood being bound for their Hawaiian vacation.

There was a baby crying incessantly since it was past her bedtime, and she was being kept awake. When her eyes met Marie's, she saw a face so funny she quit crying for a second. Marie made other faces at her, and soon she was laughing. After several minutes of faces, talking, and even crooning, Marie had the child fast asleep on her mother's lap.

The flight was smooth, and Marie slept most of the way to Hawaii. Upon arrival, she went directly to her hotel to check in and freshen up a bit. Then she went to the restaurant for breakfast. During the meal, many people came and went, but six men, one of whom wore a turban, sat at a nearby table. At various times one or another of the men glanced at Marie.

By the time she was finished eating, Marie was a nervous wreck. She returned to her room to call Anna McGruder. She dialed the number, and the phone rang five times before Anna answered it.

Marie introduced herself then explained that she was working for a group of scientists who were studying a strange thing going on at Anna's property south of Binghamton.

"Oh my! Oh my!" Anna said. "I hoped I would be gone before the world learned about that. I guess I have to face the music now. Can you come here to see me? I don't want to talk about this on the phone. I am on Maui in the town of Pukalani. This rest home is on the south side of the road, just before you enter town. If you are near the airport on the big island, it won't take long to fly here. The taxi ride is short from the airport on this island."

As Marie made arrangements for her flight to Maui, she was wondering why Anna seemed to feel guilty about the bare spot. She boarded a small plane with seven other passengers, and the flight was short but bumpy. The plane rattled and shook and made several quick altitude changes before landing on Maui. Marie decided it was much more fun than the big airliner. It flew much lower too, and she could see boats on the ocean below.

Anna was waiting at the front entrance of the rest home. After introductions, they walked to a park bench to talk. Anna seemed fearful and apologetic. Marie was determined to find out why and then put the old lady at ease. She decided the direct approach was best.

"Anna, why do you seem to be afraid of me?"

"Because you are here to arrest me, aren't you?"

"No, of course not. Why would I want to arrest you?"

By now the old lady was crying. "When I was a young girl, I was in love with an Indian boy, and I became pregnant. When he found out about the baby, he wanted no more to do with me. The baby was born in the woodshed behind my parents' house. It was three months early and was stillborn. After I cleaned myself up, I took my baby into the woods and buried it under a big pile of loose dirt, rocks, and bones. Ma and Pa never knew I was pregnant. They didn't miss the soiled clothes that I threw away, but Pa did miss the shovel that I left at the big pile. Soon after, I started hearing horrible tales about that big pile of dirt out there. I guess I started something really bad. I knew I would pay for it someday."

"Oh, Anna, you didn't start anything. I am sure you conceived that child in love, didn't you?"

Sniff. "Yes, I did. I loved that boy with all my heart. I gave him all of me. But he didn't love me. I was only twelve, and the curse had only just started in me. I did finally marry McGruder, and we had six kids together. All my life I have lived in fear because of what I started in the woods. You say I didn't start anything?"

"No, Anna. That was started by the Indians hundreds of years ago. That pile of bones and dirt is where they buried their people who were 'confused.' We think God is so disgusted with 'confused people' that he has abandoned that big pile. The pile is gone now. It just disappeared. In fact, there is a depression there now, and it is as big as this lawn here."

"What do you mean by 'confused'?"

"I mean homosexual. They didn't know if they were men or women. There were so many of them in that small tribe that the tribe died out. I met the last remaining member, a woman named Dancing Star."

"I knew her," Anna said. "She was the mother of the boy who made me pregnant." That was the last thing Anna said for quite a while. She was crying, rocking back and forth on the bench. She cried for several minutes then finally hugged Marie. She asked between sniffles, "Have you eaten anything lately?"

"Yes, but I am still hungry. I passed a restaurant down the street. Let's go there."

"Oh, I would love that. Should I call a cab?"

"No, I rented a car at the airport. We can drive ourselves there. Then after we have eaten, we'll explore the island."

"Oh, that's wonderful. You make me feel young again, Mary." Anna smiled brightly. "I feel young, alive, and free and light. All my life I carried that burden, and finally I am free."

At the restaurant there was more small talk, about Maui mostly and how the island came to be. Marie noticed a man who came into the dining room after she and Anna were seated. He looked vaguely familiar, and Marie felt a bit ill at ease but didn't know why.

After their food was served, Anna asked, "Mary, if I didn't start that mess at Binghamton and you aren't here to arrest me, why are you here?"

Marie anticipated further correspondence with Anna after their meeting, so she thought it best that Anna know her name. "My name is Marie, Anna. It is like Mary, but ends in *ie* instead of *y*."

"Oh, I am sorry, Marie. I guess I don't hear very well," Anna apologized.

"That I can understand, but I think I will wait until we are in the car to answer your question. Do you have many friends here on the island?"

Marie didn't want to talk loudly about the mission she was on for fear of starting panic, and that strange man glanced her way several times, making her nervous. They discussed Anna's friends in the Red Hatters Club and the senior citizens club. The senior coordinators were a young couple who were full of energy. They took the group off the island to the other islands and to the mainland, and even to Europe, Australia, Japan, and other interesting places.

When they left the restaurant, Marie turned right on the first street she saw then left on the next one. She made several more turns until Anna finally asked, "What are you doing, Marie?"

"I think we are being followed," Marie answered. "At the restaurant and at the hotel on the big island, some strange men kept looking at me. When we left the restaurant, a man got up and left too. He started to follow us in a car, but I think I lost him."

"Oh, this is getting exciting," Anna said gleefully as she turned around in her seat to search for any cars that might be following.

Marie was not so happy about it. She found a small park and hid the little car between two big ones. They stayed in the car, and Marie explained her mission to Anna. She told about the slow disintegration of the woods and that the best scientists in the world were trying to learn why it was happening. She told how the discovery of the thing started with Aaron Fisher's toe.

She also told how the scientists were about to give up on the project because it seemed to be an act of God, an act meant to eliminate the human race. Perhaps God had given up on them because of their horrendous behavior.

"They did discover a way to stop or at least slow down the thing until we can find a way to eliminate it," Marie explained. "That is where you come in, Anna. We need your help."

"I'm just a little old lady. What can I do?" Anna said with a slight tremor.

"You own the land where the big bare spot is," Marie reminded the old lady. "We need to construct a really big magnet over the spot or around it. That means we need to bring big construction equipment there and build a road to the spot. We need your permission to do all that."

"Oh my! I wanted to keep the woods like the Indians found them so little children could play there and explore. But if it isn't safe, I guess children shouldn't be there." Then Anna got a stern look on her face and said, "I heard on TV about scams pulled on old folks. How do I know I can trust you? Do you want to build a big shopping center on my property?"

Marie was taken aback a bit. She was always truthful and honest. She never expected to be suspected of any nefarious motive. "Anna, do you remember Henry and Donna Fisher?"

"Oh yes. Donna's mother was from the tribe of Indians that lived around there. She and I used to play together a lot. Her daughter ran off to college and came back with a renegade Amish man. He is quite a man and a good farmer too!"

"I have their phone number. It is their son who was first infected by the thing," Marie said gently. "Please call Donna, and she will tell you who I am."

"Oh, I will as soon as we get back to the home. I didn't know that you know Donna and Henry. How is their little boy? Is he still alive?" Anna asked.

"He sure is! That little boy has more life in him than ten other boys. He is a budding scientist. He collects anything he finds, but he doesn't just throw things into a box. He mounts things on a display and labels everything. He has a friend, a little girl named Lorraine from Hawleyton, and between the two of them, they can think of more mischief to get into! Tony and I just love those kids.

"Aaron," Marie continued, "stubbed his toe on a rock in the middle of that big bare spot. His toe was slowly disappearing until Dr. Staneck stuck a magnet on it. That stopped the toe from disappearing altogether. We hope to use the same technology on the big bare spot to stop the thing from eating New York and Pennsylvania."

Anna's eyes showed surprise when Marie mentioned Dr. Staneck. "Would he be Dr. Joseph Staneck?" she asked. "A Dr. Staneck took out my appendix about sixty years ago. I was young, and he was a romantic and handsome man, even if he was Polish and could hardly speak English. Of course, I fell in love with him, but then my heart got broken when I learned he had a wife."

Marie smiled and said, "His wife's name is Sophie. She is a very nice woman."

"You should have seen her sixty years ago. She was a knockout! And yes, a lovely person too. How does a magnet stop the thing? What is the thing anyway? Is it like cancer? How do you know it will work in the woods?"

After Anna's barrage of questions, Marie answered simply, "I don't know. In Chicago there are over one hundred scientists trying to find answers to all your questions. The thing is growing so fast that we have to try to stop it while we work to discover just what it is.

"Anna, that is the reason we need your help. We need written permission to build a road to build a big magnet and a power line to keep the magnet working. If we don't stop it soon, we never will. There will be no property, no Hawleyton, no Binghamton—"

"Oh my! Oh my! Let's get back to the home. I need to make a phone call or two, then I'll sell the place to you or whatever..." Anna trailed off.

Marie had no idea where they were, but after she found a major thoroughfare, Anna was able to direct her back to the rest home.

Anna did indeed call Donna. They had a long discussion about old times, Aaron, and finally Marie, Tony, and Dr. Staneck. When she finally concluded that call, she called her attorney and made an appointment. Then they began a frantic search for a key to Anna's safe deposit box at the bank. She finally remembered that the key was in a cookie jar in the kitchen.

Anna directed Marie to her bank, and there she removed a deed from the deposit box. Then they rode the elevator to the eighth floor where her attorney's office was.

The attorney was reluctant to draw up any papers because he was suspicious of Marie. Neither she nor Anna was eager to explain the thing to him. Finally, Anna just said, "Now listen, young man, I know I am not being snookered here. I have completely checked this woman out. Besides, all we want is to give her power of attorney over a patch of woods, not Fort Knox."

The papers were drawn up, and to satisfy himself, the attorney even included a clause prohibiting the building of any commercial enterprise. The deed was returned to the safe deposit box, and the ladies returned to the home. Anna made coffee, and they talked for several hours about Donna, Henry, Aaron, Dr. Staneck, and the area south of Binghamton.

When Marie finally left, it was a tearful good-bye. Marie promised to bring Tony down to meet Anna after the thing had been stopped and the two young assistants could take some time off.

Back at the hotel, Marie called Tony and told him she had power of attorney over the land, so construction could start immediately. She also mentioned the strange man at the hotel and on Maui.

Tony said, "Get back here as soon as possible. That sounds scary."

Tony relayed the news to Hans and Emil. Within one half hour, Marie received a phone call from the local FBI office. She was advised to stay in the hotel, either in her room or in plain sight of other guests. There would be uniformed local police near her until she departed Hawaii.

Marie thanked the lady who called then smiled with satisfaction and thought, *Good old Emil. He is looking out for me.*

Later at dinner in the hotel restaurant, the same group of strange men were together at a table across the room. Finally one of the men walked over to Marie's table. She could see two police officers move closer to her table too.

The man introduced himself as an employee of the sheik. He informed Marie that the sheik had decided that Marie would accompany him to Paris. She was to pack her bags immediately and be ready to depart on a private airplane in one hour.

Oh no! Not another one! Marie managed not to laugh at the man but informed him that she was going to Chicago, not Paris.

"No! You are going to Paris. You have no choice! You are only a woman, and the sheik has decided you are to be his wife."

The man was becoming frustrated and looked fearfully at his boss. Marie could not restrain herself any longer. She informed the man that she was an American woman. She could go anywhere she wanted to go and go with whomever she pleased. She definitely did not wish to go to Paris with a stranger or to join his harem!

At that point, the two uniformed officers approached Marie's table and asked if there was a problem. The strange man retreated to the group at his table with his head hanging low. Marie pictured his head on a platter. She also said a silent thanks to Emil.

The next morning when Marie left her room to get breakfast, there was an officer at the end of the corridor, and he accompanied her to the dining room. He had breakfast with her and even escorted her to the airport security gate where Marie thanked him for his help.

Later, on the airplane, Marie's seatmates were startled when she suddenly began laughing. She laughed at the poor lackey who failed his mission, and she laughed at the frustrated sheik. She laughed until she thought how horrible life must be for Arab women or any women who were treated like cattle.

Marie did not know that many Arabian people are actually Christians. It was only after Mufid's activity in the laboratory that she became interested in the people of the Middle East. To her, anyone from that region was classified as Arabs.

She explained the situation to her seatmates amid peals of laughter. It opened conversation with the people around her, and it was a very enjoyable flight.

LIGHT

Meanwhile back at the farm in New York, Aaron was doing some experimenting on his own. He placed stakes around part of the bare spot and made measurements many times each day for a week. He noticed that on clear sunny days, the spot did not grow at all. He checked again and again to be sure of his observations. After a trip home and back again, he laid heavy brown paper over the ground alongside of the bare spot and partly over the edge of the spot. After a week he removed the paper with sticks and found the spot had grown to the shape of the covered area. Aaron repeated the test and got the same results.

Next, he and Lorraine carried a lantern to the site and illuminated part of the spot and the area around it. The battery lasted through two nights, and each morning the children measured the growth in the illuminated area. There was no growth!

Aaron called the temporary lab in Chicago and asked to talk to Hans. He told the scientist what he had done and what he had found. Hans was speechless! He thanked Aaron politely then duplicated Aaron's tests in the lab. Aaron was absolutely right. Light energy also prevented growth of the thing.

Several days after this discovery, Lorraine approached her mother and asked, "Mom, are you busy?"

"I'm just making dinner, honey. Do you have a problem?"

"Yeah, I'm worried about Aaron."

"Why? What's wrong?"

"Do you know what is wrong with his toe?"

"No, I don't know any more than you do. I thought Dr. Staneck had that problem solved."

"Well, maybe he does. It quit getting smaller, but Aaron was acting weird today. I asked him if something is wrong, but he didn't answer me."

"What makes you think he is acting weird? Is it because he didn't answer you?"

"No, but he had this really weird look, like the way he looks when something is wrong that he can't figure out. Today we walked along Avignon Road to the swimming hole, and he kept turning around to the left for a while, then to the right for a while. Then he walked sideways like a crab and kept looking down at his bad toe.

"When he took off his shoes to go swimming, he just looked at that stub of a toe and kept touching it. He did that five times on the left of it, then five times on the right. He just barely touched it. After we went swimming and were coming home, he did that crazy dance again. But he still wouldn't tell me what is wrong. Mom, Aaron always tells me everything, just like I tell him. But not today. I think something is bad wrong. I'm scared, Mom!"

"Well, just give me a few minutes to get the rest of the stew into the pot. Then I'll call Aaron's mom."

"Donna, this is Mary. I just talked with Lorraine, and she is troubled by Aaron's behavior. They went swimming today, and Aaron did a strange kind of dance or something while they walked to the pond and again on the way back. He kept looking at his bad toe. Lorraine is really upset because Aaron wouldn't talk about it."

"Did she say what the dance was like? I have seen him turn to the left then turn to the right. Once he turned around several times then did the left and right thing again. He kept looking at something in his hand, but I didn't think there was anything wrong. I just figured he is being a boy. But if Lorraine is concerned, then maybe I better call Doc Staneck. I think Lorraine knows more about my boy than I do."

"That's why I called. She was crying as she told me about this, and Lorraine doesn't cry very often. I have never before seen two kids who know each other like these two. When they can't communicate, there is usually something wrong. I expect there will be a big change in their friendship whenever they reach the age when they know they are different. They won't change for a few years yet, will they?"

"Oh, Mary, I don't think it is that far away. Lorraine could start her periods in about a year. Some girls do start early, like ten or eleven, but I don't think that is bothering her yet. I don't know why Aaron won't tell her if something is wrong. Maybe he doesn't even know he is doing something strange. You know how his brain is always thinking about the way things work. I'll call Doc about it, but I don't think it is too serious. Aaron seems normal otherwise. I'll call right now, then I'll call you back."

"Okay, Donna. Bye."

After several minutes, Dr. Staneck came on the line, "Good afternoon, Donna. Sophie tells me you have a problem with Aaron. Is it his toe?"

"Well, I don't know, Doctor, she said. He has been doing a strange kind of dance or something lately and won't talk to me or Lorraine about it. Those two kids are closer than sardines, and when Aaron won't talk about something with her, there must be something wrong with him."

"Hmm? When is his next visit with me?"

"Not until next month. Could I bring him in to see you today? I'll tell him those old guys in Chicago want to know something so I don't scare him."

"Yes, bring him in. I'll have a man-to-man with him, in between a broken arm and stomach ulcers."

"Oh, Doctor, there's nothing like that wrong with him—oh, I see what you mean. I'll round him up and bring him in as soon as I find him."

"Good, Donna. I am looking forward to seeing Aaron again. He always brightens my day. Bye."

Donna found Aaron in front of the barn, where he and Henry were cleaning the old manure spreader. She made him take a bath and put on clean clothes, so they got to town a little later than planned. The ulcer case had just left the doctor's office, and Doc was checking a sore throat. Aaron had to wait a bit. Donna was worried that Aaron still smelled of manure.

Aaron was wondering what the old guys in Chicago wanted this time. He was also trying to decide what flavor of ice cream he wanted.

Finally, Dr. Staneck called him in and checked the normal things a doctor always checks: weight, blood pressure, etc. Then he asked Donna to step out for a bit so he could have a man-to-man talk with Aaron.

"Aaron, do you still see a lot of Lorraine?" the doctor asked.

"Yeah, almost every day. Sometimes like today I didn't 'cause I had to help Pop clean the old manure spreader. He got the crazy idea to paint it up and park it at the end of the lane. Is there something wrong with her?"

"No, but she is concerned about you."

"Why? Ain't nuthin' wrong with me since you fixed my toe."

"She told her mother that you have been acting strangely lately. She said you have been doing some strange dance or something when you walk with her, but you won't discuss it with her. She said you two talk about everything, but not what is wrong with you now."

"Oh, that! There ain 't nuthin' wrong. I just noticed somethin' about my toe, but I'm not sure I'm really feelin' what I think I feel. I need to check it out more, that's all."

"What is it that you are feeling, Aaron?"

"Well, I said I have to check it out some more, so don't laugh at me. First I have a question. Where are the poles on that magnet you put on my toe? I tried to figure that out by using my little toy dog magnets. But the one on my toe is too strong, and the dogs don't know which way to turn."

"Is one of those dogs white and one black? I haven't seen those toys for many years. Where did you get them?"

"They were Pop's when he was little," Aaron said.

"Well, the magnet on your toe is lined up with the poles on the sides."

"I thought so. When I turn around slowly, I can feel the pressure on my stub change. I can tell which way is north by the pressure on my stub. When I face east, like this, the pressure is greater on the left side of my stub. When I face west, the pressure is greater on the right side. I took off the magnet, and then I couldn't feel anything. I thought everyone would think I am nuts if I told about it. Do you think I'm nuts?"

"No, I certainly do not! I think you are a very observant little boy. Is that why you didn't tell Lorraine?"

"No! She knows me. She would not think I'm nuts. I just wanted to be sure of the feelin' in my toe. Sometimes it feels different or itches or somethin', but so does all of me. I just wanted to be sure this feelin' wasn't somethin' that will go away in a day or so, that's all. I have been feelin' it for about two weeks now, so I guess it is here to stay. My toe is now a compass. I'll always know which way I am going."

"Aaron, that is remarkable! You should be a scientist. Lorraine was crying when she told her mother about your strange dance. She thought there was something very wrong with you, but I can understand your wanting to be sure of that which you have observed."

"It ain't no big deal. It's just somethin' I noticed, that's all. It's nuttin' to bawl about."

"Well, tell her about it," Dr. Staneck insisted. "I can't think of any way to confirm your observation, but I believe that you can indeed feel the change in pressure. You are certainly not nuts! I have never before met a boy with your ability to observe things as you do."

"I know a way to prove I am right about this. Put a blindfold on me and spin me around a few times, and I'll tell you which way I am standing."

Dr. Staneck got a roll of gauze and wrapped it around Aaron's head several times so he could see nothing at all. Then he turned the boy around several times. Aaron stood still a minute or two then slowly turned until he faced north. The test was performed two more times, and each time Aaron faced north when he stopped turning.

Dr. Staneck called Donna back into the room. He also called his receptionist in and asked them to be very quiet. He then repeated the test, and again Aaron faced north when he stopped turning.

None of the four people could think of any scientific or commercial use for this bit of information, but later on, Aaron and Lorraine used the foot compass to find their way around in the parts of the forest they had not explored before.

By that time, Aaron and Lorraine knew enough about the affliction in the toe. They knew that as long as the magnet was there, Aaron was safe from whatever it was that made his toe disappear.

Again Lorraine cried. She cried with relief that Aaron was well. She also cried because Aaron didn't trust her enough to explain his odd dance. Maybe, she thought, she didn't know him as well as she had thought. She just wasn't sure.

Aaron stopped walking and just hugged her. He explained that he had said nothing because he wasn't sure about his feelings in the toe stub yet.

Just as Aaron took Lorraine in his arms to hug her, Bill Priss and his wife Mabel passed by in their car on the way to canasta club. Mabel Priss was the town gossip spreader. She urged Bill to hurry on to the meeting. She couldn't wait to tell the other women about the disgusting behavior of the two children. By the time the story got around several times, Aaron was on top of Lorraine, and both kids were without clothes! Finally Henry heard the story and repeated it to Donna. Donna called Mary, and at that time, both kids were in her kitchen helping her can grape jelly.

Mary was surprised to hear the story. In her normal direct way of solving problems, she asked the kids if they had been lying naked in the ditch along the road yesterday.

"What would we do a dumb thing like that for?" both kids asked at once.

"Were you together on the road at all yesterday?"

"Yeah," Aaron answered. "We went for a walk after I went to Doc Staneck the day before. Doc told me about Lorraine bawling about me being sick, and I just explained that there wasn't nothin' wrong with me. We were not in no ditch!"

Lorraine remembered that just as Aaron hugged her, a car went by and splashed water from a mud puddle on the kids. She had been so relieved to know that Aaron was well that the splashing was indeed a small problem. Neither child was sure who it was that splashed them, only that it was a blue car.

They were not sure, but they thought it was an old car. Mary knew that Bill Priss drove an old blue car, and she put two and two together. She told Donna that Mabel probably saw the kids hugging. Both mothers knew of Lorraine's worry over Aaron, and they both laughed about it. Donna mentioned that it was probably time to explain the birds and bees to the kids.

Actually, both kids knew about reproduction and how it was accomplished because they lived in farm country. But they knew nothing about adult sensitivities. After hanging up the phone,

Mary explained to the kids about how wild imaginations could get. Aaron had a hard time understanding because he always double-checked anything he saw or heard.

"Besides," he said, "if we were going to try to make a baby, we certainly wouldn't do it on the road!"

The story went around and around several times until it finally faded away when Sam Gill broke his neck in a fall from the barn rafters. By the time this bit of news was told and retold, the story was that he had been pushed off the rafter by another suitor for Betsy Groff. That story went around and around too, even though that other suitor was in Florida when Sam fell.

MAGNETS

While Marie was in Hawaii, Tony kept busy by visiting every craft and hobby store he could find. He bought every little magnet each store had in stock. His car soon had so many magnets in plastic bags that the weight of them made the old car groan. Tony had to take his harvest to the lab several times to unload. He piled them up in a corner. After the third load, Tony wondered how they would get the magnets through the woods to the bare spot.

Meanwhile, Hans and Emil were busy too. They called Henry and asked him to find a local contractor to build a road through the woods to the bare spot.

Henry called Joe, who had a friend with a bulldozer. The kids had started school, so the men waited until after school to ask Aaron his idea for a route for the road. They all met with Tom, the dozer operator, at Aaron's chicken house museum. There on the wall was a map of the area with the path to the spot well marked. There were little yellow and green dots on each side of the proposed road.

Henry asked, "What are the yellow and green dots for?"

"We already staked out the road. The yellow marks are yellow ribbons we tied around the stakes on the high spots. The green ones are low spots. We picked this route 'cause it's short and not very thick with big trees," Aaron answered.

Tom was amazed. "I know that woods too, and I agree. The kids picked the best route. When can I start building the road?"

"I guess we have to wait for those scientists in Chicago to give us the go-ahead signal," Henry said.

"Okay, Henry. I'll build it as soon as you tell me to. I'm ready to go," Tom said.

The experiment with the little magnets, the core drilling, and Hans's new plan to use light all had to wait for the road to be built. The road had to wait for Marie's report. She had called Emil and told him she had the written power of attorney, but both Hans and Emil wanted their attorney to make it official before road building could commence.

Tony collected magnets! He collected so many magnets he nearly filled a storage closet in the office. He collected magnets morning, noon, and night! He collected magnets until Hans and Emil had to disable his car. As they were discussing Tony's obsession with magnets, Emil suddenly began laughing.

Hans stared at his friend then asked, "*Varoom sind sie erfreulich?* [Why are you so happy?] What's so funny?"

"Tony is lovesick! If he has nothing to do, he worries about Marie! I don't think he ever stops thinking about her! That boy is so much in love that even being shot didn't distract him much." Emil laughed.

"I think you are right, old friend. May God bless them with much happiness and many children," Hans pleaded. Then he too laughed and said, "She is on her way home. Maybe the magnet flow will stop soon!

"Another young person has humbled me. Our friend Aaron has made a discovery that the greatest minds in science failed to see. He discovered that light also prevents growth of the thing. The boy is only nine years old! Never in my life have I been so humbled! I confirmed his finding in our laboratory. If for no other reason, we have to stop this monster so the boy can mature and take us through a century like no other in history!" Hans declared.

Emil, also feeling humble, asked, "How did Aaron make that discovery?"

"The boy is very diligent. He made many measurements and recorded everything, even the current temperature and cloud cover. He noticed that on bright, sunny days, there was little growth. He confirmed it by covering with paper a small area adjacent to the spot. That area became infected when the rest of the good ground was protected by sunlight. Then he did the reverse. At night he put up lights to illuminate a small area, and there was no growth there. Test and confirm! The boy is a natural scientist!

"He is such a simple boy. His language is quaint, to say the least. He does not puff himself up, and what he says, he means. He sees that which he sees. He does not see something, then analyze it or modify it or explain it away. He simply sees and records. His little girlfriend is amazing too. She is also very observant, and from what I understand, she drew that map of the spot. What an amazing pair of kids. What a future they have if the onset of puberty doesn't change them too much. I love those kids."

Emil asked, "Hans, why did we not see the effect of light months ago?"

"Ach, Emil, we know too much! We should have seen this when Cushman and his wife sent us their report on their experiments on the free unit negative charges and masses in the ionization produced by x-rays and ultraviolet light. These charges are small indeed, not more than $1/1837^{th}$ of the mass of the lightest known atom, that of hydrogen. But the team could measure no charges at all when they bombarded mass affected by this weird phenomenon—none. They tried many frequencies within the spectrum and still could measure no charge at all. Cushman even told us in his report that the mass of the tested material did not change. I got too interested in duplicating Millikan's oil drop experiment and experimenting with photons, the localized electromagnetic energy traveling through space and its effect on electrons that absorb it. That is all basic science, but I missed the simple fact that the tested mass ceased to change as the light was focused on it. It took a simple little boy to see the significance of that!"

"Hans, I missed it too, so don't feel bad. Also, that little boy is not so simple. He reminds me of the twelve- and fourteen-year-old boys who composed the classical music that is still popular today, after three hundred years or so. I think maybe the Cushmans, Marie, and Aaron are closest to the solution of this whole thing, but they are looking from three different directions at the same thing."

"Emil, we spent too much of our time and energy trying to learn how the sample of Aaron's toe affected that electron microscope," Hans said. "That device employs an electron beam that is accelerated by a voltage of one hundred thousand volts or greater to a speed approaching that of light. We assumed that somehow energy or whatever the thing is traveled through that stream of electrons back to the circuits that created the beam and destroyed some components. I have come to the conclusion that the microscope failure was merely a coincidence. If the operator had removed the sample and the slide it was on while he analyzed his problem within the circuits, he would still have his scope. I think that capacitor failure was merely a breakdown of the electrolyte between its plates, resulting in a short circuit that greatly increased the current through the resistors. It was just a normal failure that often happens in electronic equipment using high voltage.

"Mr. Sczymzack spent much time trying to fix the scope then went about other activities and didn't return to the scope for nearly twenty-four hours. That was time enough for the thing to do its dirty work. We were much too engrossed in our science to see the simple fact. I think that is why Marie is always one step ahead of us. She approaches problems in a simple uncomplicated way, just like she reads the Bible. It just is!"

"Hans, several months ago you told me you are working on a theory. Did you ever confirm that theory?"

The old German scientist went to the chalkboard, erased part of a large and complicated formula, and wrote "$E = MC^2 = GOD$."

Hans sat down and said, "Think about it. Does this not fill in many of the holes in our scientific theories? Does this not bring reality to God? Einstein said that men see natural occurrences in different ways. That which happened, happened in only one way, and that doesn't change. Our observations vary, but not the actual fact. So it is with God. God is! God created us. Men see God in different ways and call him by many different names, but God is and does not vary. There should be no controversy between God and science. Science only explains the way God does things.

"Prayer is not voodoo worship of some spook. Prayer is the most powerful force we can apply to any problem, although I suspect we waste a lot of this tremendous energy on trivial problems or rather in trivial ways. For instance, why pray for a miraculous cure of cancer in a man whose body is so riddled with the curse there is no hope for recovery? Rather, we should ask God to guide us to a way to eliminate cancer altogether. If we must pray for that condemned man, let us pray that God sees the good in his soul so that he isn't dumped into a lake of fire! These laws of physics, that you and I have studied all of our lives, were written by God, but they are only of secondary importance to our creator. The laws of physics were written only to provide and protect the physical containers for our souls. I think that the soul of man comes into existence even before sperm meets egg.

"Genetics determine the shape of the nose and perhaps susceptibility to disease and maybe even habits, but the soul controls its own destiny, no matter how birth or death occurs.

"The important laws that God wrote are written in ink in a book called the Bible. The very first of these important laws were written in stone. These laws guide and nurture that which is really important to God, the soul which is in his image. Look at what happened when your government took God out of schools.

Children began to shoot each other, and a deranged truck driver killed several girls in a one-room school, and teachers are afraid of students. If your government takes God off of your money, your economy will disintegrate.

"Emil," Hans continued, "we have broken all of these laws so many times that I am afraid God has given up on us. I think he has left us, and the effect was first seen at that mound of dead bodies in that forest in New York."

Emil stared at the formula for several minutes then asked, "Are we doing any good here? Have we accomplished anything?"

"Not a thing here! All that we have learned we learned from Joseph, Tony, Marie, Aaron, and Lorraine. I think maybe Tuesday we will all be here. My niece will be back from Darmstadt, and Said should be back from Hadithah. Marie is in the air now and will be back today. Tony is somewhere in Chicago. Were there any other of our scientists flying around somewhere?"

"No, not that I know of. Marie keeps track of them. She can round them all up by Tuesday, I think. What do you have in mind?" Emil asked, even though he was quite sure he knew what Hans was thinking.

"I am going to call a meeting of everyone, including Joseph, Aaron, Lorraine, and their parents. We are going to end this big project, give everyone a doomsday lecture, and send them all home. If they want to keep trying to catch the thing, they can do it in their own labs. They all know the danger by now. In spite of the fact nothing was done here, they are all the best scientists in the world and will be careful not to contaminate their part of the world.

"I am convinced that this thing is an act of God. An act meant to destroy the planet Earth and all of us. I think the only solution is to beg and plead for forgiveness and for another chance. I am an old man and probably the worst sinner of the world. I don't know if I have the ability to convince the world, or even this bunch of scientists, to reform, but I have to try. Do you agree, old friend?"

Emil answered, "I agree with you that we have to inform the world and try to convince them to change, but I don't agree that you are the worst of sinners. Thousands of us still living did horrible things. Both sides committed great sins in that war era. The number of people who died by your hand is quite small when compared to the millions of children who are being murdered before birth by their mothers. Is what you did any worse than a man begetting a child then abandoning the child and its mother? Or are you worse than the man who gets so deeply involved with his work that he ignores his wife and children? Or even a person who openly praises another while thinking in his mind how to destroy the other? No, old friend, you are not the worst sinner. We are all rotten! We have all fallen short of what God had in mind when he created us.

"Hans, I have to agree with you that we can do nothing about this thing in this great laboratory. All the greatest minds in the world are here, and we have found nothing. It is an act of God. There is no doubt about that. But there is something we can do about it. Every problem we have encountered, we have researched extensively. We have studied all the thinking of Einstein and even Aristotle for answers to physical problems. Perhaps we have to study another source to solve this great mystery."

Hans, still upset and frightened, replied, "I assume you mean the Bible, the *b*asic *i*nstructions *b*efore *l*eaving *E*arth. I have read parts of that great book, but I find it extremely confusing. The religion scholars can explain everything, but they are the same gang that wanted to put Galileo in a noose because he said the earth rotates around the sun. If we had listened to those guys, we would have no America as we know it today. There would be no satellites in the sky and no man on the moon. Those guys are still adamant about everything being created in just six days.

They even believe that the dinosaur bones we find are only a few thousand years old or are from beasts that still roam the earth.

"I am fully convinced that we will find an answer in the Bible, but I think we have to study it ourselves to find it. I think that some of our religious scholars are still influenced by pagan practices that were in existence before Jesus came along. We shall have to study the ancient scrolls and other writings found around the world. I never fully trusted the translators, especially those monks who wrote the King James Version. Can a man living without sex really think straight? How can he make conclusions about life when he knows nothing about getting up at three in the morning to feed an infant or the strange behavior of a woman who is about to start her period?

"The Bible itself is very confusing. For instance, in Jeremiah 7:22, God is telling Jeremiah that when he brought his forefathers out of Egypt, he did not give them commands about burnt offerings. They were to obey him, and they would be his people, and he would be their God. I have been reading a later translation that is easier to read, but how do we know that the translator did not change any meanings?

"I do not know why those early Christians missed the boat on the shape of the earth when it appears right in the Bible. Isaiah 40:22 talks about God sitting enthroned above the circle of the earth. Maybe they thought it is shaped like a pizza pie. They sure misunderstood a lot of other stuff. The super religious church-going saints living in the south of your country still think that black people are not children of God. I guess they are like the rest of us. They believe whatever they want to and distort the rest."

"Hans, you can't blame only the people in the south of America for our disgraceful treatment of black folks. I'm afraid that is all over this country. But you really surprised me with your knowledge of the Bible. I didn't know you even read that book at all, and here you are quoting chapter and verse!"

Hans said, "I sure do not claim to be any kind of authority on the Bible. I have never consulted it to find the atomic weight of an element or the exact way an element might affect an organ in a human body. But that certainly does not mean that I cannot see where an element came from. Any fool or any genius knows that God created everything. Exactly how and when and how long it took, we do not know beyond what the Bible says. When that information becomes useful to us, God will reveal it.

"Those religious scholars think that we scientists are so cold and calculating that we cannot possibly believe anything in the Bible or any other book of religion. You and I know differently though. Those guys we have in those two Muslim labs back there can't get much done because they can't concentrate on any problem. They are too busy watching the clock for the next time to get down on the floor and worship Allah.

"Besides that, if I had no conscience and no belief in God, the horrible stuff I did in Germany and Poland sixty years ago would not bother me now, but it surely does. God tells us over and over to love each other, but look at all the horrible murders that were committed in the name of Christ. The crusades were an excuse for slaughter. The witch hunts in Salem were done in the name of Christ. The millions of murders committed before and during World War II were done in the name of religious purity. Even I believed in that horrible atrocity.

"Perhaps we scientists are wrong in our belief in evolution, but every day we do learn more and more about this earth, the universe, and even the human body. Those brilliant religious scholars have been studying the same three or four books of religion for several thousand years, and they still can't get it! The dummies are so caught up in what clothes we should wear, what words we should use to worship God, how many candles we should burn, and even the size of sugar scoops that women are required to wear on their heads. They can't see that all those religious writings were made to teach us how to live together in love. None of them has it right. People keep going from one religion to another to find answers. The only churches or other religious groups that stay big are the ones that carry a big club and use it frequently.

"The actual getting along with each other is left to our young men who are especially trained to either control or kill. Unfortunately, this is worldwide, and these young men are either soldiers or policemen. Religion itself has been a total failure because of the inability to agree on anything. Is it any wonder that God is so angry with us that he is not even waiting for the events in the book of Revelation to occur? Is there to be no Rapture? Are we all doomed? I know I am because of what I did years ago, but what crimes have little babies committed? Our Marie is love itself. What has she done wrong enough to deserve to be just wiped out of existence? What has Aaron done? That boy has to be the finest little boy in the world. He doesn't deserve this."

"I don't know, Hans, but there has to be some way to change God's mind. It has been done before, but we sure are not going to find the solution in a beaker or under a microscope. Ah, Marie is back. I can hear both her and Tony in the office." As he said this, Emil touched the intercom button and then said, "Tony and Marie, come in here please."

Tony's grin disappeared as soon as he saw the look on Emil's face. He and Marie exchanged glances, and together they said, "Uh-oh." Tony added, "Did my mother die or something?"

"Tony, what do you think the thing is?" Hans asked. "And you too, Marie. What do you think?"

Tony replied, "Well, I don't think God went to the local drugstore for glue to hold things together. I think the thing is the absence of God. I think he has given up on us."

"What about you, Marie?" Hans asked.

"I'm afraid I have to agree with Tony. I think we had better start praying nonstop. We might be able to delay the disintegration of earth with science, but prayer is the only thing that might save us. Even that is a long shot. God gave us the ability to make our own decisions, and we have made all the wrong ones. We have failed miserably. Selfishness, greed, and hate rule our lives. The devil has won this round, I am afraid.

"Moses was able to change God's mind," Marie continued, "when he was about to wipe out all of the Israelites when just two of them sinned. God opened up the earth, and it swallowed those two, their families, and 250 others who were in cahoots with the two. He did spare the rest of the people. I have total faith in God, but not in us. There is not one of us who has not sinned. Not one! If there is any chance at all for us, we had better start to pray now. What religion's prayers should we use? I don't know. Religion has been around since the creation, but it has apparently failed. There are so many of them! Which is right? I would bet that Adam argued with Eve about that."

Hans frowned and said, "We have almost every religion on earth right here in these labs, plus a bunch of atheists from every country. I do not think we can convince them all of this conclusion we have reached, but I want to try. How was your trip to Hawaii, Marie?"

"It was wonderful, but I will never go anyplace without Tony again. I had a man stalk me the whole time I was down there. He finally ordered me to accompany his boss, some kind of sheik or something, to Paris where we were to be married! He said I had no choice! I straightened him out good and proper. We were in the hotel restaurant, and the whole roomful of people heard me. The poor man looked like a whipped puppy when he crept back to his boss's table. They all learned a lot about American women! I'll be glad when this project is complete. That is the second one of those Arabs that tried to run off with me. Maybe I should auction myself off for the most millions. I don't think the first kidnapper had any money though."

When the laughter subsided a bit, Tony asked, "Didn't that hombre know I already staked my claim on this piece of property?"

"Property, my eye!" Marie replied as she punched Tony on his sore arm! He winced and cried, "Ouch!"

Marie was instantly sorry and apologetic. Hans and Emil laughed at their antics.

Finally Hans said, "We are going to dismantle this lab and tell the world of the existence of the thing and that prayer, universal prayer, is the only solution. I want you to call a meeting of all of our scientists and also Joseph Staneck, Aaron and Lorraine, and their parents. It is to be Tuesday at 9:00 a.m. Can we get everyone here by then?"

Marie had to think a bit then consulted her laptop computer. Nodding her head, she said, "Yes, all the scientists will be here by then, but can I call one more person?" She remembered her promise to Robin, the reporter at the Binghamton newspaper. She asked, "Are we ready to tell the world about the thing?"

Hans and Emil both said, "Yes, it is time."

Marie and Tony both went right to work. Tony sent the meeting notice to all of the scientists' computers. Just to make sure they all got the message, he made hard copies, which he hand-delivered. Each copy was in the language of the senior scientist at each location in the temporary lab.

Marie called Joseph Staneck, Donna Fisher, and Joe and Mary to inform them of the meeting. When she spoke to Henry and Donna, she told them they could start the road building.

When Tony came back into the office, he made calls to people with trucks for sale. He arranged to buy six old semi trucks. They would be making one last trip from Chicago to a location south of Binghamton, New York. Next he located two hundred wooden pallets and rolls and rolls of shrink-wrap.

When Marie called Robin, the reporter was covering a city council meeting that was of much interest to the citizens of Binghamton. It involved the possible annexation of real estate south of town.

Robin hesitated to answer her cell phone. She placed her fingertip over the mute button but changed her mind for some reason and answered the call. When she recognized Marie's voice, a thrill of anticipation went through her.

"Hi, Marie. Are you calling to spill the beans?" she asked cheerfully.

"Yes, I am," Marie answered. "Can you be in Chicago Tuesday morning, or better yet on Monday evening? That way Tony and I can fill you in on what this is all about. Robin, do you go to church?"

"No, not to church, but I grace the halls of my synagogue every week and in between too."

"That's good, Robin. You will need your faith big time. I'll arrange a room for you then call you back to give you the location. In the meantime, book a flight. Book it early, Robin. This trip will be worthwhile for you. I promise. You are the only reporter I am calling, so bring a good recording machine and lots of notepaper."

Robin said, "Book two rooms if I can bring my photographer. No. Just book one. I'm trying to get the big lug to marry me, but he is such a big dork. He just doesn't get it. I love the big dork. He's a good photog, but he doesn't like playing second fiddle to a reporter."

MARIE'S REVELATION

Marie promised to book two rooms, and Robin could tell him just one was rented. If things wouldn't go well, she would have an escape.

"But, Robin, after you know what is going on in your backyard, your personal problem will be very small indeed," Marie advised. "You can fax your story from here so you will have an exclusive."

Next, Tony and Marie began calling for temporary workers to dismantle and package the lab for shipment to Binghamton. All the temp companies were very enthusiastic until told about the hazardous nature of the work, the need for special clothing, and very careful handling for their safety. Tony finally had to call a major company that had experience cleaning up atomic bomb plants and chemical warfare plants.

Hans and Emil talked to the salesperson then agreed to a meeting. The dollar figure mentioned was far more than expected, and Hans wanted a chance to whittle it down.

Tony and Marie spent the rest of the day trying to find an alternative. All this time Tony kept thinking that maybe, if all the scientists helped, they could do the job themselves. Hans was doubtful of getting the scientists to help but promised to ask them at the meeting.

Throughout all of the work involved in preparing to tell the world of the imminent disaster and initiating the dismantling of the labs, Marie had a personal problem. Tony talked all day of his eagerness to spend the night with her, but it had been nearly two weeks since she had been home. Her mother had called several times and was just being a good mother. She was warning of dire consequences if Marie didn't come home and stop her wanton behavior.

Marie's period had not yet started, and she was waking up feeling ill the last few days. She was sure she was pregnant. Her mom was a very emotional person and did not seem to like Tony much. Marie was tired of the stress and decided to take the bull by the horns and end the problem.

Tony was getting a drink of water when Marie said, "Tony, we are going to my house tonight. I am going to tell Mother that we are getting married and that I am pregnant."

Tony choked on the water. His face turned red then changed to white as he coughed and choked and sputtered. He finally managed to ask, "What did you say?"

"I said we are going to my house tonight. Mom is driving me crazy. I have to tell her that her baby is leaving the nest. Oh yeah, I said that I am pregnant too!"

"Oh, Marie, are you sure? I can't believe I'm to be a father! Are you really sure?"

"Yes, I am sure. I bought an EPT at the drugstore. It confirmed my pregnancy."

"Oh *wow*! Holy cow! Me, a father! I can't believe it. Oh, Marie, are you all right? You are working much too hard here. Do you feel okay? Can I get you anything? What can I do?"

"Well, you can marry me for one thing," Marie answered.

"Must we do it today? Did you call the preacher? What will your mom say? What will Emil say? Oh migosh! Oh good grief! I don't know how to be a father. How soon will the baby be here?"

"Tony! Tony! Relax! You will be a great father. Everything is just fine. In fact, it is great! I have never been happier. You are a scientist. You know the baby will come in nine months. We have lots of time to get ready for him or her. Let's tell Emil and Hans and then plan a date for our wedding."

The two old scientists were delighted. They all discussed the imminent work of dismantling the lab and the one at Kilabrew and decided the wedding could be in two months. If the work were still going on, the wedding would be a good break for them all. The date selected was Wednesday, September 8.

Marie was now ready to confront her mother. When she and Tony entered the house, both her mother and father jumped up from their chairs. Her father asked Marie, "Are you all right?"

Her mother asked, "Where have you been, girl? We thought you were dead or something."

"Mom and Dad, please sit down. We have much to tell you. Some of it you must keep to yourselves until Wednesday. By then it will all be on television, newspapers, and everywhere. Tony and I have been to Binghamton, New York. Tony got shot there and was in the hospital for a while. I have also been to Hawaii to visit an old lady there, but mostly we have been at work in that big warehouse downtown."

"What?" her mother asked. "You work where they transport people to Mars, experiment on babies, and use cosmic rays? What has become of you? You were in Hawaii? I always wanted to go there, but Ed never made enough money. Tony, are you all right? What is going on?"

"Oh, my word!" Ed managed to say.

"Tony is just fine now, Mom. South of Binghamton, New York, a tribe of Indians once lived. They were a small part of the Seneca nation at one time. For some reason many of those people were homosexuals. The tribe kept getting smaller and smaller because not enough babies were being born to maintain the tribe. When the confused people died, their bodies were thrown on a big heap. Over the years the heap grew to about four meters, uh, about twelve feet high. Then years after the tribe was gone, for some reason that pile of bones and dirt slowly disappeared. That process is still going on. A little boy stubbed his toe on a rock that had been part of that pile, and now his toe is nearly rotted off. So is every medical tool or instrument that came in contact with the toe. Even a million-dollar electron microscope that was used to look at the toe fell apart and eventually disappeared. That is where Tony and I came in. We received a piece of that scope to analyze.

"We couldn't figure it out, so we gave it to our boss, Emil, to analyze. Emil couldn't figure it out either. He called Hans, a scientist from Germany, and he couldn't figure it out either.

"That place in New York that is disappearing grew from the size of a small haystack to the size of two football fields in only about three years. If it keeps going, there will be no New York or Pennsylvania or anything!

"The little boy's doctor found that putting a magnet on what is left of the boy's toe stopped it from disappearing altogether.

"Emil and Hans built a laboratory inside that big warehouse, and there are over one hundred scientists trying to find out what is going on. Hans has come to the conclusion that it is an act of God. He has given up on us and is simply abandoning us."

Interrupting, Ethel asked, "Who is this Hans? Emil is your boss. Did he give up on you too? That clerk job at Woolworth's is still in the paper."

"No, Mom," Marie continued. "Hans and Emil did not give up on us. I meant that God gave up on us all. He first left the most disgusting abomination of all—that pile of bones of 'confused people.' We are going to build a huge magnet to put over that spot. Hopefully that will stop the spread of the thing. I had to get permission from the owner of the land to build a road to the spot and then to build the magnet. That's why I was in Hawaii."

"But why did Tony get shot?" Ed wondered.

Tony answered that one. "Oh, that was an accident, sorta. After we got that piece of scope to analyze and couldn't figure it out, we wanted to know more about what happened to the electron microscope. The guy that owned it was afraid to go near it anymore, so he stayed away from his lab. There was a letter telling about the sample that destroyed the scope."

"Sample of what?"

"We didn't know that either, so Emil sent Marie and me to Binghamton to try to find the letter that came in with the sample."

Marie took up the story again and described their buying old clothes and burglar tools and changing clothes in the car.

Then Tony told about their entrance into the building, and the hole in the floor, and finally the terrorist invasion, with the poor soul who didn't know the difference between a gun and a pair of pliers.

"He came to the hospital to visit me the next day. He turned out to be quite a guy, and we became friends."

Marie took up the story again. "At the hospital I also met a newspaper reporter from the Binghamton paper. I promised to give her the first news about all this. On Tuesday, Hans and Emil are calling a meeting of all the scientists. Robin is going to be there to break the story to the world, so please don't tell anyone about this until you hear it on television or read it in the paper."

"What if that big magnet doesn't work?" Ed asked.

"Dad, there will be no New York or Pennsylvania, and eventually the whole earth will simply disappear. That is what the big meeting is about. Hans is going to tell the whole world that asking God for forgiveness and another chance is the only thing that can save us."

"Oh my! Oh my! What has happened to my daughter? How did you come up with such a wild story? Are you pregnant? You didn't have to concoct a tale. It will show soon anyway. The whole world can see that!"

"Oh, Mom, it is not a wild story we made up. It is true. Yes, I am pregnant. Tony and I will be married in two months. I am not ashamed of that."

"Marie, you not only disgraced me and Ed, but just look at what you did to Pastor Lewis. How can you face him?"

"Oh, Mom, I can't think of any place in the Bible where Jesus condemned anyone for getting pregnant before marriage. Look at Betsy Reiner. Pastor Lewis married her to Sam, and they were both virgins at their wedding. Betsy's father spent thousands of dollars on that wedding, and there were two hundred or more people there. Betsy never got pregnant for two years, and when she did, Sam disappeared. He did not want to raise any children!

"Tony can't wait to be a father. He loves me, and he already loves our baby, even though it is just a little blob now. Which is worse? Tony is already pestering Emil for a raise so he can buy a crib and diapers and stuff. Tony and I are committed to each other forever. We spend hours talking about the 'for better or worse, for richer or poorer' stuff. We have made the commitment to each other and our children.

"I have never been happier in my life, but all we told you is true. We wanted you to know about all this before you see it on TV. Oh migosh, Tony, I forgot something! Once the news people get hold of this, reporters will probably be here asking Mom and Dad about me and you and stuff. They can be really obnoxious sometimes.

"Mom, you should hear some of the questions they ask us whenever we go in or come out of that warehouse building. They want to know if we are doing experiments on babies and other dumb stuff."

"When is your baby due?" Ed wanted to know.

"About the end of March," Marie answered.

"Next March I'll be a grandfather. How about that!" Ed boasted.

"In March the neighbors will put two and two together and know you were pregnant at your wedding. I'll be disgraced! How will I feel at my canasta club? How can I go to church?"

"Oh, for Pete's sake, Ethel, shut up about your damned image! This is one of the happiest moments of my life, and you're bitchin' about timing," Ed commanded.

Ethel fumed for a while. Ed, Tony, and Marie talked about the thing and how it was affecting their lives. Ed was proud that his daughter was involved in such a great undertaking and was the one to find the only solution—prayer.

After a few minutes, Ethel finally asked if Marie and Tony had names picked out for the baby. The conversation turned to things like diapers, car seats, etc.

Ed wanted to know more about the thing and how long it would take to destroy the whole earth.

"It really isn't a thing, Dad. I just gave it that name when we had no idea what it was. Now we are pretty sure it is a lack of something, namely God! I think we can save ourselves by learning to love each other. I mean every one of us, including the bum sleeping on the sidewalk and even Democrats."

Ed was a Republican committeeman, and he made an ugly face when Marie mentioned the Democrats.

Ethel found fault with everyone and could not imagine loving perfect strangers.

"We are not all perfect strangers, Mom. We are all children of God, and none of us is perfect. We have got to try to be, and we need to criticize only ourselves. We need to help each other get through bad times. Always seek out the good in other people."

Ed and Tony often worked together on Ed's old car and on landscaping around the house. Ed realized that he never really thought much about Tony being part of the family. When they all got up to go to bed, he embraced Tony and welcomed him into the family.

Ethel wondered how long the marriage would last. She rolled and tossed long after Marie's bed stopped squeaking. Ed slept like a baby.

AN UNEXPECTED VISITOR

The next day, the two lab assistants reported for work two hours early to help set up the big auditorium for the meeting. Robin, the reporter from Binghamton, was early too. She was very excited about her big scoop but at the same time noticed the air of doom and depression that seemed to pervade the building.

The scientists began arriving at seven thirty, and by eight o'clock, everyone was seated. Robin and her photographer had front-row center seats. As they were setting up their equipment, Marie noticed that both of them were smiling constantly and often exchanged sly glances. They were the only two who didn't feel the atmosphere of doom. Marie was sure that only one hotel room was used. Mike must have forgotten his foolish pride and male ego. When Tony and Marie briefed them on Monday, the outlook for the world was certainly gloomy, just like the day when President Kennedy and Khrushchev were holding atomic bombs over each other's heads during the Cuban missile crisis.

The grim news did indeed change Mike's attitude. During their long discussion of Marie's revelation, Robin and Mike decided that Marie's optimism gave reason for hope. Mike asked Robin to marry him, and of course, Robin said yes. Even the doomsday news could not deter their happiness.

The auditorium was quiet. Only a few murmurs were heard. When Hans, Emil, Tony, and Marie walked onto the stage, the room was completely silent.

Hans called the meeting to order, but Emil did most of the speaking because Hans had a very strong German accent. They wanted to be sure everyone understood everything.

"Ladies and gentlemen, we have made many fine discoveries that can probably be put to commercial and medical use, but we have failed in our mission. We have not discovered what is destroying a forest in New York and everything that touches that big bare spot in the woods. We do not know what is destroying a little boy's body. We have spent millions of dollars and thousands of hours and still do not know why molecules are simply disappearing. None of our known laws of physics or chemistry seem to apply to this problem.

"We have, however, discovered a way to slow down the thing. As we speak, a bulldozer is building a road through the forest south of Binghamton, New York, to the big bare spot that is growing relentlessly. The growth is vertical as well as horizontal. What was once a four-meter-high pile of human bones and dirt is now a one-meter deep crater. Horizontally it has grown from the size of a haystack to several football fields. If this growth rate continues, the small town of Hawleyton will disappear in two or three years, Binghamton in about forty years, New York and Pennsylvania in two hundred years.

"We have worked with small samples of the soil that Hans and I brought back from the spot and with instruments that are disappearing because of contact with that spot. Now I want to put a human element in the spotlight. Aaron, would you come up here, please."

Aaron looked at his parents and asked, "What's he want with me?" But he got up and walked to Emil's side on the stage.

Emil continued, "This remarkable young man has lost part of his big toe to the thing. Aaron, why don't you tell about your loss?"

Aaron took the microphone and began his account, "Me 'n' Jinx, my dog, were walking in the woods looking for stuff. I walked across a big bare spot about ten or twelve feet in diameter when I bumped my toe against a rock. I cussed at it—oops! Sorry, Mom—but kept going. My toe kept hurting a bit, and when I looked to see if there was blood coming out, I noticed it was changing color. Later I noticed my toenail was smaller. After a couple days my toe looked kinda stubby. Mom took me to Old Doc Staneck.

"He didn't know what was wrong, so he started carving up my toe like a Christmas turkey and sent slices of me off to some laboratory. Then he made me go to a hospital and get into some big machine called MRI.

"After that the toe quit getting smaller for a few days. Then it started to get smaller again. Doc made me get in that thing again, and the toe quit getting small again. Doc tied a magnet to my toe, and it ain't got smaller since. That magnet feels kinda weird, but I got used to it. I have to wear shoes all the time though to keep the magnet on. But the toe is still there—some of it anyway. That's all."

Aaron started to leave the stage, but Hans stopped him and, making a huge effort to control his accent, said, "That is all we know about Aaron's toe, but we know much more about Aaron. This is a remarkable young man. The stuff that Aaron, his girlfriend Lorraine, and Jinx found throughout the forest is all on display in his chicken house museum. Everything is accurately and precisely labeled.

"This boy is a natural scientist. His measurements and observation led him to discover that light also stops the thing from growing. This is a fact that all of us top scientists from around the world failed to see."

Instantly, the room was filled with a cacophony of muttering that went on until Hans banged his cane on the podium.

"It was Marie, Emil's assistant, who told us to look for something missing rather than something that is there. Marie's observation and Aaron's experiments show us that the thing is the lack of energy. We cannot create energy nor can we destroy energy.

So where has it gone? What is energy? Einstein showed us that energy is mass times velocity of light squared, but where is the mass in the bare spot? It used to be a big pile of bones and dirt, and it had no velocity at all. It wasn't moving at all. I can only conclude that energy is God. God is love, and we have lost God's love. He it is that is leaving us to—"

There was a bright flash of light. It was so bright it made the lights from Mike's video camera look dark. There was no sound of thunder, only a bright flash of light. An instant later, a man appeared between Emil and Hans. That is, all of the men among the scientists and visitors saw a man. All the women saw a woman. When she spoke, all of the Americans and all of the British people heard her, or him, speak English. Hans, Emil, Annamarie, and all of the other Germans heard German. All the Italians heard Italian. Each scientist heard his native language.

"Good morning, Hans. Good morning, Lars. Good morning, Ivan." There was just one "Good morning" but in multiple languages, and everyone heard his or her own name.

"I am surprised you figured that out, Hans! Marie has known for weeks, but she has faith enough to know she can change my mind, faith enough to conceive a child. By the way, Marie, he will be a fine healthy man you can be proud of.

"Oliver, why do you look around for projectors? I am not a hologram. I am not some new electronic marvel. By the way, you left the coffee pot turned on in your hotel room."

An instant later, he was beside Olga in the tenth row. He removed her rather flamboyant hat and handed it to her. "Hold this in your hand. People behind you can't see the stage through this thing."

Then he was among a group of Japanese scientists. One of them looked like he had had no sleep for a week. "Masuto, why do you weep so, and why don't you sleep? Your child is cured. Call your wife and tell her to take him home from the hospital.

"Hans, that which you did was horrible, but your sins are forgiven.

"Aaron, take off your shoe."

Aaron removed his shoe, and the magnet that Joseph had fashioned for him fell out. The toe was completely restored!

"Marie, you were right when you told your parents that I first left that pile of bones in the forest. God does not hate homosexuals. It is the affliction that is abominable. You people, all of you, live in those bodies, male and female. I live in you, not in your body, but in you. I merely created the body to be a container for your soul. But if there is no body, there is no soul. The body must be used properly to carry souls for me to inhabit. Male and female create new souls, not male and male, not female and female.

"But lest you all condemn homosexuals, listen to me. Finally listen to me if you want to save this world and this human race. I created sex to create souls to inhabit. It is the only way I can live and grow. Every abortion you do is a fatal injury to a human being, to a soul, and to me. Every condom used is a fatal injury to me. Where can I live on this misguided planet? Why do you permit starvation, genocide, and disease in Africa? You Americans and Europeans have it in your power to feed and educate the people of Africa and other less-advanced nations.

"I suffer along with the unfortunate couples that desperately want children but, for one reason or another, can't conceive or carry. Often things go wrong. Is every potato perfect? Does every acorn produce a new tree? I feel the pain of barren couples, but my love for them is just as great as for childbearing couples.

"Your wise seers worry about excess population. You think famine, war, and genocide control population. I ordered you to fill the earth. Is not your ability to grow food in the west, and in vast Russia and Australia, constantly increasing? You scientists right in this house know ways to greatly increase the world food supply. You can feed the entire population of earth. Only stupid governments cause famine. Storms may make people hungry for a while. But when I live in you and you listen to me, you can get food to stricken lands. All can help. Even the widow's mite given can help get food to needy people. That is how the system should work!

"You worry about needing space for an increasing population. You have plenty of space on earth for years.

"In Lima, Ohio, there was a scientist conceived who would discover a propulsion system not yet dreamed of on earth. There were people conceived in Colorado who would control that propulsion system to travel to other stars, even other galaxies, to find other planets humans can inhabit. I am waiting there on those planets, but guess what! Their mothers aborted all of those scientists before they were born!

"I worked for centuries of your time to create a visionary leader to take humans to a new level of conduct. It never happened because her father wasted the sperm cell I worked so hard to create on another man.

"You people here are the most mentally developed people on earth. I have worked for centuries to develop your brains, but even you scientists use only a small portion of your capacity.

"You must take this message to all the people of earth. I gave you the Bible, the Talmud, the ancient scrolls, and other books that tell you how to live. But you choose to read my word and interpret it. Don't do that! Read what is there! Accept my word as a small child does.

"Remember, I need you as much as you need me. I cannot exist without souls to live in, and you cannot exist without me. Yes, Hans, I am love, and love is energy. It was love that created the first two bits of mass and brought them together in the vastness of space. As mass grew, love grew. But to grow to completion, I need souls. Don't worry so much about how I created it all. Do worry about how to sustain the growth. For that I need your help, and without it, I must scrub this project and try again with another creature.

"I did give up on you! The thing, as you call it, is the result of my leaving this planet. The love of Aaron and Lorraine, Tony and Marie, Joseph and Sophie, and others like them who love unconditionally, held me here. I could leave in a puff of smoke, and that is all there would be of earth.

"You do not need to believe in me. Know that *I am*, and without me you cannot live.

"Don't change my word. Don't add to it. The first time I became a man to set you straight, you clowns nailed me to a tree. That hurt! How can I live in people who would do that to me? How can I live in people who murder their own babies? How can I live in men who put their seed in other men or women who will not accept a man's seed? Remember that if I can't live here, neither can you.

"Take this message home to your leaders. Convince them. Most of the world leaders are egotistic blockheads. It may take a big mallet or a bulldozer to drive anything into their heads, but do it! You must do it!

"By the way, don't build a big magnet on the bare spot. Build me an altar there. Use it to educate the world.

"This building is now free of the thing. It is safe to remove your laboratory. I would allow the whole building to be consumed to be an example of my leaving your presence, but the people of Chicago would just blame you. There would be no message. Instead, the microscope lab in Binghamton will disappear.

"Allow it to become a crater ten meters deep, then stop it with lights or another source of energy not yet discovered. It will take one hundred years to reach the depth of ten meters. That should be enough time to enlighten enough people to the danger of not obeying me.

"I am not a figment of someone's imagination. *I am*—like the bricks and mortar that are this building. In fact, without me, bricks cannot exist.

"You have seen this. You have seen what happens when I am not present. Go home. Tell your people. Tell them to forget their differences. Tell them to love all men. That's love, not lust after. Tell them to help one another. You Arabs and Jews have been fighting ever since you were brothers. That's about seven thousand of your years. Get over it already! There is too much to be done for you to waste any more of your time fighting!

"Men, love your wives. Wives, love your husbands, and both of you love and nurture your children. Teach them all things. Don't teach them that sex is bad. How can it be bad? I created it! Instead, teach them how to enjoy it and to give most joy to each other. Teach them the responsibility that comes with it! Teach them that there is no greater endeavor than bearing, educating, and nourishing children. Teach them about me, that I am love, and without love nothing can exist. Teach them to love each and every person. Teach them to seek out the good in others. Usually it is there.

"Don't look for miracles! I do them only to make a point or to prove that *I am*. None of you now living on earth will see the results of your efforts to change the way you live, but you must begin now to change. The results will take time. Nothing is perfect. Does every seed bear fruit? Does every raindrop fall where it is useful? Does any person live their life without making mistakes? No! Not even you, Annamarie! But I cover mistakes. Love covers mistakes.

"You are here only a short time. Enjoy that time. Help those around you to enjoy their lives. Learn love now. After you no longer live in those bodies, it will be too late. Those who are a positive force to me will join me forever. Those that are a negative force will be discarded in a lake of fire!

"Robin, your recording machine will play back only gibberish. It will be useless to you, but do not throw it away. There will be one born in the future who will build a machine to reproduce my speech in any language. I hope his mother does not abort him!

Write your notes quickly. Then write your story and publish it after Mike takes pictures of the lab here and in Binghamton and of the spot in the woods. Do an interview with Dancing Star too. I want this published worldwide soon. It was two or three hundred years before people wrote about my last visit. I think you call that writing the New Testament. During those years, much of what I taught you was forgotten or changed.

"Robin, do not interpret what I say. Write only that which you hear. Do not analyze it. Do not change it. Your hand is shaking as you write. Be calm. I am controlling your accuracy. Do not change anything you are writing. Do not allow your editor to change this message.

"None of you be pompous. As I promote you in your field of endeavor, remember that I also increase your responsibility, not your greatness.

"It is written that if a man remains celibate so that he can better serve me, he will be blessed. So be it—but be sure the motive is to serve me, not to hide your inability to live with a spouse of the complementary sex.

"Be honest! Be humble! Remember that as you increase in rank, you must increase your effort to serve me. Look down on no one! Love among people, all people, is most important, not wealth or intelligence. These are but tools to aid in spreading love. Love promotes life and easier life for all people. Being pompous serves no purpose—none. Remember the poor widow is as good to me as a rich man or an official in government or religion!

"My final words to you are 'Love one another as I love you.'"

There was a bright flash of light again and then complete darkness. For thirty minutes there was no light in the auditorium. There the darkness was instant, but throughout Chicago and all the rest of the world, the darkness fell slowly. People driving cars found that their headlights had no effect. Light simply disappeared from earth completely for thirty minutes. No vehicles moved on earth. Aircrafts continued to fly but were not guided by sight or radar. There were no crashes anywhere—none. There was fear. Great fear was in all the earth. The fear was greatest in educated people who knew there was no eclipse of the sun. They could not come up with any theory to explain the darkness and the complete failure of every communication system on earth. This was a fear greater than any ever felt on earth before.

People like Marie, Tony, Aaron, Lorraine, Hans, Emil, and others who knew God felt no fear—only wonder. Fear was greatest in people who denied that God exists. There was no reason for the darkness. They could not control it. They could not deny it. They could not explain it. There was much crying, weeping, and wailing among those scientists and atheists who knew there was no god. Among those who finally got it, there was peace and a huge feeling of relief.

As the darkness continued in the warehouse and in laboratories around the globe, scientists, doctors, technicians, and even politicians became aware of solutions to problems that had evaded them before.

One Muslim scientist working on the thing with Hans and Emil had come to America not to help Hans, but to learn how his team in his own land could use his knowledge of the thing to serve Allah by killing more Americans or even all of the infidels. During the darkness, he realized who had been talking to him and the message he had heard. At first he was overcome with fear. God had promised him eternity in a lake of fire. As the darkness continued, he became aware of his duty to his fellow Muslims throughout the world. His job was to warn his brothers and sisters that their founder, Mohammad, never intended his followers to be a band of murderers. It was during this time of total darkness that a solution to his problem entered his mind. He remembered the book he found in his hotel room, a Bible, left there by a group called the Gideons.

This scientist vowed to start such a group in his own land to distribute and encourage the reading of the Koran and the Sunna.

He knew this to be the right path to follow because a great feeling of peace enveloped him as he thought it. He planned how to start the group, who should be in the group, funding, and other problems to be solved.

All the scientists in the warehouse had similar thoughts about how to reach their fellow citizens back home. They had to convince them that they should forget the vague and varied parts of their religion. They needed to concentrate on the one most important command that came directly, not through a vision or dream, from God: "Love one another."

None of the scientists in the auditorium were aware that the darkness they experienced covered the whole world. They didn't know that at that moment, the entire population of the world was prepared for their message of love that came from God himself. The scientists' sudden change from studying to broadcasting that which they had just seen and heard did not happen fast enough. They used too much time to think about it. They couldn't take advantage of the universal fear.

Among that group of scientists assembled in the warehouse, there were no longer any atheists—none. There were many before that visit, but not afterward.

Aaron was awed. He had gone to Sunday school all his life. He often thought the people he learned about did a lot of really stupid things that got them in trouble with God, and now he knew he was right. He always believed, without question, that which he read in the Bible, but some of the lessons in the Sunday school books seemed to miss the point. Teachers and authors seemed to take a verse or a chapter from the Bible and twist it around a bit.

Aaron wondered if other religions did the same thing and if that was the reason for all the strife in the world. He knew nothing about any other religion, so he knew he couldn't judge them at all. He just knew that his own ideas about life and religion were not changed at all. He felt he was on the right track. He did vow to clean up his language a bit. He realized it hurt his mother whenever she heard him cuss.

Lorraine thought about all the things her father taught her about the old tribal ways. She now understood why Joe never killed a deer without first thanking the deer for its gift to him. She understood all the little courtesies he practiced that came from the tribe. She vowed to always tell her mother where she was going and with whom, even though it was almost always with Aaron into the woods.

Every scientist there realized that if they were to change the world, they first had to change their own treatment of those closest to themselves.

Hans could not remember anytime in his life that he felt happier. The heavy burden had been lifted from him. His mind was finally clear. Many things he had not known before were now clear to him. During that half hour of total darkness, Hans was already thinking of ways to use his intellect to end strife in countries torn apart by civil war and to educate people so they could live peacefully and feed themselves.

Emil decided to repair the building that housed the Kilabrew Lab then sell the property and retire. His next endeavor would be to build the altar that God had asked for at the bare spot. Tony and Marie could help with that project then see where they were led to next. What form would the altar take? How could it educate? These questions filled Emil's thoughts.

Neither Tony nor Marie was concerned about their future or how they would provide for their child. Their problems were more immediate and tactical. They had to help find transportation to homes around the world for the hundred or so scientists and their families then find contractors to dismantle the laboratory.

Annamarie was almost in shock. All her life, almost from the day of her birth, she was taught that belief in gods and spirits was nothing. It was but foolishness dreamed up by people who were failures and had no self-confidence. Superior people like herself did not need an unseen god to guide them.

But today she knew she had met God face-to-face. No figment of imagination could have restored Aaron's toe. No one, not even Hans, could have known the things about her that she was reminded of today—dumb things she had done as a child and as a young woman. She vowed to buy a copy of the book, which she had spent a year of her time while in the Communist youth movement finding and destroying. She had burned several hundred bibles. She destroyed not only the books but also hopes, dreams, and even memories. In many of the bibles she burned were family histories going back several hundred years. Annamarie's remorse and grief nearly crushed her as that half hour of darkness wore on. It was a half hour when even a burning match produced no light. Just before the lights came on, she thought that maybe, just maybe, even her sins were forgiven. She hoped she would not have to endure that lake of fire.

When the light returned, there were seven scientists in the room with their cigarette lighters ignited, but fire couldn't be seen until all the lamps were emitting light. Two of the scientists had burned themselves though.

There was silence except for an occasional cough or movement until Hans approached the podium and said, "Ladies and gentlemen, let us go home. I think we all know what we must do now."

Slowly and politely, everyone left the auditorium. Some went to their lab to shut down experiments, but most went back to their hotel rooms.

Outside the lab complex, the scientists met a confused and fearful world. The light was returning slowly. Most of the radio stations were either silent or playing soft music. Fear and confusion filled the air. There were still no vehicles moving. Taxi drivers who happened to see that the scientists came from the warehouse refused them entry into their cars. They locked the doors in fear. They knew that those weird scientists caused the strange darkness. So great was the fear in Chicago that guns were being carried in plain sight. That increased the level of fear, but rather than causing mass murder and bedlam, the fear brought about cautious behavior. Everyone was very polite, but the atmosphere was explosive.

Those scientists that were refused transportation reentered the warehouse and located Hans and Emil. They were surprised to learn that the darkness occurred throughout Chicago. Tony ran to his office and turned on his radio.

AFTER THE VISIT

There was no music on any station by that time—only news of complete darkness everywhere in America, and it soon became known that it was worldwide.

Tony, Marie, Emil, Joe, Mary, Henry, and Donna all got on the phones and the Internet and began calling every clergyman they could reach. The lines of communication were slow to respond. Some did not work at all for about fifteen minutes. Satellites had to be repositioned. Switches had to be synchronized. When everything began to work again, the systems were overwhelmed by calls from people needing to know of the welfare of relatives and friends.

Eventually, everything did return to normal, and every leader of every religion (Christian, Judaism, Hinduism, Shintoism, Taoism, Confucianism, Buddhism, Sikhism, and Zoroastrianism) that they could find phone numbers for was called. The callers gave only a brief message that it was extremely important that they all meet as soon as possible.

Hans knew that the warehouse the scientists had occupied would not be able to accommodate this meeting because the labs took up most of the building, and their removal was going to take too much time. Also, the level of fear and suspicion was so great in Chicago that another city would be necessary. Finally the Vatican was chosen because security was in place, and the pope was too frail to travel.

The meeting was held within a month. The message was unanimously rejected. Every one of the religious leaders had an easy life with thousands or millions of believers who supported them in grand style. Not one of them wanted to have his boat rocked. None believed that God would appear personally to a group of scientists rather than to heads of religion or state. The Christians were so upset to hear that the earth was around more than seven thousand years, even though dinosaurs are dug up all over the earth, that they walked out of the meeting.

Robin was unable to file her story for three days. She tried several times to fax it to her editor and tried many times to phone it in, but the communications lines were still a jumbled mess. Finally she and Mike rented an old car that did not have a computerized engine but had plugs, points, and a distributor and drove home to Binghamton.

The editor liked Robin's work. She was precise, accurate, and prolific. But this story was just too unrealistic. Robin was so excited to turn it in that she was just bubbling over with additional information and enthusiasm. The poor editor just didn't know what to do with it. He finally put it on the religion page, between stories about promotions and ordainment of gay ministers.

Robin was heartbroken and confused. She quit her job three weeks later. The newspaper company got recycled into a weekly that covered sporting events, and eventually that failed too.

Robin's newspaper article that warned the world of the thing was so well hidden in the religion pages of the Binghamton newspaper that it was missed by almost everyone. It was totally ignored by those who did read it. The total reaction to that article was "Oh no! Not another crackpot." The story died there.

In Chicago, promoters and citizens who wrote letters to the editor expressed disgust that the big warehouse was still unusable. A sportswriter from the newspaper wrote a long story about a public building that was put out of use until it could be certified safe to use for dogfights, cockfights and wrestling matches. The writer called for stiff fines to be levied on the group of weirdos that rented and trashed the building.

Hans and Emil were working full-time to get every bit of material and every splinter of wood out of the big warehouse. Tony, Marie, Aaron and his parents, and even Joe, Mary, and Lorraine were helping. All of the other scientists had gone home. Trucks and carpenters had to be hired from out-of-town companies. The rumors of sacrificing children and transportation by osmosis were much more believable than Emil's press release warning the world of the need to pray for forgiveness. All of the Chicago citizens were afraid to go near the building until it was certified safe.

After several hours and many beers in a local bar, the full-time custodian who worked at the warehouse was holding court with his drinking buddies. "It ain't no wonder that place is still not ready. Them crazy scientists spend so much time on their knees or even facedown on the floor praying to some god that they have no time for work. I heard one old geezer that talked funny, complaining that everyone who had been supporting their madness wanted their money back. That's why the old goat has to do so much work by himself. He can't pay no one. I ain't helping. I take care of the building but not the crap they dragged in."

Nationally, the House of Representatives had passed on to the Senate a bill prohibiting all states from restricting same sex marriages. The bill also had a rider that provided a flat tax of one hundred dollars on all weddings. The funds from this tax were to pay for special insurance to cover AIDS treatment and research to discover the cause of the proliferation of that disease. The Senate and the president were both expected to pass this legislation.

Finally, Emil and Hans held a press conference in which they declared the big Chicago warehouse building to be free of their laboratory. Emil declared that every splinter of wood and every wire and nail had been removed. He also informed the public that all the scientists who had worked there were the best in the world. None of them was insane and, in fact, among them they had won thirty-seven Nobel Peace Prizes.

Then Emil pleaded with the public to pray to God for forgiveness. "We scientists failed to stop a destructive force, or rather the lack of it, from destroying the earth. The force that is missing is God, and only our combined prayers can save the earth from complete disintegration."

Halfway through that plea, the three television and two radio stations cut for commercial break. The print media reporters scratched out what they had written.

In Denver, Colorado, a serial rapist who had killed two policemen during his capture was released from prison. His appeals reached the Supreme Court, which determined that his conviction was in error because the five witnesses, all victims of his, had sworn on the Bible to tell the truth. The court determined that using a work of fiction like the Bible was unconstitutional. Following his release, five more girls were raped. Two of them were murdered.

Six months after Emil's press conference, the government released new money to the banks. The statement "In God We Trust" had been replaced with "In Gold We Trust." Within three days, the price of gold hit six thousand dollars an ounce. Inflation hit 200 percent, and within three more days, every CEO of every financial institution in America and Canada had disappeared. Also missing were billions of dollars in euros. Violent fights were breaking out in grocery stores all across America. Grain elevators were now guarded night and day.

It had been hinted that all of these problems were caused by those nuts in that warehouse in Chicago. It was hoped that the removal of liquor and tobacco taxes and gambling restrictions would restore stability to our markets. America was the strongest nation on earth and would soon recover from these problems.

America was now the fairest nation as well since corporal punishment of children was now illegal in the home as well as in public. Our children were now free to study in school without being exposed to references to any kind of god that can't be seen or touched. Laws against homosexual activity, food and drug laws, and other restrictions had been removed. Safe and sanitary home abortions were being taught in sex education classes, which now began in third grade.

The release of all persons charged with using or selling any kind of drugs would free up the jails to handle criminals who try to inflict upon us any kind of story about a dead man who got out of his grave and is alive again. Drug use had been determined by the courts to be a personal choice. However, any attempt at mind control had been determined to be a public matter and a real nuisance.

Freedom from drug and so-called sex crime prosecution would free up the judicial system to determine the causes of the horrendous school dropout problem, murder, rape and robbery rates, and the extremely high vehicle accident rate. Great progress was being made on the accident problem since the president of a major tractor manufacturing company was now in jail. He failed to provide safety warnings on a bulldozer that demolished a twenty-unit apartment building. As soon as the operator of that machine would get out of drug rehabilitation, the trial could begin.

In the months after the meeting of the religious leaders, many of the scientists who worked in Chicago on the project to identify the thing were in jail. Several simply disappeared, and three were publicly hanged.

Tony, Marie, Emil, and even Aaron and Lorraine planned and built the altar that they had heard God order. They built a church around the altar to be a teaching facility. The altar was built directly over the spot where Aaron had stubbed his toe on the rock.

Marie had started a journal of all the events that the thing brought about. She consulted with Tony, Aaron, Emil, Lorraine,

Hans, and everyone else involved in the project to make sure all the writing was factual. The journal was written in the form of a story, and several hundred copies were sent throughout the world to all the scientists who had worked on or knew of the thing.

Those scientists were blamed for the half hour of darkness and loss of control of every system made by man. Marie's book was banned in every library in the world. Congregations of each religious order were split into many smaller groups of those who believed the story, those who didn't, and those who wanted to excommunicate the scientists among them. Some even wanted to hang them.

Hans and Emil both retired and spent the rest of their lives building the altar and trying to convince people that the story Marie had written was indeed true.

Tony went to work for a big international pharmaceutical company and became a well-known scientist. He also studied magnetism and other forms of energy.

Marie gave birth to five children. One of those children, the firstborn, spent his life trying to prove Marie's story was true. His younger brother became a monk and spent his life trying to disprove everything his brother said.

Aaron spent all his free time helping to build the altar. He finished high school then attended a local college where he earned a BS degree in chemistry. He then went on to the university in Chicago, where he earned a master's degree, then a doctorate in biochemistry. Lorraine also earned a master's degree in biochemistry with minors in philosophy and religion.

Both Aaron and Lorraine had romances that nearly became marriages but always seemed to fail. One Christmas they were both at the altar in the woods, and there they began to renew their childhood friendship. They married two years later. Together they were credited with many discoveries that proved beneficial. Lorraine took up Hans's old project of trying to discover why some people are afflicted with homosexuality. They had three children. Two were boys who were both killed in a stupid religious war, and their daughter married a guitar player whose music drove Aaron crazy.

When Lorraine died at age eighty-one, Aaron took up permanent residency at the altar and became caretaker. Aaron tried constantly to arrange a meeting of the remaining scientists who had worked on the thing, but all of them were too frightened of their governments to ever assemble again. They always refused.

Finally, only Aaron and Marie's firstborn child remained. Damian was still in the womb when the Chicago meeting was held, but he was able to quote the entire speech that God had made to the scientists. Damian was able to quote the speech in any language.

HOPE?

The inventor who would build a machine to decipher Robin's tape recording of the meeting was yet to be born. Robin had put the tape into a special box to preserve it. Just two weeks before she died, she gave it to Aaron. He kept it in a safe at the altar.

These two old men—Damian at a rest home in Binghamton and Aaron at the altar—knew they alone could keep alive the memory of God's appearance. Even more important was his message. The world was in a very sorry state and needed to hear the Word. It was so bad that even the Gideons and the group that distributed the Koran were both forbidden to do so anymore. No woman or girl anywhere was safe from rape, beatings, and muggings. Only the strongest and biggest of men succeeded in business. Judicial systems were so entangled in technical jargon that justice was nonexistent. Judges were threatened. Witnesses were badly beaten or simply disappeared.

Liquor stores, bars, and sex clubs did well. Aaron's son-in-law played guitar in a strip joint in Jamestown. Aaron pleaded with his son-in-law to stop his wild behavior and join in the effort to reform the world. They needed to convince people that the group of scientists, which had met in Chicago nearly one hundred years earlier, really did have a visit from God.

What Aaron didn't know was that Jacob's wildness was already near its end. Jacob was well aware of the huge responsibility that was waiting to fall on his shoulders. He was trying to delay having to carry that huge load. He had read the story Marie had written and believed every word of it. Many times he and Aaron discussed what had happened. He was aware that God had told that group of scientists that none of them would ever see the results of their efforts, and that included Aaron. But it did not include Jacob and his wife (Aaron's daughter) and their children. One other possibility could be Tony's great-great-grandson, but Aaron had already contacted Charlie and his wife. So far they had shown only a minimum of interest. Aaron decided to call them one more time. If he could just make them curious enough to visit the altar and read Marie's writing, maybe they could turn the tide. Maybe they could convince the world to change and stop the growth of something that is causing five buildings in five different parts of the world to slowly just crumble and disappear.

ANOTHER CHANCE

"Charlie, this is really weird. Do you think this stuff actually happened?"

"I don't know, Barb. But if it did, it started right here. It says that Aaron kicked that rock right under this altar. Is that old man the Aaron in the story? He must be more than one hundred years old!"

"He probably is. Most people live past one hundred now. Did you notice the big toe on his left foot looks different from the one on the right? It looks like a much younger man's toe. Charlie, I have the spookiest feeling that this story is all true."

"Yeah, and I have a terrible feeling that old Aaron is going to tell us we have to convince the world of that."

"Well, you did say that you don't want to spend your whole life selling satellite interfaces. I guess we have a goal now."

"But how can we do it? Aaron couldn't and all those scientists couldn't, even after the whole world went dark and scared the people half to death. Just what is it we are to convince people of? I think I have to read this thing several times to understand it. Why me?"

Just then, Aaron approached and said, "You, Charlie, because you could sell a refrigerator to an Eskimo or a furnace to a man in Key West, Florida. I think God prepared you for the job. We scientists know the facts of how things are, but none of us has your ability to relate to people the way you do.

"To answer your question, yes, I am the Aaron in the story. I stubbed my toe on a rock, there under the center of the altar, almost a hundred years ago.

"Charlie, I want you to scoop up some of the soil around here. Notice that nothing is growing in it. Lorraine tried for years to grow grass and flowers. Nothing grows. God stopped the growth of the dead area, but he didn't restore the soil that is around this church. Take some of it to a laboratory and have it analyzed. You will have the same results that your forefathers had—none.

"There are five different buildings in five different cities around the world that are slowly disappearing from the top down. No bricks, mortar, glass, or steel falls to the ground, but the walls, windows, floors, and roofs are just disappearing. Two of the buildings are courthouses where scientists were sentenced to prison for telling the story you just read.

"One building has completely disappeared. It was the prison where three scientists were hanged for heresy. After that hangman tripped the lever to kill the last of those three scientists, he disappeared instantly. Two hundred people saw him disappear. He didn't move left or right, up or down—he just disappeared. There was a loud pop as the air filled the space where he had been. The witnesses were threatened with death if they informed the world of the disappearance.

"None of this has ever been reported by any news agency still in existence. One television station that reported the disappearance of the prison burned down. Their license was revoked, and the reporter was never heard from again. Charlie, no government in the world and no religion will ever admit that God is as real as water or wood or steel or bread. No leader wants to give up his status. They depend on a belief in a vague invisible god, not the real physical God, which is love. Love is the energy that is a part of mass, the part that holds mass together, and the part that holds us together. Love created us.

"Of course, God is a spirit. Remember, he made us in his image. We have bodies, male and female. That is necessary for reproduction, but are those bodies us? No! We live in the bodies. We are spirits too, but we are just an image of God. Think how much greater the real thing is!

"Barb and Charlie, I am asking you to take up the biggest, hardest chore ever undertaken by anyone. You must convince the world that God is as real as you and I and that we must begin to obey him. There was much rotten, evil, conniving treachery revealed in the Bible. It is a history book of man's base nature, but there is also the message of love. When God became Jesus, he told us his mission was not to change the law but to fulfill it. He was indeed the Messiah, predicted and hoped for by many generations of people. But people were thinking of a physical leader who would give great wealth and perfect health to everyone. That is exactly what Jesus did promise us, but not in these bodies and not without our effort.

"We can't even imagine how great our lives will be in heaven, but we have to deserve to be there. We not only have to accept that Jesus is God, we also have to accept what he taught us: God is love.

"The first of two most important things we must learn is to love God. If God is love, then we are to love love. No amount of intelligence, political power, physical strength, popularity, honesty, or any other quality can compare to love.

"The second is to love one another as we love ourselves. Charlie, just think what we could accomplish if everyone would love everyone else, and we would all help each other. In a large store chain, all the associates are as helpful to the customers as they can be, but that is an artificial helpfulness. It is intended to encourage the customers to spend money in the store. That helpfulness disappears when the employees' work time is ended. Think what we could accomplish if we would all love one another and help each other, with no expectation of return. God is love. Let him live in you!

"If we do not learn this lesson, those five buildings that are disappearing will only be the beginning. We will all disappear, and we will not end up in heaven. We will be discarded in a lake of fire. Why should God hang on to a project that just will not work? I have thrown away many projects and experiments that didn't work for me. God is much more patient and tolerant than I, but he is getting fed up with us humans.

"Go to work now, Charlie and Barb, but don't expect any results until after I have passed on. God himself said that none of us at that meeting in Chicago would ever see the results of our work. You have the whole world to teach, but only two things to teach. The first is to love God. The second is to love each other. That's all. Carry on. Maybe this time we can make the world understand. Maybe this time."

CPSIA information can be obtained at www.ICGtesting.com
Printed in the USA
LVOW01s0939021213

363508LV00001B/128/P